WITHOUT A GRAVE

The new Hannah Ives mystery

Hannah's in paradise, enjoying Bahamian island life. When controversy arises over the construction of a luxury resort that could devastate the coral reef, Hannah dives in. Acts of vandalism, a deadly wildfire, a missing scientist – Hannah suspects a connection, but her investigation stalls when Hurricane Luis slams into the island. Before the skies clear, a dynasty is threatened by a venomous sibling rivalry, environmentalists face off against progressive island fathers, and death pays a call...

Marcia Talley titles available from
Severn House Large Print

DEAD MAN DANCING

WITHOUT A GRAVE

A Hannah Ives Mystery

Marcia Talley

Severn House Large Print
London & New York

This first large print edition published 2010
in Great Britain and the USA by
SEVERN HOUSE PUBLISHERS LTD of
9-15 High Street, Sutton, Surrey, SM1 1DF.
First world regular print edition published 2009 by
Severn House Publishers Ltd., London and New York.

British Library Cataloguing in Publication Data

Talley, Marcia Dutton, 1943-
  Without a grave.
  1. Ives, Hannah (Fictitious character)--Fiction.
  2. Resorts--Environmental aspects--Bahamas--Fiction.
  3. Sabotage--Fiction. 4. Hurricanes--Bahamas--Fiction.
  5. Detective and mystery stories. 6. Large type books.
  I. Title
  813.6-dc22

  ISBN-13: 978-0-7278-7890-8

Severn House Publishers support The Forest Stewardship Council
[FSC], the leading international forest certification organisation. All
our titles that are printed on Greenpeace-approved FSC-certified paper
carry the FSC logo.

Mixed Sources
Product group from well-managed
forests and other controlled sources
www.fsc.org Cert no. SA-COC-1565
© 1996 Forest Stewardship Council

FSC

Printed and bound in Great Britain by the
MPG Books Group, Bodmin, Cornwall.

*To the most critically endangered horses
in the world, the Abaco Barbs.
May you always run free.*

www.arkwild.org

Roll on, thou deep and dark blue ocean, roll!
Ten thousand fleets sweep over thee in vain;
Man marks the earth with ruin – his control
Stops with the shore. He sinks into thy depths
with bubbling groan, Without a grave,
unknell'd, uncoffin'd, and unknown.

Lord George Gordon Byron, *Childe Harold's Pilgrimage*, Canto iv, Stanza 178–179

Acknowledgements

Thanks to:

My husband, Barry, whose love of sailing first took us to the Bahamas where I fell in love all over again.

Pattie Toler, who invented the Cruisers' Net, on the air in Abaco every day, rain or shine, for eighteen years. She graciously stepped aside to allow Hannah to fill in as moderator, and cheerfully answered my endless questions.

Milanne 'Mimi' Rehor, whose love and unqualified dedication to the Abaco Barbs has brought them back from the brink of extinction.

To Brent Morris for Paul's project.

To Ben Stavis, captain of *Astarte*, a Rhodes Reliant 41, for *Wanderer*.

And to Chris Parker, for the weather.

To the Annapolis Writers' Group – Ray Flynt, Lynda Hill, MaryEllen Hughes, Debbi Mack, Sherriel Mattingly and Bonnie Settle – for tough love.

Author's Note

The islands of Hawksbill Cay and Bonefish Cay are not on the charts. I have taken the very great liberty of sandwiching them between Scotland Cay to the north and Man-O-War Cay to the south while pushing Fowl Cay a bit further out into the Atlantic Ocean. I apologize in advance for any inconvenience this will cause, especially to cruising sailors.

In the Bahamas, Cay is pronounced 'Key,' never 'Kay'.

It would be impossible to set a book anywhere in the tiny out-island chain known collectively as the Abacos without including local personalities like Pattie Toler, Mimi Rehor, Troy Albury and Vernon Malone. While these people actually exist, I have written a work of fiction. Their roles in this book, and the words and deeds attributed to them, are entirely figments of my imagination and should in no way be construed as fact.

The Abaco Wild Horse Preserve and Conservation Area is located on the island of Great Abaco in the area of Treasure Cay, but if you try

to follow my directions, you will not find it. For the protection of the horses I have left my descriptions purposely vague. If you'd like to visit the Preserve, Mimi Rehor will happily be your guide. Contact Mimi at:
http://www.arkwild.org/visitbarbs/visit.html

And while you're there, give a buck for the Barbs!

One

AT TWO HOURS AFTER MIDNIGHT APPEARED
THE LAND, AT A DISTANCE OF 2 LEAGUES.
THEY HANDED ALL SAILS AND SET THE TREO,
WHICH IS THE MAINSAIL WITHOUT BONNETS,
AND LAY-TO WAITING FOR DAYLIGHT FRI-
DAY, WHEN THEY ARRIVED AT AN ISLAND OF
THE BAHAMAS THAT WAS CALLED IN THE
INDIANS' TONGUE GUANAHANI.
Christopher Columbus, *Journal of the First
Voyage*, October 12, 1492

We'd lived on Bonefish Cay for a week before
it occurred to me. Take your clothes off, Hannah. Swim nude.

On a jagged limestone bank behind me,
Windswept Cottage hunkered down in clumps
of sea grape and towering palms, their fronds
rattling softly in a brisk, offshore breeze. Our
landlords, a pair of crackerjack attorneys from
New York City, had bought up the property – a
cottage and two outbuildings – as well as the
vacant lots on either side to 'help out' a client in
the wake of an ugly, divorce-spawned fore-

11

closure. Barring curious fishermen with binoculars, or a bored passenger on the occasional passing cruise ship, there was no one to see me as I shook off my flip-flops, eased my cut-offs down to my ankles and stepped out of them on to the sand. With a swift, cross-armed motion, I hauled my T-shirt over my head, exposing my body, not exactly as Mother Nature intended – there'd been too many surgeries for that – but in all its post-op, what-you-see-is-what-you-get glory.

I stood for a moment on the narrow strip of beach, eyes closed, face to the sky, wiggling my toes deeper into the sand. The sun had been up for only an hour, but it had already taken the night's damp chill out of the pink, sugar-fine grains. It warmed my eyelids, my cheeks, too, as I surrendered to its rays and to the kiss of the wind as it lifted my curls and caressed my body gently, like a lover. Not for the first time, I was thanking whatever gods had led Paul and me to this tiny Bahamian island, an unpolished gem in the Abaco chain just one hundred and fifty miles – as the seagull flies – off the coast of Florida.

Not the gods, exactly, I corrected as I stepped into the curling surf and waded in up to my knees, but the chair of the Naval Academy math department and the Academic Dean who'd granted my husband a six-month sabbatical at full pay. Paul was writing a textbook that would revolutionize the way geometry is taught in high schools, the perfect text that would open the door to advanced calculus for thousands and thousands of college students. He'll explain it to you, if you ask, but prepare yourself for folding three-dimensional paper figures that don't hold up very well in the humidity. The price one pays for working in paradise!

That the property became available was another miracle wrought not by the gods, but by our family attorney, Jim Cheevers, who represented the occasional investment banker with a second home and a three-count conviction. Jim had once engineered our getaway to a secluded cabin on Deep Creek Lake in western Maryland, but if anyone ever ran a vacation rental sweepstakes, *Windswept* would be first prize.

I turned my back to the sea and studied our home-away-from-home, a pale-aqua board-and-batten octagon cantilevered over the Sea of Abaco. Wooden windows all around afforded a three hundred and sixty degree view. We kept the windows flung open to the trade winds, flipped up and hooked to the underside of a generous roof that extended at least ten feet over the wrap-around porch. With typical Bahamian efficiency, the roof collected every drop of rain that fell from the tropical sky, carrying it through a series of gutters and pipeways into a concrete cistern, our only source of fresh water.

I'd left Paul on the porch with his laptop on his knees, happily Skyping with his buddy, Brent, back in Maryland about their hero, mathematician Andrew Gleason. Paul took full advantage of the on-again, off-again unprotected wireless signal drifting our way from some good Samaritan in the settlement across the channel on Hawksbill Cay.

Hawksbill settlement: year-round home to two hundred souls, serviced by a marina, two boat yards, three churches of unaffiliated (but competing) denominations, a tiny branch of the Royal Bank of Canada, a hardware store, the Cruise Inn and Conch Out restaurant, and Harbour Market, the grocery store where we bought most of our supplies. Rush hour on Hawksbill Cay was two golf carts passing on the six-foot wide ribbon of concrete grandly named The Queen's Highway.

On Bonefish Cay, where we lived, there were no roads.

Parking my swim mask on top of my head and leaving my snorkel to dangle loosely by my right ear, I turned and waded out in the direction of Hawksbill Cay, toward a white scar on the otherwise verdant shore less than a half-mile away where construction had already begun on a controversial resort. The offending slash was a runway, built to accommodate the Piper props of the poodle and pedicure crowd. From its denuded banks silt bled into the sea, an almond-colored cloud that flowed toward Hawksbill reef slowly but relentlessly, like lava, threatening to smother it. I prayed wind and tide would keep it well away from our little corner of paradise, pristine Bonefish Cay.

Through the gin-clear water at my waist, I noticed a starfish, tangerine-red and the size of a dinner plate, ghosting along the bottom on little tube feet. I held my breath, bent down and picked it up. The starfish felt hard and spiky under my fingertips as I turned it gently, admiring the intricate lines and dots that both delineated and decorated its five, perfectly symmetrical arms. Paul tells me that if enough of the central disk is included, a whole new starfish can be regenerated from each severed arm. Very cool. Too bad the same thing doesn't apply to women, and breasts.

The drone of an engine shattered the silence. Wouldn't you know it? The first time I decide to do something even remotely risqué, a plane flies by. I scrunched down, heart pounding, hoping the pilot was too far away to notice that I was naked. As I cowered in the water, the little Cessna strafed the palms on nearby Beulah Point, then skimmed the Sea of Abaco like a red and white dragonfly before alighting on the unfinished runway across the way. Danger past, I stood up, then laughed out loud when I realized I still held the starfish in front of me like Gipsy Rose Lee performing at Minksy's. I released the remarkable creature and watched it drift to the bottom where it could get on with its work.

Fish, I understand. Starfish, I admire.

I adjusted my face mask over my eyes and nose, wrapped my lips around the mouthpiece of my snorkel and swam out, stroking steadily, toward Barracuda Reef. Beneath me, the sand gradually became a meadow of undulating sea grass. Above me, at the water's surface, a ghostly school of trumpetfish parted politely to let me pass, then regrouped and continued on their way.

Before long, the reef came into view; a grey-blue mound at first, then a yellow splash of brain coral emerged, a red tree sponge, a purple fan. I trod water for a moment, gently bobbing, then kicked hard and swam off in a clockwise direction. I preferred to approach the reef from the east where a splendid rack of elkhorn coral arched, forming a natural gateway to the wonderland beyond. Carried by the tide, I drifted through.

Sun and clouds above, light and shadow below. I smiled inside my mask. It was like living inside the Monterey Aquarium, only a thousand times better. I floated over the secret underwater world until its inhabitants began to take me for granted.

Ink-black sea cucumbers waved at me from their crevices. Yellowtail damselfish frisked about, their electric-blue spots twinkling like jewels. A bright-orange squirrelfish, his eye a black-ringed target, pecked at something in the sand.

But I was looking for my friend, Big Daddy.

He was hard to miss, Big Daddy, a two hundred and fifty pound grouper as big as a college linebacker. I swam on, checking behind an outcropping of brain coral, peering down into ragged holes that damaging storms had torn into a delicate organism already bleached out and weakened by global warming. Corals grow slowly, painfully slowly, some no more than the width of a dime in a year. If something isn't done...

I shook away the thought as a splash of green caught my eye. A moray eel gaped at me from his hidey-hole like a malevolent snake, displaying an impressive set of needle-like teeth. I gave the eel a wide berth, and swam on, still looking for Big Daddy.

I found him a few minutes later, lurking territorially behind a purple fan coral. He floated there soberly, considering me with large, lugubrious eyes, mouth turned down in a perpetual frown, like Winston Churchill after the Blitz, but without the cigar.

A school of yellow jacks flashed by; Big Daddy ignored them. He ignored a pair of stoplight parrotfish, too, as they nibbled away on the coral – algae for breakfast! – with an audible click-click-clicking sound. Suddenly Big Daddy shied away, ducking, squeezing his enormous body – unsuccessfully – under an overhanging coral shelf.

I barely had time to wonder what had spooked the big fellow when something flashed in the periphery of my vision. A dark shadow was speeding in my direction, sleek as a dolphin, fast as a shark.

I froze, heart pounding, wishing I had worn my swim fins so I could paddle out of there in a hurry.

False alarm! No need to panic. The newcomer

was my husband, wearing only a mask, flippers and a weight belt, and carrying a Bahamian sling, the slingshot-like speargun locals used for fishing.

When Paul surfaced next to me, I yanked the snorkel out of my mouth so I could say, 'I thought you were working.'

Paul grinned, his cheeks creasing handsomely around his face mask. 'I got bored.'

'You? Bored? With your buddy, good old Andy Whatshisname?'

With his free hand, Paul caught my arm and pulled me gently toward him. 'It might have had something to do with looking out the window and seeing a naked woman on the beach.'

He planted his lips firmly on mine and drew me under the water. When we came up for air, I said, 'What will Big Daddy think?'

'I don't know,' Paul said. 'Let's try it again and see.'

I waved him off, indicating the speargun. 'What's that for then?'

'Dinner.'

I splashed water in his face. 'As tired as I am of frozen, oddly shaped cuts of could-be-pork, could-be-lamb, if you shoot any of my friends...'

'Don't worry,' Paul said. 'Until I get the hang of this gizmo, your friends are perfectly safe from me.'

An hour later as I was standing in the outdoor shower, rinsing off salt and sand under a jet of warm water, Paul called to me from the other side of the latticework screen that separated me from the outside world, in the unlikely event that peeping Toms were lurking in the mangroves.

'Mutton snapper!' he crowed.

I rinsed shampoo out of my hair and reached over the door, groping blindly for the towel I'd left draped over a hook on the dry side of the screen. 'Mutton?' I asked, thinking I hadn't heard him correctly. Eventually, my hand made contact with the towel and I was able to drag it into the enclosure with me.

'It's a beauty,' he said. 'Come see.'

I toweled off vigorously, wrapped the towel around my body and tucked the loose end under my arm to secure it. When I stepped out on to the concrete apron surrounding the shower stall, Paul was standing so close that I nearly ran into the catch of the day. He held the fish by a gloved finger hooked into its open mouth and was turning the creature slowly, giving me time to admire its size, and the way the sun glistened on its iridescent, peachy-gold scales. 'Ten pounds if it's an ounce, Hannah. Dinner enough for four.'

'You, me and who else?' I wondered.

'Someone's home at *Southern Exposure*,' Paul said. 'Must have arrived on the ten o'clock ferry.'

We'd met only a few of our neighbors, the island being largely deserted during hurricane season, but I knew from the printout our

19

landlords left tacked to the wall next to the telephone, that a family named Weston owned *Southern Exposure*, and that they came from somewhere in North Carolina.

I squinted eastward over the mangroves and fringes of casuarina that separated our compound from the Weston's and noticed the Bahamian flag – turquoise, yellow and black – flying from what had been a bare pole that morning. As a courtesy to the host country, it was customary to fly the Bahamian flag any time one was in residence. A similar flag was beating itself to a frenzy on our flagpole at that very moment.

An odd custom, I'd thought, when we first arrived on the island. Why announce to potential thieves, once the flag was pulled down, 'Hey, fellas, we're gone! Come help yourselves.' Good thing crime was practically unheard of in the islands. Hawksbill Cay had a constable, though, uniform and all. I'd seen him. He ferried over from Marsh Harbour, the capital of the Abacos, every Wednesday from ten to two, the only hours in the week that the bank was open.

Nevertheless, it paid to be careful. That's why homes owned by foreigners had caretakers, a hereditary position often handed down from father to son.

The caretaker for *Windswept* was Forbes Albury; his family had lived in the settlement at Hawksbill Cay ever since 1780 when great-great-great-something grandfather Albury was shipwrecked on South Man-O-War reef during deadly hurricane San Calisto. Mr Forbes (as everyone called him) took a proprietary interest in the property, not surprisingly, since his father, Mardell Albury, had constructed it for a Canadian horticulturist, nail-by-nail and board-by-board, back in the mid-sixties. Mr Mardell and his father before him, Mr Bertram, were legendary shipbuilders. Mr Forbes was married to Mrs Ruth; Mr Ted, who owned the grocery, to Mrs Winnie – on an island where more than half the phone book was taken up by Alburys, what was the point of a last name?

Leaving Mr Paul to pound his chest manfully in celebration of his triumph over Mother Nature, I, Mrs Hannah, dashed barefoot to the orchard and snatched some underwear, clean shorts and a T-shirt off the clothesline. Hopping around on the front porch a few minutes later with one foot in and one foot out of my shorts, I called over my shoulder, 'You caught it, you clean it, sweetheart,' then trudged off through the casuarina and dense mats of Bahamas grass to introduce myself to our neighbors and see how they felt about joining us for supper.

Two

HAVE A GOOD DAY! UNLESS YOU HAD OTHER
PLANS.

> Doc Thomas, aboard *Knot on Call*

The moon woke me, shining so brightly through the window that I thought it was already dawn.

Wearing the oversized T-shirt that was about as sexy as my sleep wear got in the Bahamas, I padded to the kitchen and punched the button that would turn my coffee pot from an inanimate chunk of glass and plastic into a magic elixir machine.

Alerted by the gurgle, Dickie, the stray tabby we'd adopted, emerged from under the back porch, stretched luxuriously, then waited patiently at the back door for his morning bowl of kibble. A hard-knock-life cat, Dickie was difficult to approach, but I was gradually making headway. Strangely, I'd never heard him meow.

After feeding Dickie, I carried my coffee to the front porch, settled into the overstuffed cushions tied to the wicker love seat and waited for sunrise, sipping slowly. Across the harbor, boats rocked gently on their mooring balls and somewhere in the settlement Radio Abaco was playing gospel music, a raspy voice so amplified as it drifted across the water that I could make out every word: *Never would have made it, Never could have made it without you.*

The moon floated low in the western sky as the east became tinged with gold, and then peach, and then pink merging with a swathe of red so intense and so bright that the whole horizon appeared to be on fire.

'Oh, wow!' I commented to the cat. He'd finished his breakfast, padded from the back porch to the front, and plopped himself down at my feet. He began cleaning himself with elaborate tongue strokes, straightening his fur, stripe by stripe after a hard night's work in the orchard.

'Catch any Bahamian ground squirrels, Dickie?'

Dickie paused in mid-lick, favored me a languid stare, but otherwise didn't comment.

'Squirrels?' Paul appeared out of nowhere, settled a kiss on the back of my neck, slopping coffee on to the wooden deck as he did so. 'Oops, sorry.' He tried to erase the spill with the toe of his deck shoes. 'I didn't know they had squirrels in the Bahamas.'

'They don't.'

'Don't? What are you talking about, then?'

'Rats. Fruit rats. *Rattus rattus*, if you want to get technical.'

Still holding his mug, Paul walked to the bench-like wooden railing that separated the porch from the sea and sat down on it. 'I haven't seen any rats.'

'That's because there's a bumper crop of oranges in the orchard. Why would they go out for hamburger when they can have steak at home?'

Paul laughed out loud. 'Remind me about *Rattus rattus* the next time I'm harvesting oranges for your Bahama Mamas.'

The oranges in our orchard were bumpy-skinned, large and plump, far seedier and juicier than their Florida counterparts, but way too sour to eat. We used them in drinks, and for cooking, just as you would a lemon.

'You, sir, are the hunter-gatherer. The fish last night, for example. The vote is in. Delectable. I rest my case.'

'Nice to get to know the Westons. Too bad they aren't staying longer.'

Nick and Jenny, we had learned at dinner, were just down for a long weekend, preparing the house for the arrival of Nick's mother, Molly, in a few days' time. Molly, her daughter-in-law claimed, was a sprightly seventy-two. Molly'd been coming to the Abacos since the mid-fifties when her parents first sailed there in a fifty-two foot wooden ketch. I looked forward to meeting her.

Paul turned a chair to face the sunrise, and sat down. He propped his feet up against the rail. 'Red sky in the morning, sailor take warning, red sky at night, sailor's delight.'

'Huh?' I'd been distracted by the cat who had gone from a sprawl into a crouch, his rear in the air, tail switching. He'd spotted a curly tail, and if the silly lizard didn't move, he was going to be somebody's breakfast.

Paul gestured with his mug. 'Red sky. Maybe rough weather ahead.'

I scanned the sky from horizon to horizon. 'There's not a cloud in the sky, Paul.'

'We'll see what Barometer Bob has to say about the weather on the Cruisers' Net, then,' he said, checking his watch. 'An hour to go.'

'Do you have anything that needs washing?' I asked, thinking that if all that red-sky foolishness came to pass, I'd better run a load through and get it hung out to dry while my solar dryer – the tropical sun – was still operational.

'Plenty of time for that, Hannah. Come on.' Paul grabbed my hand, pulled me to my feet, and led me down to the end of the dock where *Pro Bono*, the little outboard that came with the rental, was tied. There was a wooden bench there, too, with *Windswept* stenciled in white letters on the side facing the harbor, so people could find us. Houses had names, not numbers, in the Bahamas.

It was our habit to take our morning coffee on the bench, admiring the passing show, and we were seldom disappointed: night herons, sea turtles, the occasional dolphin or two. A magnificent eagle ray cruised by, white spots freckling its inky-blue body. As he broke the surface,

I recognized him by a nick on his right wing: 'Ray' we had named the big one. His wife 'Marlene' sleeked along behind, followed by two smaller rays that we imagined were their children, 'Dick' and 'Jane'.

After some impressive acrobatics, Ray and his family moseyed on.

Paul and I sat in companionable silence until the first workboat of the day steamed into the harbor at high speed. As it neared our dock, the vessel slowed its engines politely, then chugged past, leaving a wake that gently licked the sandy shore. The open-deck boat was packed with Haitian workers from Marsh Harbour, laborers who constructed the island's homes, built its boats, and tended its gardens, sweating all day in the hot sun until the boat took them away exhausted at five.

'Does Daniel come today?' Paul asked. Daniel was the gardener employed by our land-lords to keep the tropical vegetation under control.

'What day is today?' I wondered. It's easy to lose track of time in the islands.

'Hmm.' Paul closed his eyes as if a calendar was written on the inside of his eyelids. 'I think it's Thursday.'

'If it's Thursday, it's Daniel.'

'Do you want to pick him up, or shall I?'

I patted my husband's bare knee. 'I don't mind. I rather fancy a boat ride this morning. Besides, we need eggs, and the grocery opens at eight.'

We carried our empty mugs back to the house where I changed quickly into shorts and a T-shirt. A few minutes later I was back at the end of the dock slipping my feet into the bright-orange Crocs I kept in a plastic milk crate under the bench. I untied the rope that held *Pro Bono* to the dock, slipped a loop around the piling, then climbed down the wooden ladder into the boat. I twisted the throttle to the full position, and pulled the starter cord. The engine sputtered to life on the first go. I flipped the rope off the piling and rammed the gear into forward, setting off across the narrow channel at a pretty good clip. Once I reached Hawksbill harbor, I eased *Pro Bono* into a space at the government dock between two rubber dinghies, cut the engine, climbed up the ladder, and made the boat secure.

Daniel Noel, a tall, ebony-skinned Haitian dressed in clean, but well-worn chinos and an open-neck shirt, was waiting for me as usual, leaning against a telephone pole in the shade of a sapodilla tree. He carried his lunch in a blue and white Igloo Playmate.

'Bonjou, Daniel.'

'Bonjou, Missus.' Daniel picked up his Igloo and waited politely for me to proceed down the dock ahead of him.

'Komon ou ye?' I asked.

'N'ap boule.'

I raised a finger. 'En minit,' I told the gardener, not completely exhausting my Creole vocabulary, but close. 'J'ai besoin des oeufs,' I

27

said, switching into French. 'Eggs,' I added in English to cover all bases.

Daniel touched a finger to his ball cap, nodded in acknowledgement, and headed toward *Pro Bono* with a loose-limbed stroll.

At the end of the dock where it T-bones with the Queen's Highway, there's a vacant lot. Well, not completely vacant. Twisted tree stumps languish among waist-high weeds, and the cinder block foundation of a house sits on the corner, with five concrete steps leading up to nowhere. Victims of hurricane Jeanne. I stopped for a moment, puzzled, because the yard looked more vacant than usual.

The signs. That's what was missing. Protest signs hand-painted on plywood sheets of varying sizes that until recently had been nailed to the tree stumps and propped up against the stairs.

SAVE HAWKSBILL CAY REEF!

SHOW THE DOOR TO EL MIRADOR!

OUR HERITAGE IS NOT FOR SALE TO
FOREIGNER DEVELOPERS!

RESPECT THE LOCALS!

Ninety-eight percent of Hawksbill Cay residents had petitioned against the development, so sentiments ran high.

Still wondering what had happened to the

28

signs, I turned left and followed the road one hundred yards or so to the Harbour Grocery, a building the size of your average two-car garage and painted Pepto-Bismol pink. Neatly stocked, the Pink Store, as it was known, carried just about anything you'd need, and if they didn't have it, Winnie Albury would order it for you. I'd already put in a request for disposable diapers (Huggies, size three) for when my daughter, Emily, and her brood came to stay over the Christmas holidays.

I opened the glass door, appreciating the blast of air conditioning that immediately enveloped me, then browsed my way along the neatly stacked shelves. Pasta and spaghetti sauce, soups, olives, jams. I remembered I needed tomatoes, so I picked up a can, then turned the corner, snagging a box of Dorset cereal, before hustling to the end of the aisle where the six-packs of soft drinks were stacked. 'Boat came in yesterday,' Winnie called after me.

Oh, joy! I knew what that meant. Half and half. I passed up the sodas and opened the sliding glass door of the fridge, selected a pint of half and half – ultra-pasteurized, but who was complaining? – clutched it lovingly to my bosom, then added a pound of bacon to the pile. On my way past the vegetable cooler, I seized on some fresh strawberries.

Winnie kept the eggs out, British style, un-refrigerated. I plucked a carton off the shelf, added them to my stack, and laid everything on the checkout counter where Winnie rang them up. 'Ives,' I reminded her.

'At *Windswept*,' she said with a smile, easing open the drawer where she kept the receipt books. She extracted the book with 'Ives' printed in block capitals on the spine, added the total '12.35' to the figures already on the page, then rotated the book on the counter so I could initial the entry. At the end of the month I would visit the store with my checkbook and pay our bill in full. I liked that in a grocery.

'What happened to the signs?' I asked Winnie as she tucked the box of cereal into my bag and snuggled it up to the cream.

'Vandals broke 'em up, set 'em on fire,' she explained in a lyrical island drawl. A little bit Southern with a touch of Merrie Olde Englande.

'Kids?' I was appalled.

Winnie shook her head, raised an eyebrow and fixed me with a look that seemed to say, *Our kids? Wouldn't put up with any of that foolishness, I can tell you.* But Winnie was a woman of few words. 'Wasn't, was it?' she said.

'Who, then?' I asked. It was hard to imagine any churchgoing, law-abiding grown-up on Hawksbill Cay stooping so low. Nobody even locked their doors in the settlement.

Another customer had come in, so I stood at the end of the counter while Winnie rang him up, punching the keys on her adding machine a bit more energetically than absolutely necessary. She jerked her head in an eastward

30

direction. 'Someone at that development, I reckon.'

She was referring to El Mirador Land Corporation, the developers of the Tamarind Tree Resort and Marina, the people responsible for the naked slash that spoiled the view of Hawksbill Cay from my living room window. 'Is anyone going to replace the signs?'

'Wood's expensive.'

Too true. *Everything* was expensive in the islands. From groceries to engine parts to generators and refrigerators, all had to be brought in by boat. And the Bahamian government added insult to injury by tacking a 30 percent duty on to items imported from non-Commonwealth countries. That's why we suffered without Cheerios and Fritos and bought Irish Gold butter for one-third the price of Land O' Lakes.

'That's the second time it's happened,' Winnie said after the other customer had left the store.

I picked up my shopping bag and adjusted the loops over my shoulder. 'Has anyone complained to El Mirador about it?'

Winnie plopped down on her stool, slumped against the wall, looking small and defeated. 'What good would it do?'

If it had been up to me, I would have marched out to the Tamarind Tree Resort and Marina, demanded an audience with the manager and insisted on an explanation. There might have been some finger pointing and fist shaking

31

involved in the confrontation, too. I wondered who was in charge over there.

'I'll look around *Windswept* and see if there's any spare plywood lying about,' I said as I went out the door. 'Could you use it?'

Winnie crossed her arms over her bosom and smiled. 'Could do.'

Daniel was waiting for me in *Pro Bono*, reading his Creole Bible. He'd had a hard-knock life, too – leaving a wife and two daughters behind him in Haiti when he immigrated to Abaco looking for work. Meanwhile, he was living in a migrant workers' community on the outskirts of Marsh Harbour, a community with a name that pretty much said it all – The Mud. No tourists of my acquaintance were standing in line to acquire a foothold in paradise by purchasing property in The Mud, or in Pigeon Peas either, the other area of the island where foreign workers were allowed to build their shanty towns.

Yet Daniel always seemed happy. Perhaps his faith kept him going. He certainly carried that Bible with him everywhere. One day at lunchtime I'd come upon him sitting on the porch of the bunkhouse, reading it aloud: *Seyè a se gadò mwen, mwen p'ap janm manke anyen.* I'd majored in French at Oberlin, so I picked up the gist of it: *the Lord is my shepherd, I shall not want.* From Daniel's lips, the Psalms of David. I had hurried away before he noticed the tears in my eyes.

'Votre famille va bien, Daniel?' I asked as I joined him aboard *Pro Bono*.

'Tre byen,' he answered in Creole.

I cranked the engine to life, and before long, Daniel and I were racing back across the harbor in *Pro Bono*, the wind tearing at our shirts.

'Quel beau jour!' I shouted in French over the roar of the engine.

'Bel jou, bel jou,' he agreed.

At *Windswept* Daniel swung his Igloo up on the dock, climbed the ladder with the rope in his hand, looped it around a piling in a neat half hitch, then waited for me to climb the ladder, too. Then he picked up his Igloo and headed in the direction of the tool shed where he kept the machete, rakes, and shovels with which he held the tropical vegetation at bay. Daniel didn't need any instruction from me. He'd been working steadily at *Windswept* for over a year.

I found Paul in the dining room tucking into a bowl of generic cornflakes. The VHF radio was on and tuned to Channel 68. It sputtered to life every minute or so as cruisers and local businesses called in to request spots on the Net. I toasted a slice of coconut bread, slathered it with butter, then sat down next to my husband to listen.

'Good morning, Abaco! This is the Abaco Cruisers' Net, on the air every day at this time to keep you informed with weather, news and local events. This is Jim Thomas aboard *Knot on Call* broadcasting from our peaceful anchorage in Marsh Harbour.'

'Where's Pattie?' I pouted, disappointed that the regular anchor, Pattie Toler, wasn't moderating the Net that day. VHF radios are like glorified walkie-talkies: you can pick a channel, but only one person can talk at a time. And everyone tuned in to that channel can hear everyone else, like an old-fashioned party line. Pattie, who invented the whole Net idea back in the mid-1980s, famously kept everyone organized, and was a natural-born comedienne, too.

'Pattie's dealing with potcakes,' Paul told me.

I'd enjoyed many Bahamian dishes during our time in the islands – like boil fish and souse and Johnny cake and guava duff – but I'd never heard of a potcake. 'What's a potcake?'

'It's a dog,' Paul explained. 'A mongrel. A mutt. Heinz 57. Some creep abandoned a couple of potcake puppies behind the Buck-a-Book trailer a couple of weeks ago. In an incredible downpour, too. Pattie's delivering them to adoptive homes in Ft Lauderdale.'

Poor potcake puppies. Did everyone have a hard-knock life in the islands?

'Someone figured Mimi would take care of them,' I said. Mimi Rehor's passion was the wild horses of Abaco. The Buck-a-Book used bookstore – a dollar a book – helped to support that effort. But she took in stray dogs, too.

'Gentle to moderate breezes, southeast to southwest at five to ten knots. Scattered clouds. High 86, low 72. Same for tomorrow. And the day after that. But what else is new? It's July in the Abacos.'

34

When Jim moved on to the ocean passage reports, *Latitude Adjustment* called in from the Whale where the waves could be high and the going pretty tough if the wind and the tide were against you. But there were no worries that day at the Whale. 'Flat calm,' the caller reported. 'You could waterski through there.'

'Guitarist Clint Sawyer at Curly Tails on Friday night,' Jim announced, continuing with local events. 'Come hear the "Music Man" and watch the sun go down.

'Steak BBQ at the Jib Room on Saturday. Music and dancing to follow.

'Sunday pig roast at Nippers Beach Bar and Grill, starting at 12:30!

'Nightlife as usual in the Abacos.'

I had moved away from the table and was busying myself with the breakfast dishes when an announcement on the Net caught my attention.

'Here's your invitation to an arts and crafts show and wine tasting this coming Saturday at Island Designs in Marsh Harbour. Starting at two thirty it continues till – well, until you're done. Wine is provided courtesy of Brenda Claridge at Tupps, and Cassandra from the Cruise Inn and Conch Out is cooking up a storm, so bring along your appetites. You'll find Island Designs near the turn-off to the Abaco Beach Resort, just down the road from Ziggy's. No tickets required, just show up. US dollars, Bahamian dollars, or max out your credit cards. Be there or be square.'

Paul read my mind. 'That sounds like fun, Hannah. Want to go?'

I shook out the dish towel and draped it over the oven door handle to dry. 'You bet.' The last event I'd attended in Marsh Harbour was a session at the Anglican Parish Hall on the predatory lionfish. It concluded (unexpectedly, at least for me) with a lesson on how to cook the critter without getting stung by its poisonous spines. Too much information, to my way of thinking.

'A rubber dinghy lost somewhere between Hope Town and Matt Lowe's Cay.

'A boat seat cushion found floating at the entrance to Marsh Harbour.'

And the Net, for that day, was done.

Paul gathered up his papers and his laptop and headed off to the porch while I checked the water level in the cistern, the 30,000 gallon concrete tank that was under the front porch. This involved getting down on my hands and knees, lifting the two-by-two-foot hatch and peering into the dark, drippy depths where water bugs the size of mice were likely to play. Nearly full. So I washed a load of laundry and hung it out in the orchard to dry.

While Paul worked, I spent the rest of the day lying in the hammock reading and feeling guilty. But not very. I'd had a bit of a hard-knock life, too. I gazed over the top of my book, past my bare toes and beyond to the porch railing where a curly tail crouched, puffing up his red throat to attract the attention of some

36

invisible lady lizard. In the front yard, Daniel was raking, drawing lines and gentle swirls in the sand, like a Zen garden. It was therapeutic just to watch him. Past Daniel was the beach, and beyond it, the vast turquoise expanse of the sea.

Yes, I thought, after all you've been through, you deserve a little time in paradise, Hannah.

Three

HOW CHEERFULLY HE SEEMS TO GRIN, HOW
NEATLY SPREADS HIS CLAWS, AND WEL-
COMES LITTLE FISHES IN WITH GENTLY
SMILING JAWS!
　　　　　Lewis Carroll, *Alice's Adventures in
　　　　　　　　　　　　　Wonderland*, 1865

Saturday dawned sunny and warm, but the
wind was piping up. With my morning coffee in
hand, I stood on the porch and stared out at the
white caps that were chasing from one
shoreline to the other across the Sea of Abaco.

'That's a pretty good chop,' Paul said behind
me. 'I don't think we'll be taking *Pro Bono*
over to Marsh Harbour today.'

I agreed. The thought of powering an
eighteen-foot outboard into the teeth of the
wind, slamming into the waves – *thwack,
thwack, thwack* – taking spray across the bow
until water was ankle deep in the cockpit, made
me shudder.

At eleven fifteen, Paul tuned to Channel 68
and hailed the ferry. We waited for the boat as
usual at the end of *Windswept*'s dock.

The *Donnie X* was bang on time, with Brent Albury at the wheel. We watched, marveling, as Brent reversed engines and backed the big vessel slowly up to the dock where it idled, gently kissing the pilings. We hopped aboard.

I plopped down gratefully next to my husband on one of *Donnie*'s vinyl-covered benches, joining a group of passengers that swelled to thirteen as we stopped for pickups at Hawksbill and Man-O-War Cays. Brent went easy on the gas as he guided the vessel gingerly between the narrow cut that formed the entrance to Man-O-War, but juiced it up to full throttle when he reached the open sea. *Donnie* seemed to revel in the freedom; the boat reared up and roared through the channel between Sandy and Garden Cays, cutting through the chop like a hot knife through butter. Even the waves seemed to lie down before him.

Twenty minutes later, Brent eased the ferry into its regular slip at Crossing Beach just east of Marsh Harbour. We stepped off, strolled past the long line of cabs waiting for passengers and walked west on the main road, covering the half-mile or so to Island Designs in about ten minutes. Cars drive on the left in the Bahamas, so we walked to the right, facing traffic, taking advantage of the sidewalk – where there was one. When it inexplicably disappeared, we walked in the street, expertly dodging puddles and speeding cars as all the locals do.

Behind the banana-yellow wooden building that housed Island Designs and two other shops, a huge tent had been erected. Paul and I followed a pod of camera-bearing, flip-flop-wearing, German-speaking tourists inside.

Just to our left, Andy Albury's hand-carved half-ship models were for sale, the natural beauty of their grain enhanced by what must have been hours of sanding and varnishing by hand. The booth next to Andy's had been reserved by his daughter, Sonya, who was holding up one of her signature straw totes to give a customer a closer look. We passed up the artist who seemed to be specializing in celebrity portraits on black velvet – Puh-leeze! Will they *never* go out of fashion? – in favor of Kim Rody's vibrant acrylic-on-canvas seascapes. Whether painting sea turtles, blue-striped grunts, angel fish or rock lobster, the Fishartista's swirling brush strokes seemed to imitate the movement of water. Two booths down, I got distracted by a necklace to die for by Linda Schleif – an artist who lived on a boat in Hope Town marina – and when I looked up, Paul had gone. Promising Linda I'd return later, I went off in search of my husband.

I caught up with Paul at a booth displaying large, sofa-sized aerial photographs of the Abaco islands. Smaller versions of the photos, the vendor's samples, were encased in plastic sleeves and stored in notebooks, one for each island group. Paul was flipping through the one labeled Man-O-War. 'Check this out,' he said when he noticed me breathing down his neck.

Sandwiched between Man-O-War Cay to the

east and Scotland Cay to the west, little horse-shoe-shaped Hawksbill Cay stood out like an emerald in a sapphire sea. Bonefish Cay, our island home, lay to the south-east, a half moon that formed a natural, protective barrier for Hawksbill's harbor. If I squinted, I could make out our cottage on tiny Beulah Bay, and to the south of it, the speck of light blue that was my favorite swimming ground, Barracuda Reef.

I ran my fingers over the plastic-covered image of our little piece of paradise. 'Buy this for me?'

Paul, bless him, produced his credit card and arranged to have a sixteen by twenty inch copy of the photograph packaged and shipped back home to Maryland where our godson was house-sitting for us.

'Thank you!' I gave him a peck on the cheek.

'This is thirsty work,' Paul said, as he tucked his credit card back into his wallet. 'Do you think you can locate the bar?'

It wasn't hard. That was where the line was. When our turn came, Paul bought us each a glass of Sauvignon Blanc. We carried our glasses outside into the sunshine where another line had formed in front of a booth bearing the sign:

Hors d'Oeuvres Compliments of
'Cruise Inn and Conch Out'
Visit Us on Hawksbill Cay
We Monitor Channels 16 and 68
www.cruiseinnconchout.com

Paul and I were making do with pineapple and cheese on a toothpick, and engaging in idle chit-chat while waiting for the line to go down so we could get a crack at some of Cassandra's amazing conch fritters when, behind me, somebody laughed.

I turned to see a woman wearing a flowered, halter-top sundress and strappy sandals talking to a guy in a white polo shirt and chinos. The woman I recognized from a picture in *The Abaconian*, Pattie Toler, goddess of the Net. Her brown, shoulder-length hair glinted with red highlights in the sun, and she'd caught it back at the sides with tortoiseshell combs. I had no idea about the guy, except to say that he was tall, bronzed and drop-dead, be-still-my-heart gorgeous. Think James Bond, of the Sean Connery persuasion, except Hispanic.

I elbowed Paul. 'That's Pattie Toler,' I whispered. 'I want to meet her.'

I was insanely curious about the guy she was talking to, too, but I didn't think it wise to mention it.

I waited, watching for an opportunity to interrupt their conversation, twiddling my empty toothpick. Pattie pulled a cigarette from a pack in her purse, paused – presumably to ask the guy if he minded – before she put it between her lips and lit up. Pattie inhaled deeply, turned her head politely to the side to exhale, then continued talking.

Meanwhile, I polished off two carrot sticks

and a piece of celery. When Paul took my wine glass away for a refill, I muttered, 'Screw the wait,' and wandered closer to Pattie and her companion. I hovered silently, but conspicuously at her elbow.

She acknowledged me immediately, almost as if she were glad for the interruption. 'You look like you could use some champagne.' She toasted me with her empty flute.

'I could. Thanks.'

Pattie glanced around the tent, raised her glass and, as if by magic, a server materialized, carrying a tray of champagne. Parking her cigarette between her index and middle fingers, Pattie set her empty flute on the tray and snagged two fresh ones. 'Here,' she smiled as she handed me one of the glasses. 'I'm Pattie Toler. *Blue Dolphin*.'

'I figured,' I said, returning the smile. 'I'm Hannah Ives. My husband and I...'

I was about to add our particulars, but she already knew. Pattie Toler, moderator of the world's largest party line, knew everything. '*Windswept*, on Bonefish. You're the ones who found that stray dinghy last week, right?'

'Guilty. It fetched up against our dock one morning. Belonged to one of the cruisers in Hawksbill Harbour who was very surprised to wake up and find himself stranded in the middle of the harbor with no way to get ashore.'

'Except swim,' drawled her companion.

'There is that,' I said, turning to study the speaker more closely. Movie-idol good looks,

43

impossibly white teeth. The kind of mature guy who always gets the girl.

Pattie slapped a hand to her forehead. 'Where are my manners? Hannah, this is Rudolph Mueller. Rudy owns the Tamarind Tree Resort and Marina. Been gone for a few weeks. Flew in on Wednesday.'

'Testing the runway,' Rudy grinned. He took my hand in his cool dry one and gave it a gentle squeeze. 'I hope we'll have the pleasure of entertaining you at the Tamarind Tree some time.'

'We've been meaning to...' I sputtered, my knees suddenly turning to jelly as Rudy's dark-chocolate eyes augured into mine. 'My husband and I,' I stammered. 'Uh, maybe for our anniversary.' I'd become a gibbering idiot. Had Rudy peered out his cockpit window and seen me naked? He certainly was giving me the impression he had.

He still had hold of my hand. 'We're soon to open the restaurant, Hannah. May I call you Hannah?'

I nodded stupidly.

'We've gutted and completely remodeled the old Tamarind Tree. And I've hired the chef from El Conquistador in Fajardo.'

'Fajardo?'

'Puerto Rico.'

'Ah.'

'He starts on Emancipation Day.'

'Oh.'

'August first.'

'Right.' I couldn't put two words together to make a sentence.

'So we're having a banquet,' Rudy continued, finally releasing my hand. 'Prix fixe. Forty dollars. Benicio...' He paused, smiling. 'Our chef, Benicio Escamilla Ávalos, perhaps you have heard of him?'

I shook my head.

'Well, no matter. What's important is that Benicio prepares the best crack conch you will get anywhere.' He laid a hand on my shoulder.

An electric charge, I swear, passed from his body into mine. And, damn the man, he knew it. 'So we can count on you, then? And your husband, too?' He raised an eloquent eyebrow that hinted at *perhaps your husband will fall ill, or be lost at sea, or abducted by aliens, then fortunately we...?*

Somehow I managed to breathe. 'We'll be delighted, I'm sure. And speaking of food,' I rattled on, finding my voice at last, 'the conch fritters here are to die for.' I gestured toward the Cruise Inn and Conch Out's booth where Cassandra and Albert Sands were scuttling about, catering to the ravenous hordes.

'The competition,' Rudy added, although from his tone, it was clear that he didn't consider the Sands' modest, homestyle Bahamian restaurant any competition at all. Frankly, I'd take Cassie's fried plantain over any highfalutin Paris-trained chef who whipped up the same dish and put it on the menu as *banane frite*, but I was polite enough not to say so.

While the three of us chatted, a young, twenty-something beauty showed up at Rudy's side, hovering proprietorially. Trophy wife? She was dressed in an ankle-length floral skirt and a bright-yellow tank top that complimented her lightly bronzed skin. Voluptuous raven curls were twisted into a knot at the crown of her head and held in place with a tortoiseshell claw. When the conversation wound down, she touched Rudy's arm and said, 'Papa?' neatly trashing my trophy-wife theory.

'*Qué quieres, mi pequeña joya?*'

'I've got a prospective buyer, Papa. I could use your help.'

Rudy took his daughter's hand, tucked it under his arm, then turned to Pattie and me, bowing slightly. 'Duty calls. You'll excuse us, then, ladies?'

Pattie answered for both of us. 'Of course.'

I took a deep breath and let it out. 'Who is she?' I asked when father and daughter had disappeared into the tent.

'That's Gabriele Mueller, Rudy's daughter, as I'm sure you gathered. He's got a son living on Hawksbill, too. Rudy's wife...' She lowered her voice. 'Wife number two. She stays back in San Antonio with the twins. They must be four or five years old by now. And if they weren't enough of a handful, I hear they're adopting an infant from Columbia.'

'Speaking of adoption, how did it go with the potcake puppies?'

'Super! Both potcakes were adopted by a

46

couple in West Palm Beach. Funny little sausages. The dogs, I mean. Terrier and collie with a smidge of dachshund thrown in.'

I chuckled at the image. 'We missed you on the Net the other day.'

She waved her champagne flute. 'Someone had to accompany the pups. It's difficult to fly them out commercial, so we chartered a flight with Cherokee.' Pattie raised an eyebrow. 'Say, how long are you here for?'

I was puzzled by the non sequitur. 'Six months,' I told her. 'Paul's writing a book and he hopes to finish by December. Then we'll have the family down at Christmas time.' I managed a weak grin. 'Alas, Paul has to go back to teaching in early January.'

Pattie tapped out the months on her fingers. 'I have to go Stateside on family business in a couple of weeks and I need someone to anchor the Net while I'm away. You always seem at ease on the radio, Hannah.'

I pressed a hand to my chest. 'Me? You're kidding, right? How about that doctor on *Knot on Call*?' I paused, trying to remember the captain's name. 'Uh, Jim. He did a great job this morning.'

Pattie shook her head. 'Jim's starting back to Virginia Beach around the first. He says he can't afford the hurricane insurance for *Knot on Call*, and he's already pushed his luck by overstaying six weeks.'

'Surely there's somebody...' I began.

'It's a piece of cake,' she insisted. 'Really. I

47

give you the script, you fill in for a couple of days just to get in some practice, and then ... *voilà!*'

I felt myself weakening. 'How long are you going to be gone?'

'Just two weeks.' Her cinnamon eyes locked on mine. Her neatly groomed eyebrows arched expectantly. A friendly smile played across her lips.

I was doomed.

'Sure,' I told my new friend. 'Why ever not.'

Pattie raised her empty glass and clinked it against mine. 'I think that calls for a toast, don't you?' And with a friendly 'Don't go away!' Pattie Toler went off in search of more champagne.

A few minutes later, Pattie got cornered by a sunburned vacationer who wanted to pick her brains about ATM locations, so I took the opportunity to slip away and look for Paul. I found him back inside the tent, standing in front of a booth where the main attraction was a meticulously constructed scale model protected from curious fingers by a Plexiglass dome. A banner in the colors of the Bahamian flag – turquoise with yellow lettering shadowed in black – announced that this was the booth sponsored by the Tamarind Tree Resort and Marina.

I'd read about the controversial development in *The Abaconian* like everyone else. And I'd seen the clubhouse, too ... through binoculars. But seeing the master plan laid out before me in

48

all its ambitious and arrogant splendor was an eye-opener.

The miles of pristine sand beach were still there, but where acres of mangrove and rare Abaconian pines had once stood, there was a marina, and condos, and single-family homes, and vacation cottages, laid out on a series of man-made canals. Next to me, Paul leaned over the case and tapped the glass. 'That represents the clubhouse,' he said, 'and the swimming pool. They're mocked up in color, because they're already complete. These others here,' he added, indicating the housing complex, the tennis courts and the eighteen-hole golf course, 'are in gray, as they're still under development.'

'Eighteen holes? You've got to be kidding.'

Paul gave me a sideways-through-the-eyelashes look. 'It's supposed to be eco-friendly. Paspalum grass, run-off management, natural methods of pest control. Gabriele has been filling me in.'

'Gabriele?' So, Rudy's daughter had been a busy little bee. My husband must have been the 'hot prospect' she'd dragged her father off to see.

Paul straightened and hooked his thumbs in his back pockets. 'She's managing the project for her father, the developer, a guy by the name of Rudolph Mueller.'

'I've just met Rudy. Pattie Toler introduced us.'

Now it was Paul's turn to act surprised. 'Rudy, huh? First name basis already?'

49

I grinned. 'It's the i'lans, mon.' I lowered my voice to a whisper. 'I'm actually working myself up to hate the guy after all I've read about the evils of his development.'

Paul flashed me a crooked grin. 'Give the guy a break, Hannah. He's complied with every restriction the Bahamian government has placed on construction, and then some. It's a prime piece of property in one of the most beautiful locations in the world. Development is inevitable, and not necessarily by somebody so sensitive to the environment as this Mueller fellow seems to be.' Paul rested his hand for a moment on the Plexiglass dome. 'It's better than some alternatives I can think of.'

I scowled at my husband. 'I see you've been brainwashed.'

'Hannah, Paul. Now that you've had time to talk it over, I wonder if you have any questions?' The voice came from behind me, rich and smooth as a shot of Southern Comfort, taken neat.

I felt my face grow hot. Damn! How did Mueller sneak up on me like that? Why didn't he cough discreetly or wear squeaky shoes like everyone else? 'Paul's just been filling me in on your project here, Mr Mueller.'

Mueller held up an index finger. 'Rudy!' he reminded me.

Paul grinned sheepishly. 'Rudy's invited us to tour the Hawksbill resort, Hannah. See for ourselves what they're up to over there.'

I tried to dredge up a smile, but couldn't,

50

thinking of the destruction of habitat, the pollution, the chemical run-off from his freaking golf course that marine experts agreed would kill the fragile barrier reef in less than three years.

I must not have hidden these thoughts very well because Mueller said, 'I have a feeling you've been listening to our critics, Hannah.' He shuffled through a pile of glossy brochures that were fanned out on the table and selected one. He unfolded it to a color picture of a hawksbill turtle swimming free in the crystal-blue sea. Poor turtle, I thought, as I took the brochure from Mueller's fingers. Where will you lay your eggs when the dune buggies take over the beach?

While I leafed through the brochure, not really reading it, Mueller rattled on about reverse osmosis water plants and sophisticated sewage treatment systems. When he paused to take a breath, I said, 'Frankly, I can't see how your development differs all that much from the one up at Baker's Bay on Guana Cay and that has been an ecological nightmare.'

That disarming smile again. 'I hear what you're saying, Hannah, but we're much smaller scale than Baker's Bay.' He tapped the Plexi-glass dome. 'For example, we've reduced the size of the golf course from eighteen holes to nine. The land we save will be set aside as a nature preserve.'

When I didn't comment, he went on, 'And you've heard about our nursery?'

Oh, yes. I'd heard about the nursery, the

51

centerpiece of Mueller's so-called preservation efforts. According to something I'd read on the Internet, it worked like this: Before ordering his bulldozers out to level one of the last surviving barrier-island forests in existence, Mueller, or one of his cronies, dispatched workers to the muddy edge of the construction zone where they pried the orchids and bromeliads off trees that were about to be felled. Rare, air-breathing plants, those shooting stars of the forest that explode into bloom like Fourth of July fireworks in red, white, purple, and orange, end up in a greenhouse.

'It seems to me, uh, Rudy, that rare plants should remain in their natural habitat, not a plant zoo.'

That patronizing smile again. 'We'll be replanting them after construction is complete, of course.'

'Of course,' I scoffed. To pass the time until I could politely excuse myself, I pretended to be fascinated by a pie chart showing how many Bahamians would be employed by the El Mirador Land Corporation on Hawksbill Cay. Meanwhile, Mueller zeroed in on Paul. The next thing I knew, the love of my life had agreed to a tour.

I reached around Paul's back and pinched him, hard.

'When do you suggest?' Paul asked, unfazed by my primitive torture technique.

'Anytime.' Mueller handed Paul his business card. 'The number's right there. Call and we'll pop over in the launch and pick you up.'

I'd seen a picture of the launch in the brochure. A thirty-six foot Hinckley picnic boat that I knew cost half a million, easy. I refolded the brochure into a neat accordion and handed it back. 'We'll certainly think about it ... Rudy.'

'How about next Friday?' Gabriele Mueller had crept up on little cat feet, picking up the conversation exactly where her father had left off, almost as if she'd been eavesdropping. 'We're collecting a group at Mangoes and could easily swing by Bonefish Cay.' While my eyes engaged Paul's in a silent battle, Gabriele turned to her father, lowered her voice and said, 'Papa, that reminds me. You need to speak to high me about that.'

Mueller bowed. 'If you'll excuse me, then?' and hurried off to do Gabriele's bidding.

'High me?' I whispered to Paul.

To my embarrassment, Gabriele overheard. Or maybe she read lips. 'J-A-I-M-E,' she spelled, 'pronounced High-me. My brother hates it. When he was in high school, he wanted to be called "Duke."'

Her laugh was infectious, as effervescent and intoxicating as champagne. Not the Nobile sparkling wine from Argentina that Tupps was serving that evening, oh no. Something high-end, I thought, like Veuve Cliquot.

'Jaime is the Spanish equivalent of James. A perfectly fine name, if you ask me. But you didn't, did you?' That laugh again.

'Is your brother here today?' I inquired.

53

'He's over there.' Gabriele waved a heavily ringed hand. 'Next to the bar. That woman with him? That's Alice. Jaime's wife.'

Wife? I drew a breath. The fragile teenager who fluttered at Jaime's elbow couldn't have been more than sixteen. She was dressed like a teeny-bopper, too; white denim jeans that could have been sprayed on her rail-thin legs, and an elasticized hot-pink tube top that defied the laws of gravity. Gold hoop earrings the size of saucers banged against her neck as she tiptoed around on a pair of Tommy Bahama high-heeled slides.

But Paul's eyes were glued on Gabriele's. 'So, tell me about the tour.'

Rudy Mueller may have left the room, but he'd clearly sent in The Closer. I knew I'd never drag Paul away until we made an appointment for their stupid tour, so I acquiesced as gracefully as possible, and we settled on Friday.

'Rain or shine!' Gabriele beamed attractively, lavishing attention on Paul who was grinning like a sap.

'Rain or shine,' I repeated so sweetly that I hated myself for it. I wouldn't want to cross the Gulf Stream in an open-decked boat, but a Hinckley was so solidly constructed that it could handle such a voyage, easy. If a little rain or wind dared stir up the Sea of Abaco on Gabriele's watch, it would be small potatoes for Daddy's Hinckley.

Gabriele handed Paul a card. 'My cell, just

in case.'

Paul tipped the card to his eyebrow in an informal salute. 'Until Friday.'

She beamed. 'Friday.'

'So,' I said as we wandered out of the shelter of the tent and into the sunshine. 'You planning to buy me one of those waterfront cottages as an anniversary gift?'

Paul tugged playfully on my ear. 'Of course, darling. We must have a spare million lying around somewhere.'

'Hold that thought,' I said. 'Meanwhile, we can pray for a movie deal on that geometry book you're writing.'

By the time four o'clock rolled around, the local conch population had taken a hit. Light munchies had been replaced on the buffet by mounds of fried conch, conch fritters, conch salad, conch chowder, and conch stew. A selection of desserts had also appeared: silver dollar-sized key lime pies, pecan bars, banana cake. Al and Cassie Sands kept the platters full, shuttling back and forth from a portable kitchen set up in the parking lot.

I picked up two plates from the end of the buffet table and handed one of them to Paul. 'Conch, conch or conch?'

Paul raised a hand, palm out. 'Maybe later. Will you be OK while I go check into that snorkeling expedition I told you about?'

Earlier Paul had pointed out a booth – 'Dive Greater with Gator' – decorated somewhat hap-

55

hazardly with fish painted on pieces of drift-wood. Holding a fried conch strip between my thumb and index fingers, I used it to wave my husband buh-bye. 'You snooze, you lose, sweetheart!' I dipped the conch into some tartar sauce, and popped it into my mouth. 'Mmm,' I moaned, licking my fingers.

Paul blew me a kiss. 'You're a heartless woman, Hannah.'

From behind the buffet table, Cassie beamed.

Conch can sometimes be tough, like eating rubber bands, but Cassie's was sweet and oh-so-tender. 'What's your secret, Cassie?'

'You don't want to know.'

'Seriously?'

'Seriously. It involves ageing, like beef.'

Cassie was right. It didn't bear thinking about.

As much as I was enjoying the conch, I wondered what the Sands would do if the Baha-mas' supply of the giant sea snail got fished out. Key West, Florida, I recalled, was nicknamed the Conch Republic, but nobody'd been allowed to fish conch commercially in Florida for decades.

I was suddenly aware of somebody standing at my elbow. 'I see you're enjoying our local fare,' Jaime drawled. A younger clone of his father, Jaime's face was spoiled by a plump, pouty mouth, but he was still a dangerously handsome man, if you preferred guys with gold chains tangled up in their chest hair.

I piled spicy conch salad on a cracker without comment.

'My sister tells me you'll be visiting Hawks-bill soon,' the young man quickly added.

'That's right.' Gabriele must have sent out an all-points bulletin. Maybe they were tag-teaming me.

Jaime staggered to one side, set his empty wine glass down on a corner of the buffet table and snagged a cold Kalik from a passing waiter.

'It must be nice having a successful family business,' I said as I watched Jaime wave off the glass being offered and drink his beer straight from the bottle.

Jaime wiped his mouth with the back of his hand. 'It's just one of the projects my father has developed all over South America and Mexico. This is our first here in the Caribbean.'

Technically, the Bahamas are in the South-west North Atlantic, not the Caribbean, but I didn't feel like correcting him. The British Virgins, St Kitts, the Grenadines, the ABCs – Aruba, Bonaire and Curacao. *They* were in the Caribbean.

Jaime downed a crab ball and chased it with another swig of beer from the long-necked bottle. I was glad he wasn't my son. I'd slap him one upside the head and teach the brat some table manners.

I didn't know where Alice, his child bride, had been hiding out, but she tottered up to us then, rolled her baby-blues and whined attrac-tively, 'Jaime, I'm tired. I want to go home.'

'Not now, Alice,' her husband snapped.

She tugged on the sleeve of his polo shirt.

57

'Jaime, please...'

He jerked his arm way. 'Not now!'

Alice folded thin arms across her chest, and pouted. 'But, I...' she began.

'Shut *up*, I said!' His voice was so loud that conversation stopped all around us.

My heart went out to the child, standing quietly, head tilted to one side, shifting her weight nervously from one foot to the other. After a few moments, still eyeing the sad excuse for a husband who was making an elaborate show of ignoring her, Alice reached out a cautious hand and selected four miniature pies from the dessert tray. As Jaime droned on importantly about a development in Port-au-Prince that his father was going to let him manage, Alice studied each morsel critically, turning it this way and that, before depositing it on her plate.

Alice finally made her selection – a tiny key lime pie – and slid it into her mouth. Her eyes closed in ecstasy.

'...in the Pétionville area of Port-au-Prince, where there are more tourists,' Jaime concluded. He paused, as if expecting applause.

Dessert plate in one hand, wine glass in the other, I simply stared, dumbfounded, when Jaime bent his head close to his wife's ear and snorted, 'Oink, oink.'

Alice tried to swallow, choked, tears came to her eyes, whether from choking on the pie or on the insult, it was hard to tell, but I could guess. I was about to say something when there was a voice behind me, velvet, but firm. 'Jaime. I see you're monopolizing Mrs Ives.'

Rudy Mueller. My knight in shining armor, or rather Alice's.

'Not at all,' I lied. 'Besides, Alice and I were about to go check out some jewelry, weren't we, Alice?'

Alice's eyes darted from the uneaten desserts on her plate to me and back again. In my opinion, the skinny waif was in need of some emergency ravioli, so I said, 'Bring your plate with you, Alice.' I grasped her elbow and drew her away from the men.

'Thank you,' she whispered when we were out of earshot of her in-laws. 'I hate it when I get caught in between.'

I pointed to one of the pielets on her plate. 'Eat.'

Alice obliged. While she chewed, I said, 'Alice is a pretty name. I once had a great-aunt named Aliceanna. If I had more than the one daughter, I would have named her Alice.'

'My full name's Alice Madonna Robinson.' The girl's cheeks reddened. 'Mueller, now, I mean.'

'How old are you, Alice?'

'Seventeen.'

Alice looked fourteen, fifteen, max. I wondered if she was telling me the truth and if children were allowed to marry children in whatever South American country she and Jaime Mueller had been in when they decided to tie the knot.

'How long have you been married?'

'A couple of months. I met Jaime on a high-school graduation trip to Bonaire. After we fell in love...' She shrugged. 'I just never went home.'

'Where's home, Alice?'

'Chicago.'

'Your parents?'

'Oh, they're still there.'

'Have they...' I began.

Alice shrugged. 'They don't really care. To tell you the truth, Mrs Ives, I wasn't a very good daughter. Always getting into trouble. I think they were happy to get me out of the house.'

'I doubt that,' I told the girl, remembering how devastated we had been when Emily ran off after graduation from Bryn Mawr with the college dropout she later married. But at least Emily had graduated! The little-girl-lost standing next to me, her thin, fly-away hair floating palely above her bare shoulders, and the kind of porcelain skin that pinked up, rather than tanned, had barely made it out of high school.

'Are you happy, Alice?'

She smiled sadly. 'Mostly.' She seemed to consider her words carefully. 'Jaime's all right, Mrs Ives. It's just when he's been drinking...'

Boy oh boy oh boy. A recipe for disaster, I knew. My father was an alcoholic – is, I should say, but in recovery – but dad had been the sad sack, cry in your beer kind of drunk. Not Jaime, though. From what I'd just witnessed, booze turned Jaime into a loud-mouthed jerk. Apparently Jaime's father thought so, too, because he'd maneuvered his son into a corner by the bottled-water table, and if I read the body language correctly, Master Jaime was getting a good chewing out along with his bottle of Deer.

'Come with me,' I said to Alice. 'I'm thinking of buying a necklace and I could use your advice.'

I led the girl to a stall manned by a local woman who sold jewelry crafted out of natural materials – sea glass, coconut, tagua and other exotic seeds. I picked up a necklace made of graduated rings of polished coconut strung on twine and held it up under my chin.

Laughing, Alice shook her head no.

I picked up a smaller version, this one featuring bright-orange tagua slices and dyed bombona seeds. She cocked her head, studying the effect. 'That's better,' she said, 'but still no.'

While I was fingering another necklace, Alice spotted a pair of earrings made out of bits of colored sea glass – white, Milk of Magnesia blue, and Coke-bottle green – strung on delicate, sterling-silver rods. She held them up to her ears, checking out her reflection in a mirror that the designer was holding up for her. 'They're so beautiful!'

I had to agree. 'Go ahead. Get them.'

Alice hooked the earrings back on to the display rack. She shook her head, cheeks flushing. 'I'll have to ask Jaime. I forgot my purse.'

I didn't believe that for a minute. Unless I was way off base, Jaime kept his wife on a short leash. If she owned a single credit card, or had more than ten dollars to spend at one time, I'd have been greatly surprised. But I didn't want to embarrass her by saying so.

'How much?' I asked the shopkeeper.

'Twelve dollar fifty cent.'

I dug into my purse for twenty dollars Bahamian and handed the bill over. While the shopkeeper was sorting through her cash box looking for change, I lifted the card of earrings off the rack and held it out to Alice. 'Here. These are for you.'

Alice pressed a hand to her chest and stepped back, flinching, like a startled deer. 'Oh, Mrs Ives, I *couldn't*!'

'Yes you can. I insist.'

Alice stared at me, lips pressed together, as she came to a decision. Her hand shot out to claim the earrings, and she grinned like a six-year-old on her birthday. 'I'll pay you back some time, I promise.'

I watched as she unhooked the hoops she was wearing and replaced them with the pair of earrings I'd just bought her. She turned to face me and tilted her head from side to side. 'How do I look?'

'Beautiful,' I said. 'The blue glass perfectly matches your eyes.'

How was I to know that the next time I saw Alice Madonna Mueller, her eyes would be anything but blue?

We caught the last ferry home. Just. We'd lost complete track of time at the art show, overstaying so long that we had to hustle, blowing five dollars on a cab that dropped us at Crossing Beach with no seconds to spare. Paul pounded down the dock shouting, 'Wait! Wait!' after the departing ferry, but fortunately the driver had seen us coming, turned his side thrusters on, and eased the boat back to the dock.

We jumped aboard, and called out our thanks, barely getting into our seats before the ferry took off again, with us on it this time.

Close call. A night at a Marsh Harbour hotel, even the modest Lofty Fig, could set you back a couple of hundred bucks.

For that time of day, the Man-O-War ferry was surprisingly full. From the bags everyone carried, I deduced that half the population had been to Price Right for groceries and the other half had attended the art show, like we had.

The ferry had just nosed into Sugar Loaf channel when Paul said, 'There's somebody I'd like you to meet, Hannah.' He dragged me to the opposite side of the ferry where we sat down on the bench next to a rugged, suntanned fellow who'd spent so much time in the out-of-doors that his sandy hair, eyebrows and even his watery-blue eyes looked bleached. 'Hannah, this is Gator Crockett. He runs the dive shop on Hawksbill Cay.'

I leaned forward, my elbows on my knees, so I could talk to the fellow face to face. 'Paul tells me you're taking us snorkeling on Monday.'

'Yup. Over to Fowl Cay.'

'They say Fowl Cay's spectacular.'

Gator nodded wisely. 'Only place better is Snake Cay down Little Harbour way, but the wind's rarely in the right direction down there. Kicks things up.'

A potcake lay at Gator's feet, his wheat-gold head resting on his paws, liquid-brown eyes considering me soberly. 'Hey, pal.' I reached down and scratched the dog's ears.

'Name's Justice.'

I smiled. 'Good dog, good Justice.'

Justice rolled over and offered his stomach for some quality scratching. I obliged, and Justice's tail thumped happily until the ferry pulled in to Man-O-War and some of the passengers prepared to disembark.

Gator picked up his backpack and collected his dog. Holding Justice's leash, he stepped to the stern, put one foot up on the steps, then turned around and stuck his head back inside the cabin. 'Best not to get too chummy with Alice.'

I blinked. 'Why?'

Gator slung his backpack over his shoulder. 'Just saying.'

And he was gone.

Four

SO THEY PAVED PARADISE AND PUT UP A
PARKING LOT WITH A PINK HOTEL, A
BOUTIQUE AND A SWINGING NIGHTSPOT.
DON'T IT ALWAYS SEEM TO GO THAT YOU
DON'T KNOW WHAT YOU GOT 'TIL IT'S GONE
THEY PAVED PARADISE, PUT UP A PARKING
LOT.

Big Yellow Taxi, Joni Mitchell

How to recycle an ashtray.

In an uncharacteristic exhibition of do-it-yourself know-how, Paul had drilled three holes into the rim of a 1950-style melamine ashtray, threaded shoestrings through the holes, and suspended the ashtray from a hook just outside our kitchen window.

Voila! A bird feeder.

I'd filled the feeder with sugar water, and the bananaquits were frisking around, squabbling over a foothold on the wildly swinging perch. The yellow and black wren-sized birds were so tame that they'd sit on your hand if there's something in it for them. Try granulated sugar.

A dark shape passed over the sun, distracting

65

me for a moment from the cheerful little birds who were *squeek-squeek-squeeking* like wobbly wheels on a grocery cart. I craned my neck to see a frigate bird soaring effortlessly overhead, riding the thermals, his silhouette jet black against the blue sky. 'They've got eight-foot wingspans,' Paul informed me lazily from his spot in the hammock. 'Soar for days without flapping their wings, snatching food out of other birds' mouths.'

'I'm impressed,' I said, admiring the bird's forked tail, like a swallow, only twenty times bigger.

'That's how Man-O-War got its name, you know.' Paul swung his legs out of the hammock, stretched and shook out the kinks.

'I thought the island was named after a racehorse, or vice versa.'

Paul winced. 'A frigate is a warship, my dear, sometimes called a man-of-war.'

'Ah ha,' I said. 'Always useful to be married to someone with Navy connections.' I watched as he wandered into the back garden, picked up the business end of the hose and twisted the tap.

From the depths of my pocket, my iPhone began vibrating. 'Speaking of connections, darling, my phone demands attention.' When I pulled it out, I saw from the display that the caller was my daughter, Emily, but in spite of repeated hello-hello-hellos on my end, the signal was too weak, so I lost the connection.

Paul was conscientiously watering the banana tree, once weekly, per our landlord's instructions. Holding the phone loosely in my hand, I let him know that I was heading out to the point to see if I could get a decent signal.

I set out on the sandy path that circled behind the bunk house and led into the woods. Daniel and his trusty machete kept the path itself clear, but bushes grew tall and lush on both sides, forming a natural canopy over my head. The foliage was so dense in places that the sun could barely penetrate to the forest floor, but where it did, the delicate shafts of sunlight reflecting through the steam that rose from the rain-wet leaves made me feel like I'd wandered into an episode of *Lost*.

The path tunneled through the trees for another hundred yards or so, then opened into a clearing. Shielding my eyes from the blazing sun, I stepped out on to a jagged limestone cliff. Twenty feet below my feet the Sea of Abaco surged and foamed benignly against the rocks. I sat down on a primitive bench – two cinder blocks and a two-by-six – and punched in my daughter's number.

My granddaughter, as usual, picked up. 'Shemansky residence. Chloe Elizabeth Shemansky speaking.'

'Hey, pumpkin. It's your grandmother.'

'I know that!'

Of course she did. How many people called her 'pumpkin'?

'Did you get my postcards, Chloe?'

'Uh huh.'

'Does that mean yes?' I teased.

'The horse pictures were cool, Grandma. I like Bellatrix the best.'

At the ripe old age of eight, Chloe had two passions in life: ballet and horses. The wild horses of Abaco in particular, a critically endangered breed of Spanish barbs that had been reduced over the last century, by human intervention and habitat reduction, from a herd of several hundred to just eight – four stallions and four mares. Like the horses made famous by Marguerite Henry in her children's book, *Misty of Chincoteague*, the wild horses of Abaco had been shipwrecked on the island during the time of Christopher Columbus. But unlike Misty and her foals, DNA tests had proved that the Abaco barbs had been so isolated, their pedigree so pure, that they were unique in all the world.

'I'm looking forward to your visit, Chloe.'

'Can I see the horses?'

'Of course you can. I'll call the woman who takes care of them and arrange a trip out to the preserve.'

'Wanna know how my Brownie troop is raising money to help the horses?' Chloe asked.

'Of course I do. That's wonderful! How?'

'We baked cookies and cakes and went to the Naval Academy and sold them all to the Mids.'

It was a brilliant idea, and I told her so. Midshipmen had been known to eat just about anything, including baked goods prepared by eight-year-olds.

'We got two hundred and twenty-three dollars and thirty-five cents. When I come, I'm gonna give it all to W.H.O.A.'

W.H.O.A. The Wild Horse Preservation Society of Abaco. Never had an acronym been so apt.

'Where will I sleep, Grandma?' Chloe asked, suddenly shifting gears.

'You and Jake can sleep in the snore box.'

'What's a snore box?'

'When Bahamians need another bedroom, they don't build a room on to their house. They build a cottage nearby and call it a snore box.'

'I thought you said I could sleep in the bunk house.'

'It is a bunk house, but because people sleep in it, they call it a snore box.'

'I don't snore, Grandma.'

I decided to shift gears myself before this conversation with my just-the-facts-ma'am granddaughter started running in circles. 'Can I talk to your mother, Chloe?'

Chloe ignored the question. Something else was weighing heavily on her mind. 'Where's Timmy going to sleep?'

'Timmy can sleep in a bedroom with your mother.'

'Good,' she said, clearly satisfied. 'Well, bye!'

The line went silent for a few seconds, and then Chloe belted out 'Mommy!' so close to the mouthpiece that I feared it would rupture the teeny-tiny speakers on my iPhone. They were still working fine, though, when Emily came on the line a minute later. She told me she'd

69

arranged two weeks off from work, their e-tickets were already purchased, and all she needed was the ferry schedule. I gave her the URL for Albury's.

'We can't wait to share this magical place with you,' I told my daughter.

'It's going to be the best Christmas ever. You're terrific, Mom.'

'I may be aces in the Mom department, but I'm a failure as a housewife,' I confessed to Paul a few minutes later as we sat at the table having lunch, a couscous vegetable sauté with bits of his favorite spicy sausage thrown in.

Paul shoveled a forkful into his mouth. 'You could have fooled me,' he said, chewing thoughtfully. 'This is delicious.'

I'd planned macaroni and cheese, but mac and cheese was a challenge without milk. We'd barbecued the last of the steaks the night before and, in a weak moment, I'd fed Dickie the remaining can of tuna. Water-packed white albacore, too. I hope the greedy cat was grateful.

Tip for island living: Never run out of something on a Saturday night because the stores don't open again 'til Monday morning. Or, Tuesday, if Monday's a holiday. I was once caught for three days without eggs before becoming familiar with Bahamian holidays. Labor Day is the first Friday in June, Independence Day is celebrated on the tenth of July and Whit Monday, a moveable feast like Easter, can slide around and sneak up on you in May or even June. Hawksbill Cay residents took Sundays and their holidays seriously.

'Nothing in the cupboard for dinner, though,' I told him as I got up to clear my plate. 'Unless you want to go all caveman on me and club some protein to death.'

'Bahamian ground squirrels?' he suggested.

I snapped him with the dish towel. 'You could try fishing,' I suggested sweetly.

'I have a better idea. Let's go to dinner at the Cruise Inn and Conch Out. My treat.'

'Brilliant!' I kissed his cheek. 'I think I've tried everything except Cassie's curried crayfish.' I paused for a moment. 'Lobster's in season, isn't it?'

'August through March,' said my husband, trotting out his nautical knowledge once again. 'So unless she's got some frozen, you're out of luck.'

I folded my arms and pouted.

'Poor Hannah,' Paul said, rising from his chair with his plate in hand. It was his turn to do the dishes. 'You better call Cassie, though, to make sure they're serving tonight.'

While Paul squirted dish liquid into the sink and started the hot water going, I went to the radio, picked up the microphone and pressed the talk button. 'Cruise Inn, Cruise Inn, this is *Windswept*. Come in.'

'*Windswept*, this is Cruise Inn. Up one?'

'Roger.' I turned the dial to Channel 69 and pressed the talk button again. '*Windswept* on six nine.'

71

'Go ahead, *Windswept*.'

'Cassie, this is Hannah Ives. Just wanted to see if you were open tonight.'

'Sure thing. Just you and Paul?'

'Right. No visitors as yet, but I'm expecting our family over the holidays.'

'That'll be nice.' I could hear the clinking of crockery in the background, then white noise as Cassie released her finger from the talk button while she consulted the notebook in which she kept track of reservations. Several seconds later, she was back. 'See you tonight, then. Six OK?'

'Perfect. Thanks. *Windswept*, out.'

'Out.'

I slipped the microphone back in its slot, then turned to my husband. 'Five hours until dinner. What do you want to do in the meantime?'

Paul had been wiping the countertops down. He tossed the sponge he'd been using into the sink and crooked his finger at me. 'I have an idea.'

I walked into his open arms.

He cupped my chin, lifting it for a kiss.

As the bananaquits squabbled outside the window, I drew away and looked into his eyes. 'Uh, let me guess. Hunt for sand dollars?'

'Not exactly.'

'Hike around the island?'

'Nope.'

'I guess you'll just have to show me, then.'

So he did.

* * *

72

The sun was still high and the Sea of Abaco smooth as glass when we set out for Hawksbill Cay that evening in *Pro Bono*, dressed in our Sunday best: chinos fresh off the clothesline and long-sleeved T-shirts.

After crossing the channel and entering the harbor, Paul aimed *Pro Bono* straight for the government dock. Just as it seemed he would crash into a piling head-on, Paul shoved the tiller all the way to the right causing the boat to drift sideways where it came to rest neatly against the foot of the ladder, starboard side to. 'Show-off,' I said, as I clambered up the ladder with the painter in hand and tied the boat off. Paul followed, grinning hugely, carrying a tote of white wine.

Hawksbill Cay was dry, and you couldn't buy cigarettes there, either. There was no law against it. In this conservative, deeply religious community, it simply wasn't done. At the Cruise Inn and Conch Out, thank goodness, it was BYOB, and almost everyone except the locals did.

At the restaurant, we stepped into a blast of welcome air conditioning to find Albert standing behind the counter, drying glasses with a clean white towel. 'Hey, Al.'

'Hey!' A mountain of a man in any case, Al's ever-expanding waistline bore silent testimony to his wife's culinary talents. He wore his trademark tropical shirt tucked into Bermuda shorts belted low around his hips, Teva thongs on his feet. A diamond stud decorated his left ear.

The restaurant was already crowded, but I could see a few free tables. 'Where shall we sit?'

Al eased his bulk from behind the counter and escorted us to a table for eight near the door with a plastic 'Reserved' card propped up against the salt, pepper and D'Vanya's Junkanoo hot sauce caddy. As the popular restaurant filled up we knew we'd probably end up sharing a table with other diners, family-style, but that was sometimes half the fun.

Paul and I took seats across from one another at the end of the table farthest from the door. By the time we got settled, Al had returned with the menu, hand printed on a tall, narrow chalkboard with 'Cruise Inn and Conch Out' painted across the top in pink and orange script. He propped the chalkboard up on a chair and gave us time to study the selections while he went to fetch iced tea and glasses for our wine.

Around these parts, there are usually only four entrées: mahi-mahi, grouper, conch and lobster. It's how they're prepared that makes all the difference, and Cassie was a genius. No lobster, alas, but that night the mahi-mahi came broiled with a Parmesan cream sauce, and Al must have made a visit to the grocery in Marsh Harbour because there was a special – prime rib – heading up the menu.

No need to specify sides. I knew everything would be accompanied by coleslaw and by a rice and bean combination Bahamians called 'peas-and-rice'. Fried plantains, too, if we were lucky.

While Paul made up his mind, I looked around, checking out the other diners and admiring the décor. Plantation shutters covered the windows, with valences made of Androsia, a colorful batik woven and hand dyed on the Bahamian island of Andros, many miles to the south. Matching fabric covered the tables, which were protected from stains and splatters by paper place mats printed with a fanciful, not-to-scale drawing of Hawksbill Cay and the neighboring islands. Numbers on the map were keyed to local businesses whose ads framed the place mat.

One of Andy Albury's ship models hung on the wall over the salad bar, and paintings by other local artists decorated the remaining walls. One image in particular caught my eye, a huge satellite photo of Hurricane Floyd.

I excused myself for a moment to use the restroom, stopping on my way to take a closer look at the photo. At the moment it was taken, in September 1999, Floyd was a dense white donut almost six hundred miles in diameter, and the hole of the donut – the eye of the storm – was smack dab over Abaco. Floyd looked surprisingly benign from that altitude, yet underneath that snow-white swirl I knew that from the Abacos to Key West to Cape Fear, homes and lives were being devastated.

I found the restroom – a small room with two stalls – clean, as usual, and pleasantly pine-scented. Curtains made of patchwork Androsia covered the single window and hid the spare rolls of toilet paper, paper towels and cleaning supplies Cassie kept under the sink.

I did what I had to do and was washing my hands when the door to the other stall creaked open. In the mirror, I saw the reflection of a young woman wearing white shorts, a blue T-shirt, and a pair of oversized Jackie-O sunglasses. In spite of the sunglasses, I recognized her right away. I turned around. 'Alice!'

The girl smiled when she recognized me. 'Hi, Hannah.'

'You eating here tonight? I didn't see Jaime.'

Alice stepped up to the sink and twisted the hot-water tap. 'Nah. I was out taking a walk. Just stopped in to use the bathroom.' She put a finger to her lips. 'Don't tell.'

I laughed. 'I'm sure nobody minds.' Meanwhile, I wondered why Alice kept her sunglasses on indoors; the sun wasn't exactly blinding inside the Cruise Inn and Conch Out ladies room at six fifteen in the evening. Then I noticed a stain on her fair face, a purple discoloration that began at the corner of her eye, mutating into shades of green and yellow as it merged into the hairline at her left temple.

'Ooh,' I gasped before I could stop myself. 'What happened to your eye?'

'It's awful, isn't it?' Alice tipped the sunglasses up to her forehead so I could admire the damage. 'Jaime's got this sailboat and I didn't duck in time.' She waggled her fingers.

76

'There's this thingy that holds the sail.' She demonstrated by holding her arm out stiffly in front of her.

'The boom.'

'Boom. Yeah. It clipped me one.' She snatched a couple of paper towels out of the dispenser, dried her hands, chucked the used towels into the waste-paper basket and chirped, 'Well, gotta go. Nice talking to you.'

Leaving me with my mouth hanging open. And wet hands.

When dinner arrived at our table, Cassie served it herself.

People used to seeing Cassie standing behind a counter were often surprised by how slim her legs were, how trim her ankles. The heavy thighs and ultra-wide hips those delicate limbs supported had nothing to do with calories and everything with genetics. The islanders had been intermarrying for two centuries. Until recently, hereditary blindness had not been uncommon. After a study by the Baltimore Geographic Society early in the last century (which *still* makes the locals froth at the mouth!), the islanders had been encouraged to marry off-island, or to adopt. Cassie and Al – who were quadruple cousins – had taken this on board. Their daughters who charged around the restaurant when Cassie's mother wasn't available to rein the little girls in, were Korean, about as far off-island as you can get.

I was halfway through my mahi-mahi and

Paul was making headway on his steak when Al appeared at our table with a stranger in tow. 'Here's someone I'd like you to meet. Henry Allen, warden of the Out Island Land and Sea Park. You'll be snorkeling over there soon, I hear.'

I grinned. 'No secrets on Hawksbill, are there?'

Al grinned back. 'Henry, this is Paul and Hannah Ives staying at *Windswept* over on Bonefish. Paul's a professor at the Naval Academy in the States.'

I sighed. How about me? Did I have no identity? Not so long ago I was head of records management at a major Washington DC accounting firm. Considering the current financial climate, however, I had to confess my relief at being riffed *before* the company went belly up. So what was I now? Ex-records manager? Wife, mother, grandmother, sister, sister-in-law, friend? All these, yes, and survivor, too. But not exactly suitable abbreviations to follow my name on a business card.

'Join us, please,' said Paul while I was sitting there like a lump, feeling sorry for myself.

'What will you have to eat, Henry?' Al pointed to the chalkboard.

Henry didn't even consult it. 'The dolphin, if you've got it, Al. Broiled.'

When we first hit the Bahamas, seeing 'dolphin' on the menu had me worried. I quickly learned that 'dolphin' is dolphin fish. Mahimahi. Dorado. Weighs from ten to thirty

78

pounds, with a flat, protruding forehead. A dazzling golden, blue and green when pulled from the water, not a gray, bottle-nosed mammal like its namesake. Not Flipper, thank heaven.

'Broiled dolphin, coming up.' Al disappeared into the kitchen to turn in Henry's order.

Henry snatched off his ball cap to reveal a full head of densely curled auburn hair. He laid the cap on the chair next to him. 'There's a meeting over in Hope Town week from Wednesday,' he announced without preamble. 'A consortium of local citizens and second-home owners have banded together to try and stop Mueller's development.'

Remembering my conversation with Rudy Mueller and his daughter, Gabriele, at the arts and crafts show, I said, 'Mueller seems pretty sure of himself. He's already hiring, you know. Someone told me he's sending folks for training to one of his mega resorts in Cozamel.'

Henry moved a small bowl of butter pats aside and turned his place mat around so we could see the map on it. Using his fork, he drew a circle around Hawksbill, Bonefish, and several smaller, uninhabited cays to the east. 'This is my territory, the Land and Sea Park.' He dragged the tines down a long series of Xs that separated the islands from the Atlantic Ocean to the east. 'And this is the barrier reef.'

'I've heard it's one of the finest left in the world.'

Henry's gaze was firm, and steady. 'And I

79

plan to keep it that way.

'And, here,' Henry said, tapping a smaller cluster of Xs just to the north of Hawksbill Cay, 'is Fowl Cay where you'll be snorkeling next week.' He looked up, his bottle-green eyes alive. 'It *is* the finest reef in the world. Vertical drop offs, spectacular cuts, black coral forests, a couple of wrecks. And the sea life!' He laid down his fork and folded his hands. 'Octopus, giant grouper, lobsters as big and as tame as dogs. They've even got names.'

I nodded, thinking about my friend, Big Daddy.

With my finger, I reached across the table and retraced the circle Henry had drawn. 'But if all this area is within the protected boundaries of the park, how come Mueller's allowed to build on it?'

Henry scowled darkly. 'Grandfather clauses. The government wanted to protect the reefs, but there was no way to do it without including Hawksbill Cay where a lot of the land was privately owned. You must have noticed there's no commercial development on Bonefish Cay, where you're living.'

I nodded. 'And we like it that way.'

'A lot of the locals agree with you, but some...' Henry paused. 'Well, you can't blame them, really. It's hard enough keeping your kids from leaving the islands, deserting it for schools and high-paying jobs in the United States. And Mueller's development means local jobs, lots of jobs.'

'It's an uphill battle, isn't it, Al?' Henry continued as the restaurant owner appeared with a glass of ice and a Diet Coke and set them down in front of him. 'The development's already started. He's renovated the old Tamarind Tree restaurant. Turned it into a private club.'

'I know,' Paul put in. 'We've agreed to tour the resort next week.'

'Watch it, Ives. Mueller's slick. Before you know it, you'll be plunking down two, three million for a condo.'

I gasped. 'Two million? You've got to be kidding, right? For one of the mansions, maybe, but for a *condo*?' I'd been reading the real estate ads in *The Abaconian* – a girl can dream! – and there were a number of fine properties on the market. Custom-built, four and five bedroom homes right on the water had been listed for a hundred thou or two on either side of a million bucks. I couldn't imagine paying twice that much for a lousy condominium.

'I wish I were.' Using his finger this time, Henry traced along the southern shoreline of Hawksbill Cay. 'This is one of the finest pink sand beaches anywhere in the world. But visit it while you can, ladies and gentlemen, because if Mueller has his way, it'll soon be fenced off for the exclusive use of the American Express platinum card crowd.'

'Surely the government...' I began, thinking of the new Prime Minister's stated commitment to local rights, sustainable development and keeping the Bahamas for Bahamians.

Henry raised a hand. 'Don't get me started. The government's down in Nassau, and they don't give a shit what happens up here in the Abacos.'

I'd read about that, too, in a picture book *Windswept*'s owners kept out on a coffee table. The Abacos – deserted since the 1500s when the native Lucayans were wiped out by slave raids and European diseases introduced by the Spaniards – had been resettled in the 1780s by New Englanders coming by way of North Carolina, British citizens who had played for the losing side during the Revolutionary War. Two hundred years later, in 1976, when the Islands of the Bahamas sued for independence from Great Britain, Abaconians picked up their machetes and their pitchforks and protested. They appealed to the Queen, reminding her of their sacrifice and unflagging loyalty to the crown in 1776. But alas, the Queen and her Parliament were unmoved.

'So why?' I wondered.

The park ranger rubbed his fingers briskly together.

'Bribes?' Paul asked.

'Oh, you bet. I can't prove it – yet – but if you have some time, there's a videotape I want to show you.'

'Goody. I love home movies.'

Henry didn't return my smile. 'You know where the park headquarters are, right? On Little Hawksbill?'

When Paul and I nodded, Henry continued.

82

'We're the first cove on the Sea of Abaco side. The channel tends to silt up, so keep well to the left of the green marks. Come during the week, any time. We monitor 16 and 68, so give us a call so we know when to expect you.'

Al brought Henry's dinner, and we tucked in, chewing in appreciative silence as the restaurant filled up around us. I waited until Henry finished his slaw before asking, 'What's on the agenda for the Hope Town meeting?'

'We've got some experts coming in. They all agree that run-off from the fertilizer El Mirador's going to use on the golf course will kill the reef within three years, and the livelihood of our fishermen along with it.'

'So I heard. And the sewage from all those houses and condos isn't going to help the reef much, either.'

Henry pushed his empty plate aside. He took a deep breath and let it out slowly through his mouth. 'And the destruction's already started. Over the past several months, Mueller's workers have bulldozed acres and acres of mangrove.'

I nearly choked on the last of my plantain. 'But don't they know how important the mangroves are? When Cyclone Nargis roared through Myanmar last spring...'

Henry raised a hand, cutting me off. 'I know, I know. More than eighty percent of that country's mangrove forests had been destroyed, so the cyclone had an easy ride into the delta. An impressive loss of life, and much of it completely avoidable.'

'If there's another storm as bad as hurricane Floyd...' I paused, shook my head. 'Doesn't the Bahamian government get it?'

Henry scowled. 'I guess they have other priorities.'

'We can certainly come to the meeting,' Paul said, 'but we won't be able to vote on anything.'

'Doesn't matter. What we're looking for is a strong turnout, a show of force.'

'I can help with that.' I smiled at the park ranger. 'Pattie Toler's talked me into running the Cruisers' Net starting next Monday, so I'll plug the meeting in community announcements.'

Henry brightened at last. 'Sounds like our Pattie! Mention that Albury's running extra ferries out of Man-O-War and Marsh Harbour. No reason why folks can't make the meeting.' He laid both hands flat on the table. 'I really appreciate your help getting the word out, Hannah.'

'Do you have a website, Henry?'

'Yup. It's www.savehawksbillcayreef.com. We're a coalition of islanders and second-home owners. We can't dictate what Mueller builds on his own land, unfortunately, but where that impinges on our land, and our reef, then we have to speak up.'

I thought Henry had wound down, but he was just getting started.

'Guana Cay is on firmer legal ground, many

believe, because the Prime Minister at the time gave away, actually gave away crown land to a foreigner. Crown land is supposed to be reserved for the Bahamian people in perpetuity. For their children, and their children's children.

'Think about it this way. It's as if George W. Bush had said to some fat-cat developer in, let's say Japan, "Here's Yellowstone National Park. Take it, it's yours. Turn it into an exclusive gated community that only the ultra-rich can afford."' He picked up a fork and jabbed the air as if to punctuate his words. 'If the Privy Council doesn't find in their favor, the heritage of every Bahamian on Guana will be behind locked and guarded gates.'

He leaned back in his chair and let out a long breath. 'Good thing my wife's not here. She'd scold me for being long-winded. Just met you and here I am, already boring your socks off. On to other things. What's for dessert?'

'I have been reliably informed that it's banana cream pie.'

'Have you tried it?' When I told him no, he said, 'To. Die. For. Cassie doesn't mess with store-bought piecrusts or Cool Whip. Just bananas and cream. What a concept.' Henry waved his arm about like a schoolboy seeking permission to go to the bathroom. When he got Al's attention he called out, 'Pie all around!'

While we waited for our pie, I asked, 'Other than the experts and the folks from Save Hawksbill Cay Reef, who'll be there?'

'Officials from Friends of the Environment as

85

well as representatives of the Bahamas National Trust ... or so they say. They may just blow us off. It's happened before.'

I picked up my fork. 'Do we need to bring persuaders? Machetes? Bahamian slings?'

Henry leaned back in his chair, threw back his head and laughed. 'No. But hold that thought.'

Five

MIAMI, FLORIDA (MAR 5 2008) – SHARK-FEEDING TOURS TO THE BAHAMAS – LIKE THE ONE THAT ENDED LAST WEEK IN THE TRAGIC DEATH OF AN AUSTRIAN DIVER – ALSO POSE A THREAT TO ISLAND VISITORS NOT INVOLVED IN THESE EXPEDITIONS.

ONCE A SHARK LEARNS TO ASSOCIATE BOAT ARRIVALS AND/OR PEOPLE IN THE WATER WITH DINNERTIME, THOSE ASSOCIATIONS ARE REMEMBERED FOR A LONG TIME AND TAKEN WITH THE SHARK WHEREVER IT MAY WANDER – A RECIPE FOR DISASTER.
Bob Dimond, *Cyber Diver News Network*

At home, I typed www.savehawksbillcay.com into my browser. I couldn't believe what popped up on my screen. 'Meet Susie and her young teen friends! 15,000 pictures online! See Susie take it all off and get it on!' There was a picture of Susie, too, wearing three strategically placed daisies. She had more friends, *lots* of friends, if I'd only fill in my age and credit card number.

I stared at the URL, wondering where I'd gone wrong.

I clicked in the search box and retyped my query, this time in quotes. The site I was looking for was savehawksbillcayreef.com. Clearly, someone had hijacked Henry's URL, wanting to embarrass him. I wonder if he knew.

Putting on my researcher's hat, I went to Whois, and discovered that the imposter's URL had been registered only two months ago, to an owner who was clearly fictitious – Arthur Pendragon, 5 Butt Close, Glastonbury, Somerset, BA6, UK. Butt Close! Get real. To my absolute astonishment, however, when I googled the address, there actually was a 'Butt Close,' but number 5 was a parking lot.

Whoever he was, I felt like reformatting his hard drive using nothing but a baseball bat.

I decided to get rid of my pent-up frustration by doing something physical, so I spent twenty minutes prowling around in the overgrown lot that separated *Windswept* from *Southern Exposure*, turning up old paint buckets, battered boat dock bumpers, a ratty tarp and other tatty treasures. Eventually I found what I was looking for – a perfect, four-by-six sheet of plywood. Not sure whose property the lumber was actually on, I decided to drag it into Molly Weston's yard – leaving a drunken trail in the sand that would send Daniel scurrying for his rake – and propped the wood up against her generator shed where it could dry out.

The previous day, I'd run into Molly coming

out of the post office carrying a grocery sack of mail and a huge parcel with 'Molly Weston, Bonefish Cay, Abaco, Bahamas' printed on the side in black Magic Marker.

'You must be my neighbor, Molly Weston,' I said.

'How...?' Then she blushed. 'Might as well be wearing a name tag, huh?'

I relieved her of the package, and followed her down to her dinghy. Ten minutes later, we'd bonded instantly over tea and Scottish short-bread on the porch at *Windswept*.

Now I stood at the end of my new friend's dock where she'd hung a bronze bell of the sort used by teachers in olden days to call children in from recess. I grabbed the leather thong attached to the clapper and gave the bell a vigorous ding-dong-ding-dong-ding before starting up the sidewalk that led to Molly's deck.

'I'm he-ah!' Molly drawled from somewhere inside the house. 'Come in!'

I slid the screen door to one side and stepped into a brightly lit kitchen that opened into a pine-paneled living and dining room area offering a spectacular panorama of the sea.

Molly (or some Weston before her) certainly had a knack for interior design. A white wicker sofa and two matching chairs covered with flowered chintz and a scattering of pillows were arranged in a conversational grouping around a pot-bellied stove. Paintings by local artists decorated the walls. On a credenza behind the sofa Molly had arranged a collection of photographs. One, framed in sea shells, was an obvious family grouping. Everyone posed informally, arms draped casually around one another. I was trying to figure out where and when the photo had been taken when Molly entered the room.

'That's me at six,' she explained. 'With my mom and dad.'

'You look very tropical. I assume it was taken on Bonefish Cay?'

She nodded, pink lips parted in a wistful smile. 'A very long time ago.'

In the photograph, a muddy-kneed but otherwise immaculate Molly wore a white pinafore with red rick-rack trim, white ankle socks and white patent-leather Mary Janes. Six decades later, she seemed to favor the same color combination – white clam diggers, a red T-shirt, and white lace-up tennis shoes. Instead of pigtails, though, the grown-up Molly's hair was cut in a stylish wedge; silver strands feathered attractively over the tips of her ears.

'I found a sheet of plywood in the woods,' I said, getting straight to the point. 'I was wondering if it belonged to you.'

'Could be. There's a lot of trash in there. Found a sink once, and a rusted-out water heater.' She grinned. 'Where is it?'

'Down by your generator. Come see.'

When Molly surveyed the plywood a few minutes later, she said, 'From the nail holes I'd say it's an old hurricane shutter. Washed ashore.

Can you use it?'

'Do you mind? I promised Winnie I'd find some wood she could use for a replacement "El Mirador Go Home" sign.'

Molly's blue eyes sparkled. 'Why shu-ah. Need help?'

'Thanks. I was wondering how I was going to get it over there.'

'We can use my Zodiac. It's a little wider than *Pro Bono*. And I have bungee cords we can use to strap the wood on.'

I rubbed my hands together briskly. 'Let's do it!'

When I get to be Molly's age – seventy-two – I plan to be as spry and nimble as she. Barely one hundred pounds soaking wet, it was said Molly could single-hand her Zodiac inflatable in the worst of weathers, schlep bags to and from the grocery, and lift items so bulky that even Daniel stood in awe of her. 'Miz Molly, she work like a Haitian,' he had commented to me one day. It was a compliment.

By the time Molly and I had wrestled the plywood sheet to the end of her dock, eased it down the ladder, and secured it across the back of her Zodiac like an extra seat, Molly had talked me into a picnic lunch off her favorite beach. 'If you promise not to tell anybody,' she cautioned with a grin. 'Best beach in the world for collecting sand dollars.'

The Zodiac gobbled up the distance between Bonefish and Hawksbill Cays in half the time it would have taken me to single-hand the plywood over in *Pro Bono*. We delivered the wood to the government dock where, with Gator's help, we carried it down to the Pink Store and propped it against the bag ice machine. I popped into the store to let Winnie know where to find the plywood, then purchased sodas and chips to go along with the lunch Molly had thrown together. A few minutes later, leaving a rooster tail of water in our wake, we zoomed off in the Zodiac heading for Molly's secret sand dollar beach.

Wasn't so secret, as it turns out.

'Well, hel-lo,' I said as we neared the shore. 'Poinciana Cove, if I'm not mistaken. The very view from my porch, except up close and personal.'

Molly let the Zodiac drift to a stop about fifty yards off the beach in eight feet of water. I tied a fisherman's bend around the anchor rode, then, using the same knot, secured the other end of the rope to a cleat on the Zodiac, tying a couple of half hitches for good measure. When we had drifted well clear of the reef, I tossed the anchor overboard, and watched until it settled to the bottom and bit securely into the sand.

Molly peeled off her T-shirt, revealing the top of a dark-blue, racing-back Speedo. 'Back in the old days, twice a week sometimes three, Island Fantasy Tours would pack tourists into these honking big cigarette boats and haul ass over here from Treasure Cay. Put a lei around their necks and a beer in their hands and let them hang out barefoot all day. Dumb clucks thought they'd died and gone to Fantasy Island, for Christ's sake, with Tattoo running out of the jungle shouting, "De plane, de plane."'

I smiled, remembering that old TV show. Come to think of it, if you put Rudy Mueller in a white suit, he'd look a lot like Ricardo Montalban.

'Speaking of planes,' Molly said, pointing. 'There's the beginning of a landing strip.'

'Yeah. I can see it from our porch. You probably can, too. The silting is pretty bad, but so far, it seems to be flushing away from the reef and out through the cut into the Atlantic.' I picked up a pair of binoculars and squinted through them at the runway. 'I couldn't believe it when I noticed that Mueller's already using the airstrip. From here, it looks like it'd be a pretty bumpy ride.'

Molly snorted. 'He flies a Cessna 185 tail-dragger. Could land that thing on the back of a turtle, if he wanted to.'

We bobbed in companionable silence for a while, sharing a bag of potato chips. After a bit Molly said, 'Island Fantasy built tiki huts all along the beach. Set Porta-Potties out in the woods.' She paused for a moment to take another swig of her Pepsi. 'And a shark pen.'

'A shark pen?'

Molly nodded. 'For sixty-five dollars and change, you got to go down and feed lunch to the sharks.'

'What kind of sharks?'

'Tiger. Hammerhead. Lemon.'

What kind of crazy fool would think it was a good idea to swim with sharks? Dolphins, maybe, but *sharks*? I must have had skeptic written all over my forehead.

'I can see you don't believe me,' my friend said. 'But it's true. And there'd be somebody there to take underwater pictures of you while you're doing it.'

'Sounds dangerous,' I said.

'It is. You'd suit up in diving gear. Go down. Then they chum the water. You wouldn't have to wait very long for the sharks to show up.'

I shuddered. 'I think I'd rather walk barefoot through a nest of fire ants.'

'Me, too. There's a big distinction between feeding lunch to a shark and becoming lunch for one.' She rummaged through her canvas bag and came up with a Tupperware container. Using her fingernails, she pried off the top and stuck the container practically under my nose.

I inhaled deeply. Ginger cookies. 'It would be rude to refuse, wouldn't it?' I said, reaching for one.

'Naturally.'

'The tiki huts are gone now, of course,' Molly said, crunching into a ginger cookie of her own. 'Hurricane Ivan took care of that. Or maybe it was Jeanne. You have to admit it's an improvement.'

'It's what they haven't gotten around to doing yet that concerns me,' I said, not really expecting an answer.

Molly had finished her lunch and was relaxing against the sides of the rubber dinghy with her hands folded behind her neck. 'This place used to be a popular spot for cruising sailors.'

'I can see why. The beach is spectacular.'

Molly laughed. 'It is, but that's not what I meant. When Daddy was alive, he used to dinghy out to sailors and share his Big Secret with them.' With her fingers she drew quotation marks in the air to capitalize the words. 'He'd advise them to come ashore on the Atlantic side. Then he'd explain how to find the path that went over the hill and down to the Island Fantasy property on the Sea of Abaco side. As long as you were wearing a Hawaiian shirt and had a camera dangling from a strap around your neck, you could enjoy the luau. Who's to know you didn't come over with the powerboat crowd? You could blend, pig out all day on free food and booze, then waddle off into the sunset, fat and happy. Daddy did it all the time. Dragged me along with him, too. I thought I'd die of embarrassment.'

I laughed out loud. 'I think I would have liked your dad.'

'What happened to Island Fantasy Tours?' I asked after a while.

Molly shrugged. 'I guess they got tired of rebuilding after every hurricane. Sold out to El Mirador in 2006.' She waved an arm, taking in the expanse of beach from east to west. 'All that natural beauty under private ownership. There oughta be a law.'

Molly busied herself putting away the remains of our picnic lunch. That done, she said, 'Tide's out as far as it's going to go. Are you up for collecting sand dollars?'

I picked up the canvas bucket that held our flip-flops and snorkel gear and held it aloft. 'Ready, willing and able.'

Leaving the Zodiac bobbing quietly at anchor, we stripped to our bathing suits, clapped the snorkel gear to our faces, and slipped over the side with me carrying the bucket.

'Drift along in the shallows,' Molly instructed when we reached the beach a few minutes later. 'Reach down and comb through the sand with your fingers as you go along.' While I stood in crystal-clear water that reached halfway up my thighs, she demonstrated, coming up a few seconds later holding a sand dollar in each hand.

I waded over for a closer look. One sand dollar seemed to be outfitted in a maroon-colored suit, like a fuzzy cookie. 'This one's alive,' Molly said, pointing out the tiny spines that covered the creature, obscuring its characteristic five-pointed star design. 'We're looking for ones that are already dead, like this whitish one here.'

Before long, we'd collected several dozen of the shells, some as large as saucers, others as small as a quarter. After each find, we'd wade ashore and deposit our haul in the bucket.

'That's so much fun!' I giggled as we sat resting on the beach with waves gently licking at our toes. 'I can't wait to bring my grandchildren here.'

Molly lay back, half reclining on her elbows, eyes closed and face to the sun. 'When you get the shells home, soak them in bleach overnight. Not too strong, or you'll weaken the shells. That'll brighten them up, get rid of any algae.'

I'd closed my eyes and was soaking up the sun, too, so the next voice I heard was so incongruous with a deserted beach in paradise that I nearly jumped out of my flip-flops.

'I'm sorry, but you'll have to leave now. This is private property.'

When I could breathe again, I turned in the direction of the voice.

Standing on the beach ten or fifteen yards behind us was a long-limbed, broad-shouldered security guard wearing the distinctive Tamarind Tree Resort and Marina uniform – khaki pants and a navy-blue polo shirt with the 'TTR' logo embroidered on the breast pocket, a stylized design of a man reclining under a pair of palm trees. Strapped to the guard's belt was a holster for ... I gulped. Could have been a VHF radio, could have been a cellphone, could have been a gun. I wasn't sure I wanted to get close enough to find out.

Next to me, Molly had pulled herself up to her full five foot three and a half inches and dug her feet into the wet sand. 'Private? No. It's not.'

Had she lost her mind?

The guard stepped forward. 'Ladies, I must ask you to leave the beach at once. Please return to your boat.'

97

'Young man,' Molly bristled. 'As a non-native, perhaps you are unaware of the laws governing riparian rights in the Bahamas. In the Bahamas,' she said, taking a couple of brave steps in his direction, 'one can only own land down to the high water mark. And as you can see, we're standing *in* the water. *Ergo*, we are on public land. *Quod erat demonstrandum.*'

The guard wore a puzzled look where his eyebrows nearly met. Perhaps Latin wasn't offered at his high school. 'Uh ... look, lady. I have my orders. You and the other lady here need to turn around now and go back to your boat.'

Molly scooped up our bucket of sand dollars, looped it over her forearm. With her free arm, she hooked mine. 'Come on, Hannah. I'm in the mood for a walk, aren't you?' And we marched lock-step along the beach, splish-splash-splish, carefully staying below the water line.

'You! Ladies! Come back!'

Keeping me firmly in her grasp, her hip snug against mine, Molly leaned over and whispered in my ear, 'Keep walking, Hannah.'

I could feel the guard's eyes burning a hole in my back. I imagined him drawing his weapon and taking careful aim. When nothing happened right away, I dared to look back. He stood precisely where we'd left him, waving an arm about while shouting into a cellphone, presumably requesting instructions from the mother ship. 'Too bad he's not using the radio,' I said to Molly as we scurried around a rocky outcrop and out of the security guard's line of sight. 'I'd love to listen in.'

'My radio's back on the Zodiac,' she reminded me.

'Silly me.' I collapsed against the trunk of a palm tree, slightly out of breath. 'What do we do now?'

Molly flashed a wicked grin. 'Well, Hannah Ives. Since we are *now* standing on private land in clear violation of El Mirador's property rights, we are already felons. So I vote we go exploring. I used to know this place like the back of my hand. Come on!'

Molly tucked the bucket containing our sand dollars into a thicket of sea grape, then hiked off over the dunes, moving quickly through a stand of waist-high beach grass with me hot on her heels. Before long the sandy trail gave way to a narrow, twisted path of jagged limestone, making me wish I were wearing sturdier shoes than flip-flops.

Ahead of me, Molly trudged doggedly on. The path zigzagged crazily up a long hill and wove through a stand of palms where it split. Molly took the fork to the right and continued up the hill. When I emerged from the trees, my breath caught in my throat.

Molly had stopped on the edge of a headland that extended out over the sea. Balanced on a large flat rock, she twirled in a circle, arms flung wide like Maria on her hilltop in *Sound of Music*, and I half expected Molly, like Maria, to burst into song.

She paused in mid-spin to motion me over. 'Take a look at the view!'

It was truly spectacular. Hope Town's historic red and white striped lighthouse clearly visible in the east. The sprawl of Marsh Harbour to the south. Dusty yellow clouds to the south and west where smoke from recent slash and burn wildfires hung over Treasure Cay. Scotland Cay, green and lush, to the west and, to the north, the vast expanse of the Atlantic Ocean. Next stop, Greenland.

'There used to be a house up here called Three-Eighty,' Molly told me while I was still trying to take it all in. 'Blew completely away in Hurricane Floyd.' She hopped down from the rock. 'But they had a snore box on the Sea of Abaco side, down in a little cove. I wonder if it's still there?'

Before I could reply, Molly practically skipped down the path we'd just come, but this time when she reached the fork, she turned the other way. Soon we were scrambling down a rocky trail, grabbing at bushes and holding on to tree trunks to keep our feet from flying out from under us. 'Where's Daniel when you need him?' I said as a branch slapped across my cheek.

Ahead of me, Molly had reached the beach. 'It's still here!' Triumph in her voice.

When I burst out of the undergrowth and joined her a few seconds later, we were standing on another pink sand beach at the base of a tiny cove. Behind us loomed the headland, dark

100

and dense with vegetation. I squinted into the foliage. 'Where?'

Molly had her hands pressed together like an excited child. 'See that speck of green over there?' She pointed, but I still couldn't make it out. 'That's a corner of the porch. Let's have a look.'

Although its paint was peeling, and morning glory and love-vine had reached out to claim it, the cottage was, indeed, still there. Of typical island board-and-batten construction, its windows closed and dogged down tight, the little house huddled in overgrowth, defying decades of often savage weather. I twisted the toggles that held one of the windows shut and tugged on the handle, but it refused to budge. 'Damn. Must be hooked on the inside.'

A woman after my own heart, Molly performed a similar test on the two remaining front windows with a similar lack of success. Undaunted, she moved around to the left side of the house while I nipped around to the right.

Where I found a door. With a big padlock. A shiny, heavy-duty, spanking-new Brinks. 'Molly!'

She was at my side in a flash. 'Well, what do you know!'

I grabbed the lock and jiggled it, but it was secure. I bent down for a closer look. 'Wish it were a Sergeant or a Master Lock. I could pick one of those with a couple of paper clips.'

'Do you have any paper clips on you?'

Since we were wearing only our bathing suits

I started to giggle. I pointed at Molly's hair, stiff with sea salt and standing out from her head in punk-like peaks. 'Or, I could use a couple of hairpins.'

Molly patted her head, then began to laugh.

'If nobody lives here, why the locks?' I asked a little bit later as we sat together on the porch, our bid for membership in the Breaking and Entering Club temporarily tabled.

'Family named Kelchner used to own this property. Maybe they still do.'

I shook my head. 'Nope. I've seen the maps. Mueller's development company owns everything to the west of Hawksbill settlement, all the way out to the point. Where we were standing up there? I think that's the ninth hole.'

Molly reached out and gave my knee a pat. 'Guess we better be getting back.'

But neither of us made a move to do so. Sea, sand, sun and sky ... inertia was a powerful thing.

One grows accustomed to the sounds of the tropics: birds chittering, seagulls jeering, lizards scurrying and locusts keening. It's when you don't hear anything that you notice. All of a sudden, the silence, as they say, was deafening. 'What was that?'

Somewhere over our heads, rocks clattered and all nature stopped to listen. Someone was stumbling down the same path we had.

Molly sprang to her feet. 'Let's get out of here. Quick! I know a short cut.'

The only way out that I knew was back the

way we had come, and already they were closing in.

'Down there!' a man's voice yelled. Whoever he was, he had not come alone.

A mini avalanche of rocks. A cry of pain. A curse.

'Shut *up*, you moron! They'll hear you.'

Molly had already reached the beach. She ducked into the mangroves, as dense in places as the briar hedge that grew up around Sleeping Beauty. I followed. Shielded from view, we fought our way along the perimeter of the bay, breaking out at last on to the beach of the adjoining cove.

Where Molly's Zodiac bobbed quietly at anchor.

I bent over, resting my hands on my knees, trying to catch my breath. 'You are a genius.'

'Local knowledge,' she panted.

We ran into the water, splashing wildly. I'd swum halfway to the Zodiac before I remembered the bucket of sand dollars.

'Leave them!' shouted Molly. Holding on to the side of the inflatable with both hands she kicked her feet and surged upwards, straightened her arms like pistons, and propelled her body neatly into the boat.

'It'll just take a minute!' I turned and stroked steadily toward the beach where I scrambled ashore and retrieved the shells. A few minutes later I was back at the Zodiac, handing the bucket of souvenirs over the side to Molly.

My re-entry to the Zodiac was far less

dignified than that of my septuagenarian friend. After three attempts, I managed to hoist myself over the gunwale where I balanced ignominiously on my stomach, planning my next move. Eventually, I managed to swing one leg over and roll into the boat, flopping to the floor, panting like a fresh-caught grouper.

'That was pretty ugly,' Molly teased as she grabbed the anchor line and started hauling in the anchor, hand over hand. 'You didn't *need* to go back for the sand dollars.'

'Yes I did.' I picked up the canvas bucket. 'See this?' I pointed to the place where the name of her Zodiac, *Good Golly* was stenciled in dark-blue paint.

Molly blushed down to her scalp. 'I take it back. It was an excellent plan.'

With Hawksbill Cay receding in the distance behind us, I said, 'What do you suppose they've got locked up over there?'

Molly shrugged. 'Equipment, most likely: solar panels, generators, outboard motors and air conditioners. That's the kind of expensive, hard-to-get stuff that tends to disappear in the islands.'

'It's just that...' I paused, trying to make some coherent arrangement of the thoughts that were ricocheting around in my brain. 'Why the hell does Mueller need all those freaking guards? And did you see that guy? I think he had a gun.'

Molly shook her head. 'It's virtually impossible for a Bahamian citizen to own a gun legally, and that includes security guards.

Bahamian gun laws are among the toughest in the world.' She paused. 'At least on the books.'

'Seven hundred islands, two thousand cays and God only knows how many miles of uninhabited shoreline, some of it less than one hundred miles off the coast of Florida. Why am I not reassured?'

Molly slowed, eased *Good Golly* up to her dock, and killed the engine. We made the boat secure, then headed up the dock with me carrying the bucket of sand dollars. 'Want to come up for a drink?' my new friend asked.

'Thanks, Molly, but I'm pooped.'

She gave me a thumbs up. 'Hannah and Molly's Excellent Adventure. We must do it again sometime.'

'You bet!' I smiled and waved.

As I meandered home along the path that led from *Southern Exposure* to *Windswept*, however, the smile disappeared from my face. Excellent? I wasn't so sure.

There are only so many ways one can phrase the words, 'Shut up.'

Shut up!

Shut up?

Shut up.

Shut *up*!

'Shut *up*, I said!' to Alice.

'Shut *up*, you moron!' to his security guard.

Those two words made me almost certain that the man crashing down the hill behind us had been Jaime Mueller.

Six

IT'S HARD TO BELIEVE, BUT THE ABACO
CRUISERS' NET HAS BEEN ON VHF CHANNEL
68 AT 8:15 A.M. EVERY DAY FOR EIGHTEEN
YEARS THIS DECEMBER. THAT'S 6,570 MORN-
INGS IN A ROW – IN SPITE OF STORMS,
WEDDINGS, BIRTHS AND DEATHS THAT HAVE
OCCURRED ALONG THE WAY.
> Pattie Toler, *The Abaco Journal*,
> December 2008

Hannah Ives, Net Control.

Could I be starring in a James Bond flick? Uh, would you believe an episode of *Get Smart*?

Seven fifty a.m. With a chair pulled up to the kitchen table, Pattie's 'bible' to my left and a spiral-bound logbook to my right, I opened to a blank page. Stuck to the table in front of me were a dozen Post-its where I'd jotted down information about community events so I wouldn't forget to announce them.

Microphone in my left hand, pen in my right and both eyes on the clock. Paul minding my coffee cup, keeping it full, but adding more sugar than I like.

The digital numbers on the clock ticked from 7:58 to :59 to :00.

Show time!

'Good morning, this is Hannah Ives at *Windswept* on beautiful Bonefish Cay. I will be your Net anchor today and I'm standing by on this channel now for anyone who would like to register early for the Abaco Cruisers' Net which will begin in fifteen minutes on this channel.'

During those minutes the airways clicked and hissed and hummed as listeners called in on their VHF radios, making appointments to talk. Using my notebook, I assigned callers to slots, depending on the category – community announcements, invitations, mail call, new arrivals, departures – on a first-come, first-served basis.

As part of the fun, Paul had come up with the daily trivia question – in what year did the first Americans come to Man-O-War Cay (stubbornly refusing to share with me the answer). Meanwhile, I confirmed with Stu Lawless on *Dances with Wave*s that he'd do the weather report.

When it came to Stu, Paul had serious radio envy. Stu received his email and weather information on a single-side band radio and could download satellite maps from remote anchorages all over the world in the twinkling of an eye. We got our weather from www.barometerbob.com, a reliable source. When the Internet signal cooperated, of course.

At 8:14 I flipped to channel 16. 'Good morning, all. The Abaco Cruisers' Net presents weather and announcements now on channel 68.'

And at 8:15, back on 68 I picked up Pattie's script and my microphone, pressed the talk button, and began reading.

'Good morning, Abaco. This is the Abaco Cruisers' Net on the air every day at this time to keep you informed with weather, news and local events. This is Hannah Ives at *Windswept* broadcasting from Bonefish Cay.

'Today is Monday, July twenty-eighth. If you think you may be calling in to the Net, please switch your radio to high power now so that everyone can hear you. Remember to use your call signs when calling in, so that I may answer you. I will repeat any messages that sound scratchy, but if you miss anything, feel free to ask me to repeat. You could do the same for me. If I appear to be ignoring a call, I'm not. Your relay will ensure that everyone is included, because, after all, the goals of this Net are safety, friendship and message handling.

'Weather, the first concern for all of us. We will get an updated weather report now from Stu on *Dances with Waves*.'

While Stu reported on the weather – sunny, but the chance of squalls later in the day – I sipped some coffee, hoping the caffeine wouldn't make me more jittery than I already was. Maybe in a few days I'd be as relaxed as Pattie always sounded, able to lean back and plan what to fix for dinner that evening – chicken in the freezer, a nice eggplant, a handful of oddly shaped but flavorful heirloom tomatoes from Milo's stand over on Guana Cay – but at that moment, I was a caffeine-fueled, microphone-clutching, tightly wound spring.

'Winds three to five out of the southeast.' Stu was wrapping up. 'And if you're wondering about those smoke clouds over northern Abaco this morning, brush fires have been reported on the old Bahama Star farm, so let's hope this change of direction doesn't help them to spread. *Dances with Waves* out.'

I pressed the talk button. 'Now that we are up to date on the Atlantic seas,' I announced, 'we need to check close to home on the sea state of the Sea of Abaco. For this report we always trust Troy Albury at Dive Guana. Troy?'

If Abaco had a Man for All Seasons, it would be Troy Albury. Dive-shop owner, island council man, community activist, Troy was also chief of Guana Cay Fire and Rescue; his boat was first on the scene in any emergency. A native of Guana Cay, Troy'd been spearheading the effort to halt the Baker's Bay project that threatened to overwhelm his tiny island, working his way tirelessly and painfully up through the Bahamian court system. I wondered if he'd turn up at the meeting in Hope Town the following week. Warden Henry Baker could certainly draw on Tony's expertise for any action plan directed against Rudolph Mueller's development on Hawksbill Cay.

That morning, though, Troy was wearing his dive-shop hat, reporting calm conditions on the

Sea of Abaco, perfect for snorkeling and diving. After Troy signed off, I called on listeners all along the island chain, asking for sea conditions from Whale Cay in the north to Little Harbour in the south.

Calm conditions all the way.

'Fabulous!' I said. 'Just what everyone dreams of when you think about boating. Look out fish!'

'We have no emergency email today,' I continued, consulting my notes. 'But remember that Out Island Internet has provided a free emergency email service to listeners since 1997 – the address is cruisersatOIIdotnet.'

Gaining confidence with Pattie's script in front of me, I moved rapidly through the community announcements to headline news. I'd tapped Paul for that. He'd spent the morning checking the *New York Times* and *Washington Post* online, taking notes, so that he could summarize what was happening in the world we'd left behind.

Paul wrapped up with the stock market report, then handed the microphone back to me. I took it and gave him a high-five with my free hand.

'We pause here to let new listeners know what's coming up next on the Net. First, we will have some invitations from some great places here with special activities you need to know about. Next, are mail call, then trivia, and our open mike session...'

'Break, break!'

Someone was calling with a priority message.

I immediately interrupted the script. 'Caller, this is the Cruisers' Net. Go ahead.'

'Uh, this is the *Raging Queen* out of Key West, and I'm looking for cabin boys.'

Oh, great. I flipped through Pattie's bible, but there wasn't anything listed under 'Assholes', so I'd just have to wing it. I pressed down on my talk button, stepping on his transmission, hard. 'Well, somebody's had his Wheaties for breakfast! Moving along now ... after open mike, we have a very special section where new arrivals can announce and introduce themselves, after which we will cover departures. Finally, as close as we can make it to nine a.m. we will have a recap of today's weather.

'Our invitations are coming up first so you can plan on not missing any fun while you are here. First on the list is Curly Tails Restaurant and Bar at the Conch Inn in Marsh Harbour. Come in, Harriet.'

After Harriet finished announcing her lunch specials, I called on the other restaurants in order – Wally's, Snappas, Mangoes, and the Jib Room where Boo's description of the baby-back ribs made my mouth water.

'I don't know how popular you are back at home,' I concluded, 'but here in the Abacos, everyone wants you!'

I breezed through mail call and spent about five minutes on open mike answering questions about where to get a haircut, find someone who could repair an alternator, and to celebrate the fortieth birthday of Mindy on *LunaSea* with Net listeners each singing a line of the song, round-robin style.

'New arrivals are next. Do we have any new listeners this morning who are not afraid of the radio and who would like to take this time to introduce yourselves and tell us where you are from? Call signs twice, please.'

Not many *sane* folks invade the Abacos during hurricane season. *FunRunner*, a charter powerboat from the sound of it, had just cruised into Marsh Harbour and the all-male crew of recent graduates from West Point said they were in search of patriotic young women with no visible tan lines. Some bonehead from Key West blabbed on for so long about the 'inedible' meal he'd had at a restaurant in Treasure Cay that I wanted to break his transmitting thumb, but Mimi Rehor from Buck-a-Book did it for me.

'Break, break!'

I recognized her voice at once. This could be serious. 'Go ahead, Mimi.'

'Avener just called from the preserve saying that the brush fire is out of control. It's spreading rapidly toward the preserve, and could threaten the horses. We need help moving fences, cutting firebreaks, and beating back the fire.'

I started to hyperventilate just thinking about it. The fires in southern California had occupied the airwaves on CNN for weeks and weeks, and I pictured our precious herd of Abaco Barbs fleeing before the flames, wild eyed and

112

panicked.

While Mimi described the desperate situation they seemed to be facing out on the preserve, I flipped frantically through Pattie Toler's bible. There was information on the Buck-a-Book container and its opening hours, details on how to arrange a visit to the preserve, and how to contribute to the rescue effort at www.ark-wild.org, but nothing about wild fires. What the heck was a Net anchor supposed to do? I'd have to wing it.

I pressed the talk button. 'Mimi, this is Hannah at *Windswept*. I imagine you need to get on out to the preserve, so I wonder if there's anyone in charge of organizing the volunteers.'

Windswept had a pretty good VHF antenna clamped to the roof, but I knew it wasn't tall enough or powerful enough to reach to all the out islands, or even as far north as Treasure Cay where the preserve was located. If I was to coordinate, I'd need a relay, which would be cumbersome and result in the waste of valuable time. So, I was relieved when Mimi said, 'Anyone who wants to volunteer should contact Susan Bliss at *Outer Limits* on seven-three starting now and anytime after the Net. In the meantime we have taxis lined up to pick up volunteers at both ferry landings – the nine forty-five out of Hope Town and the eleven thirty out of Man-O-War and Guana Cays. Just show up wearing long pants, long sleeves and sensible shoes and socks. Bring a machete if you've got one.'

While Mimi was talking, I checked my watch. Two and a half hours until the ferry from Man-O-War could stop by for us.

'Can we take *Pro Bono*?' I called out to Paul who had suddenly disappeared. He was, as usual, on top of things. He emerged from the bedroom wearing a long-sleeve T-shirt, zipping up a pair of grease-stained chinos.

'Sure.' He threaded a belt through the loops on his pants, cinched it up tight and fastened the buckle. 'Where are the bandannas, do you know? If there's smoke...'

'Top drawer of your dresser,' I said. 'Bring some spares.'

My hands were so sweaty by now I could barely hold on to the mike. While I recapped the weather for the listeners on the Net, Paul pawed through the utility drawer looking for batteries for the spare hand-held radio he'd laid out on the counter. That would be for me. He'd already strapped the one we used on *Pro Bono* to his belt. If we got separated at any time during the day, we could still communicate. Paul and I had cellphones, of course, but who knew if there'd be any cellphone signal from the interior of the island. For short distances, the radios were more reliable.

I was nearing the end of the script.

'Clearing up now, is there anyone with any unfinished business for the Net this morning?' I removed my thumb from the talk button and waited, holding my breath, listening to white noise, counting one one-thousand, two one-thousand, three one-thousand, before rushing on with the rest of Pattie's script.

'Thank you for taking the time to listen. We hope that you enjoyed yourselves. Now please feel free to join our tradition of using this channel as a kind of spare calling channel, so that 16 can be used for hailing, distress and safety as intended by law. Remember to switch to another channel for your conversations and listen first. In Abaco we never switch to 22, 70, 72, 77, or 80. And 06 is reserved for taxis. Please respect these channel reservations. Don't forget to switch back to low power when calling nearby, and if there is nothing further...?' I paused, hoping I'd be done for the day. 'The Cruisers' Net is clear!'

With blood still pumping hotly through my temples, I rested my head against the back of the chair and let my breath out slowly through my lips.

'Hard work, huh?' Paul commented from behind me. He rested his hands on my shoulders and began massaging the tension out of my muscles with his thumbs.

I leaned into him. 'Wait until I get my hands on Pattie.'

'I thought she said that anchoring the Net would be a piece of cake.'

'She did, my love. But she neglected to mention it'd be devil's food.'

Seven

THE OLD SETTLEMENT OF NORMAN'S
CASTLE ... IN DAYS GONE BY ... WAS A BUSY
LOGGING CAMP, BUT IT WAS ABANDONED IN
1929. TODAY FEW TRACES OF THE SETTLE-
MENT OR THE INDUSTRY REMAIN AND THE
ONLY INHABITANTS ARE HERDS OF WILD
HORSES...
The Yachtsman's Guide To The Bahamas,
1992, p. 235

Pro Bono seemed to enjoy her outing, skipping
jauntily over the waves for the three and a half
mile journey from Bonefish Cay to Marsh
Harbour. I sat near the stern, keeping one eye
on the smoke that was rising over Abaco, thick
as Los Angeles' smog. The sun made a valiant
effort, but only managed to hang high in the
pinkish-gray sky like a pale-yellow dime.

I was excited about volunteering, but worried,
too. Everything I knew about wildfires I'd
learned from watching CNN, so I fretted about
wind shifts, sudden gusts, back drafts, and
smoke inhalation. But most of all, I worried
about the horses.

It was Chloe who told me they'd been named after constellations. Stallions Achenar, Hadar, Mimosa and Capella; and the mares, Nunki, Acamar, Acamar's daughter Alnitak, and the princess of the herd, at least in Chloe's wise, eight-year-old mind, the winsome, blue-eyed pinto, Bellatrix II. Chloe would hate me forever if I let anything happen to Bella.

Paul charted a crazy course through the maze of docks at the Conch Inn Marina, then tied *Pro Bono* to the floating dock moored in the slip closest to Curly Tails restaurant. As usual, taxi-cab vans were waiting in the parking lot that served both the restaurant and the Guana Cay ferry landing. We had already charted a course for the van nearest the road when a vehicle pulled in that I recognized. I grabbed Paul's arm. 'It's "Papa Lou".'

I have no idea who Papa Lou is (was?) but the driver of cab #11, Jeff Key, is a Man-O-War resident, a driver who'd cheerfully rearranged his pickups in order to accommodate our trips to and from the airport, or help schlep my groceries between Abaco Grocery, Price Right and the ferry dock whenever I made a major grocery run.

We were about to inconvenience him even further.

Paul quickened his pace, reaching the van just as Jeff opened the hatch to begin unloading his passengers' luggage. 'Hey, Jeff, let me help you with that.' From all the duffle bags and boxes of provisions the two men hauled out on to the

117

pavement, I guessed the passengers piling out of his cab were about to meet up with the sailboat they'd chartered.

'Where to?' Jeff asked us as the cruisers trundled away with a pyramid of luggage and groceries piled precariously in one of the marina wheelbarrows.

'Heard about the wildfires?' I asked.

'Did. Sounds serious. Usually the caretakers can handle it, but the weather's been so dry.' He sucked air in through his teeth. 'Must be bad if they're asking for volunteers.'

Something had been bothering me ever since Mimi's early morning Mayday; I figured Jeff, as a native, might know the answer. 'Where's the Treasure Cay fire department while all this is going on?'

Jeff slammed the hatch shut. 'They rely on volunteers, too. They've got one pumper truck, but they still don't have a tanker, so unless the fire's near the sea or a blue hole, not much point. Besides, if Colin's got everyone out in the boonies fighting a brush fire, who will respond in a real emergency where property and lives are in jeopardy?'

'Seems to me that saving the eight most endangered horses on the planet constitutes a real emergency, don't you?'

'There's many who would agree with you, Hannah, including me.' Jeff waved an arm toward the passenger door, still yawning open. 'Want me to take you up there?'

I tossed the canvas bag carrying our machetes

118

on to the floor of the van and climbed in. 'I thought you'd never ask.'

Jeff's cab was immaculate, smelling like fresh-peeled oranges. He drove east along the familiar road that skirted the Marsh Harbour business district, turned left at the one and only traffic light in all of the Abacos, then carried on out the S.C. Boodle Highway in the direction of Treasure Cay. After driving for what seemed like hours, we left the main road and turned on to a dirt track surrounded by pines, tall and straight as telephone poles. From my spot in the back seat, I gripped the 'Help me, Jesus' bar with both hands as we porpoised over the road, bouncing and dipping over teeth-jarring potholes so numerous they were impossible to avoid. After this trip, I figured we'd owe Jeff more than cab fare; we might have to pony up for new shock absorbers, too.

I hadn't expected an upmarket horse farm like Middleburg, Virginia, of course, but Mimi's base, when we reached it, was still a surprise. Carved out of a clearing in the middle of four thousand acres of pine at the end of an old logging road, it more closely resembled a rough-and-ready cattle station in the Australian outback. Instead of parched clay pan desert, however, the camp was dense with palm, briar, poisonwood and Brazilian pepper, luxuriously leafy, lush and rainforest green. Steam rose from the forest floor. No, not steam, I corrected. Smoke. Smoke hazed the air, obscuring the forest canopy and any glimpse we might have

119

had of the sky.

Jeff pulled in next to an outbuilding, one of three shipping containers Mimi used for storage and staff accommodations, and braked hard. Through my window I noticed an oversized dog pen where Mimi housed her rescued dogs. I recognized one of the animals from Buck-a-Book – Bianca, a laid-back potcake with more than a little bit of white lab somewhere in her family tree. 'Why is there a solar panel in the middle of the dog pen?' I asked Jeff as I stepped out of the cab.

Jeff slid the passenger door closed behind me. 'Would you steal a couple of solar panels with those fellas on guard?' He pointed to the dogs.

Solar panels. Another hard-to-get item. Silly me to overlook the obvious. 'Uh, I guess not.'

Seeing us approach, the dogs set to barking like crazy until they were shushed in rapid Creole by a Haitian dressed in a white T-shirt and torn jeans, carrying a blue, five-gallon water jug.

'Bi-lingual dogs,' Jeff commented in an aside before turning to wave at the Haitian. 'Hello, Jean! We're here to help. Where's Mimi?'

Jean set the jug he was carrying next to a couple of others, wiped sweaty soot from his face with the hem of his shirt. 'She's gone in the truck with Avener and some volunteers. They're running down the logging road, look-ing for breaks.'

Jeff hustled to the rear of his cab and wrench-ed open the hatch, reaching inside for a small duffle bag. 'The two logging roads run more or less parallel,' he explained. 'There's a crossroad cut perpendicular to the two, like an "H". The road serves as a firebreak, but it's a constant battle for the caretakers to keep it clear.'

I thought about Daniel and how hard he had to work, week in and week out, to keep vegetation from choking the modest paths around *Windswept*. I couldn't imagine how difficult a task that would be on a four-thousand acre preserve.

I watched Jeff strip off his tie and toss it inside his van. 'You staying?'

Jeff grinned, withdrew a pair of tennis shoes from inside the duffle. 'Can't leave you stranded out here, can I?'

I could have hugged the man. If he'd gone back to Marsh Harbour, our alternatives for the return trip would have been limited. I could see Mimi's motor scooter, now leaning against the wall of a shipping container; three decrepit 'island cars' of undistinguished pedigree parked higgledy-piggledy nearby; and, incongruously, a bright red BMW Z4.

I tugged on Paul's sleeve, put my lips next to his ear and whispered, 'Who owns a BMW in the islands?'

On Abaco, a hot car was a souped-up electric golf cart, shrunk down and tricked out like a 1957 Chevy Bel Air. Not much use if you lived to pop wheelies in the parking lot of A&K Liquors, but it got you from Point A to Point B with a minimum of fuss and expense.

My question was answered almost immediately when someone I recognized emerged from the bushes, zipping up his fly.

'Beg your pardon,' Jaime Mueller said with a smirk, 'but when a guy's gotta go, he's gotta go.'

I winced. 'Is Alice here?' It seemed unlikely that she would be – fighting fires can wreak havoc on your manicure – but thought I'd ask. Jaime's answer didn't surprise me.

'She's gone shopping in Lauderdale with my sister.'

How nice for her. 'Your dad here, then?'

'Nah. Flew out to Bogota this morning. Left me in charge. *A todos les llega su momento de gloria.*'

I was saved from having to comment about Jaime's moment of glory by the arrival of Mimi Rehor, riding in the bed of a moribund red pick-up, if the gasping and grinding being emitted by the engine was any indication. Once the driver had brought the pickup to a halt, Mimi hopped out and began unloading empty water jugs. She wore khaki cargo pants and a loose white shirt, both streaked with soot. Dilapidated Tevas were strapped to her stocking feet with bands of duct tape.

'The fence line is holding,' she said when we went to help her unload, 'but the stallion area is ablaze.'

I knew that Mimosa and his mares were contained in mini-pastures set up with portable fencing within the preserve. The stallions, on

122

the other hand, still lived on farmland outside the preserve. 'Are they OK?'

'Don't know yet. We're worried about Achenar. He had lung damage in the last fire, so we're hoping he and the two others can stay upwind of the smoke.' She swiped at an errant strand of blonde hair with the back of her hand. 'Thank you all for coming!'

'What can we do?'

Mimi issued instructions with the authority of a drill sergeant. 'First, we need to refill those water jugs and load them into the truck. Once we get them back down to the crossroad, I'll need half a dozen of you to keep watch along it, dousing any sparks that try to cross over. And then...' Mimi paused, as a horn toot-tooted behind me. 'Ah ha,' said Mimi. 'Reinforcements.'

I turned to see a spanking white van bearing the familiar Tamarind Tree logo lock its brakes and skid sideways in a shower of loose sand. Once it stopped moving, four darkly tanned college-aged guys spilled out of it, followed by their lobster-red, formerly fair-skinned companion who must have left his tube of SPF30 back in Florida. All wore Tamarind Tree polo shirts over their jeans.

Mimi took a moment to size up her troops. 'You!' she ordered, pointing to Jaime Mueller and his boys. 'I'll need you to pull fence. You got gloves?'

Jaime's acolytes looked helplessly at their hands, then one another.

'*Anybody* got gloves?' Mimi asked.

'We do,' Paul said, digging around in the canvas bag he carried. Before leaving the house, he'd tucked several pairs of sailing gloves into the bag. Sailing gloves had cut-off fingertips, but were designed to protect hands while pulling lines, so they'd do nicely.

'Good. Jean's got extra pairs, too.' She waved an arm, pointing Jamie and his boys in the caretaker's direction. 'You follow Jean. He'll show you what to do.'

As I watched the boys trudge down the road and gradually disappear into the fog of smoke, I felt grateful not to have pulled that assignment. Hauling and coiling thousands of feet of heavy-duty fencing line while bent over double seemed like back-breaking work better left to the resilience of youth.

My elbow found Paul's ribs. 'I'm surprised to see young Mueller here.'

'You heard the man, Hannah. It's his *momento de gloria.*'

I winced. 'Right. Wouldn't do to disappoint Papa.'

'I wonder if Mueller knows what he's signed up for,' Paul said. 'Fighting wildfires is no picnic.'

'Messes with your hairdo something fierce,' I joked, thinking about Jaime's carefully arranged locks, lightly oiled with something that smelled like coconut and swept back, except for a comma that curled artfully over his left eyebrow. My own hairdo was already beyond help,

124

squashed under the band of a Baltimore Orioles ballcap.

Mimi sent Jeff Key and another group of strapping volunteers off with machetes and weed whackers to manicure fence lines along the vulnerable eastern edge of the preserve. Meanwhile, Paul and I joined another couple in the bed of the pickup for a short ride down to the crossroad.

That's where I learned what the five-gallon water jugs were for: to refill the backpack water pumps.

I'd carried my grandchildren in backpacks. It seemed like no big deal. Once they were filled, I volunteered to carry one of the simple, but effective, fire extinguishers.

'Are you sure?' Avener asked as he lifted the tank and held it up so I could slip my arms through the harness.

'No problem.' I braced my legs while Avener adjusted the straps over my shoulders, but I staggered and nearly fell over when he let go.

What's so hard about carrying a five-gallon water tank on your back?

Water weighs eight and a half pounds per gallon, that's what. I may have had experience toting grandchildren, but I was now carrying the equivalent of quintuplets on my back.

But I'd asked for it, so I didn't complain.

Equipped with similar tanks and operating on the buddy system, we were instructed to patrol the crossroad in half-mile laps, guarding against flare-ups. The other couple who'd drawn the

125

same assignment walked east while my husband and I went west. We kept our backpacks primed with regular strokes of its trombone-style hand pump, and doused errant sparks before they could catch and take hold in the dry underbrush.

Mercifully, the wind blew the smoke away from us, but the heat remained oppressive.

'Do you think we'll get rain?' one of the volunteers asked as our paths intersected on the second round. 'Cruisers' Net predicted we might have rain.'

It seemed like ages since that morning when I first heard Stu's forecast.

Paul paused and instinctively looked up. I did, too, but if there were rain clouds gathering above the canopy of trees they were obscured by the smoky haze. 'My advice?' he said. 'Pray.'

We passed them, and kept on walking.

After an hour, I'd grown rather skillful with the nozzle, able to lay a stream of water directly on a patch of flames maybe ten or fifteen feet away. With experimentation, I found I could increase the distance to almost twenty feet by placing my finger just so over the nozzle as I pumped. I was turning into the Annie Oakley of backpack sprayers.

When I ran out of water, Paul kept an eye on the fire while I refilled my tank from one of the jugs. Then I returned the favor. And we walked on.

Everything seemed so under control that at

one point we stopped for a break, gulping down cans of lukewarm Bahamas Goombay Punch, a super-sweet pineapple-lime soda that had been left out for the volunteers near the water jugs. Not my first choice, but under the circumstances, a sugar high could come in handy. I was unwrapping a power bar, preparing to chow down, when the wind turned.

We felt the heat first, and then the choking smoke. A cinder landed on my tennis shoe, flared orange and faded to black, leaving a pinhole. 'Damn!' I said, tucking the half-eaten power bar into my pocket. Maybe there'd be time to eat it later.

As we watched in horror, the wind snatched fire from the ravaged fields, sending a wave of sparks in our direction. A fire broke out in a patch of underbrush to our left. With me screaming, 'Be careful!' at the top of my lungs, Paul charged after it, disappearing into a cloud of smoke.

'Take that!' I heard him shout, addressing the flames, punctuated by fits of coughing. 'And that!'

Something flared to my right. A line of fire was eating its way along the tree line, heading toward the road. I aimed my nozzle at the foot of the flames and fired again and again, watching with satisfaction as the fire fizzled out.

But there was no time to gloat. Just beyond the blaze I'd just extinguished, another one had taken hold, feeding on dry palm fronds and crackling merrily. I dashed over to it, drenched the palms with water, and waited to make sure it was thoroughly out before moving on to the next outbreak. No sooner had I doused one area than flames would pop up again somewhere else.

'Paul! Over here!' I yelled, but I couldn't take time to wait for his answer.

Chasing red-hot embers, I staggered over broken rocks and zigzagged through the under-brush. Vines clawed at my ankles like the devil's hands, and I tore them free. With sweat running down my forehead and into my eyes, I chased one line of fire down a rotten log, stamping on the flames in frustration as they flared up again around my feet. Sparks from the blazing underbrush spiraled up, turning to ash, disintegrating into powder which found its way into my nose and mouth. I snatched the scarf from my head and used it to mop my forehead, my nose and lips, before moving on to the next hot spot.

I tripped over a rock, staggered, and grabbed the trunk of a tree to keep from falling. Poison-wood? I didn't notice or care. Trying to keep myself between the fire and the safety of the road, I crashed through the underbrush, attacking flare-ups to my left, flare-ups to my right. Carrying the backpack grew easier and easier. I credited the adrenaline.

Where the hell was Paul?

Where the hell was *I*, for that matter?

I paused for a moment to take stock of my surroundings, but because of the smoke my world was limited to a ten-foot radius from where I stood, breathing air so hot that it made my lungs ache.

Eyes streaming, I squinted into the smoke. A wall of trees, now, fire glowing hotly at their roots. Where the hell was the road?

'Paul!' I screamed, my lungs seared with the effort. 'Anybody!'

Disoriented, I staggered away from the flames, keeping the wind at my back. But the fire seemed to be making its own wind now, first blowing this way, then that, so how could I be sure I was heading in the right direction?

I tripped over a stump and fell to my knees under the weight of the backpack sprayer. I rested there for a moment, then used my hands to push myself into a sitting position. Hot, so hot! My skin tingled as sweat evaporated almost the instant it appeared. Using a bit of my precious water, I dampened my head scarf and tied it around my nose and mouth. Annie Oakley became wild-west desperado.

On my feet again, I kept moving, using the water to douse any flames along the way, clearing my path. When water began to drizzle from the nozzle, I worked the pump harder. And harder.

Damn, damn, damn! Adrenaline had nothing to do with it, you idiot. My backpack was lighter because I running out of water.

I slipped the harness from my left shoulder, tipped the tank so the remaining liquid drooled out of the hose and on to the scarf I had bunched up in my hand.

I am going to die, I thought, as I used the scarf to wipe my face. I'm going to die, but not of the fire. I'm going to die of stupidity.

How could I have let myself get separated from Paul?

I pressed the scarf against my forehead and used it to soothe my eyes. Its coolness was miraculously calming. Spread it over your nose, Hannah. Breathe in. Breathe out. Try not to cough. Breathe in. Breathe out. Think!

You have a radio!

I worked the hand-held out of my fanny pack and pressed the talk button, silently apologizing to listeners for the call signs Paul and I had assigned to one another. 'Rhett, Rhett, this is Scarlet, come in.'

Paul answered right away, forgetting everything he knew about proper radio etiquette. 'Hannah, my God, where the hell are you?'

'I don't know exactly,' I croaked. 'One minute the road was behind me, the next it had disappeared.'

'Look around! Can you see anything?'

'Smoke.'

Stay calm, Hannah. Think. Sign on hotel-room door: *If you encounter smoke en route, crouch or crawl low to the ground.*

I dropped to my knees, put my head to the ground and squinted into the distance. 'I see a fence! Looks like it's made out of branches lashed together. Wait a minute.' Crouching, I crab-walked over for a closer look. 'And believe it or not, there's an old bathtub.'

My throat was so parched that every word was an effort. I stuck the nozzle in my mouth and sucked the last few drops of water out of my tank, then pressed the button again. 'I'm going to clap. See if you can hear me.'

I hadn't clapped so hard since seeing *The Producers* on Broadway.

My radio crackled. 'I hear you! Keep clapping!'

I clapped for minutes, hours, days.

I clapped for my life.

Eight

I'VE SEEN FIRE AND I'VE SEEN RAIN I'VE
SEEN SUNNY DAYS THAT I THOUGHT WOULD
NEVER END I'VE SEEN LONELY TIMES WHEN I
COULD NOT FIND A FRIEND BUT I ALWAYS
THOUGHT THAT I'D SEE YOU AGAIN.
James Taylor, *Fire And Rain*, 1970

I was so busy clapping that I saw it before I
heard it, growling and grinding, emerging like
an illusion out of the smoke: the old Massey
Ferguson, ropes coiled neatly on either side
of its radiator grill, with Mimi behind the
wheel.

'Heard you on the radio,' she shouted over the
clanking of the engine as I scrambled gratefully
aboard. 'Figured you'd be over here. We use
that old bathtub as an emergency watering
trough.'

Since Mimi occupied the only seat on the
elderly tractor, I sat cross-legged on one of its
steel fenders, hanging on to a rope tied to the
steel sunroof as Mimi lurched over potholes
and leaped over logs.

'You know what's scary?' Mimi shouted as

she slammed the gear shift forward.

'*This* is pretty scary!' I said, hiking out to keep my head from bashing into the sunroof as she drove over a boulder.

'It's what it says in the operations manual for this thing.'

'What's that?' I shouted back.

'"Avoid steep hills and sharp turns." So here we are, doing everything but Immelmans.'

I couldn't help but laugh.

As it turned out, I hadn't wandered very far from the crossroad at all. In what seemed like no time, we were back. Paul was still pacing, radio pressed to his ear.

When Mimi brought the tractor to a grinding halt, I hopped down and ran, backpack sprayer and all, straight into my husband's arms.

'Don't you ever do that to me again, Hannah, do you hear? You can't do everything single-handed.' He had dropped his radio and was squeezing me so tight I could barely breathe.

'No chance of that,' I muttered into his shirt. 'Your hug is going to kill me.'

From her perch on the tractor seat, Mimi said, 'I'll drive you back to the base. Other volunteers are coming in...' She paused. 'Ah, here's Avenar with some of them now. Great timing. We can take the truck.'

I shrugged out of the backpack and set it next to the water jugs for refilling, then climbed into the cab of Mimi's truck next to Paul, feeling suddenly stiff, sore and not nearly as young as I used to be. While we waited for Mimi to

133

consult with the caretaker, Paul reached over and took my hand. 'I was really worried, you know. I don't know what I'd do if I lost you.'

I rested my head against his shoulder. 'Ditto, ditto.'

I felt Paul tense. 'Jeez, Hannah! You've got first-degree burns.'

I looked down. No wonder my arms had been tingling. They were lobster red, like a bad sunburn. 'That's what aloe is for,' I said, just managing to smile.

Feeling a combination of regret and relief, I watched through the truck's scuzzy windshield as two new recruits suited up in the backpack sprayers Paul and I had so recently carried. My mind drifted, thoughts swirling like smoke. I closed my eyes, surrendering to sleep.

Something went *plip* on the windshield. *Plip-plip*, leaving splotches the size of a quarter. *Plip-plip-plip-plip*.

'Rain?' As I struggled to sit up, the drops fell faster, beating a tinny tattoo on the roof of the truck.

'Rain!' I wrenched open the door and slid off the worn vinyl seat to the ground. I spread my arms, welcoming its cooling balm. I raised my face to the sky, and opened my mouth, savoring each raindrop as it landed on my tongue.

'Rain! Rain! Rain!' I grabbed Paul's hands, dragged him out of the truck, and waltzed him around in a circle, laughing like a raving looney. 'Chaac, the rain god, has heard our prayers!'

As if to prove he was really in charge, Chaac sent thunder, too, deafening claps that boomed, rumbled and echoed across the sky. He ripped open the clouds, and the showers turned to deluge. Along with Mimi and the other volunteers we laughed, cheered and hugged one another. If some of us were weeping, it would have been impossible to tell as water streamed from our hair, down our foreheads and into our eyes. Everyone was gratefully soaked to the skin.

Down in the forest the flames sizzled, sputtered and died. The tree bark hissed and steamed.

'God be praised!' someone sang out. 'It's over!'

'It's not over until it's over,' Mimi commented as we rattled along the old logging road in her truck. She tipped her head, squinting up at the leaden sky through the swathe that the windshield wipers, set on frantic, labored to keep clear. 'Lightning is one of our worst enemies, although if this monsoon continues, I think we'll be safe for a while.'

She turned to look at me. 'You got a ride back to Marsh Harbour?'

'We came with Jeff Key,' I told her. 'He's supposed to be working on the fence line at the eastern edge of the preserve.'

'Right.' Mimi slammed on the brakes, executed a neat, three-point turn, then headed down the road in the opposite direction. 'They will have done all they can for now, may even be heading back. Wouldn't be surprised if we met them halfway.'

We had covered less than a mile before Mimi brought the truck to a halt and set the emergency brake. 'This is as far as we can go without the tractor. Always hoping someone will donate an all-terrain vehicle. Ha ha.'

The rain had let up some, so we climbed out of the truck and stood on the edge of the road. The trees that surrounded us were charred, but no longer smoldering. 'The path starts over there.' Mimi pointed. 'Fire burned through a couple of days ago, so it shouldn't be a problem.' She captured an errant shirt tail in each hand and tied them in a knot at her waist, as if girding her loins for battle. 'Wait here. I'll be right back.'

Paul gave my sleeve a surreptitious tug, locked his eyes on mine. I'd been married to the man for too long not to know what he was thinking. Mimi might heft five-gallon jugs, pull fence, convince a wild horse to stand still while she trims its hooves, leap tall buildings in a single bound ... but he was too much of a gentleman to let her go off into the woods on her own. 'Mind if I come along?'

Mimi shrugged. 'If you'd like.' She turned to me. 'Hannah?'

'I'd rather stay in the truck, if you don't mind. I'm a bit chilled.'

Paul's face was inches from mine, concern written all over it. 'Are you sure, Hannah?'

'Of course, I'm sure. I'm feeling chilly, is all.'

I waved him off. 'Go! I'll be fine.'

After they left I huddled on the seat, hugging my knees with Mimi's towel wrapped tightly around my shoulders, like a shawl. I stared out the window through a thin curtain of rain. My breath was fogging the inside of the window, so I used a corner of the towel to clear a peephole in the glass.

To my right was the forest, to my left the fence line, and beyond it, a vast expanse of field I assumed to be part of the old Bahamas Star Farm property. It must have been the fence line Mimi had been talking about. A strip about six feet wide had been cleared along the fence as far as I could see in both directions.

Through the trees, charred and smoking, an oasis of green that had miraculously escaped the flames stood out like an emerald on a lump of coal. I climbed out of the truck and jogged over to the fence for a closer look. In the thick foliage, something moved. A flash of brown? I wiped the rain out of my eyes. Yes, and a glint of white. Could it be the horses?

Ash covered the forest floor like snow, but the rain had turned it into gray mud that sucked at the soles of my shoes as I ran. When I got back to the truck, I climbed into the flatbed and hoisted myself on to the roof. I stood on tiptoe, shielding my eyes from the downpour, scanning the bushes for any sign of the horses.

And then I saw them, the stallions Hadar and Achenar, grazing happily on poisonwood. The horses had survived!

I clambered down from the truck and ran back through the soggy, still-warm undergrowth to find and tell Mimi. In my haste, I tripped over a log, falling headlong into the mud. I swore, picked myself up and wiped my hands on my jeans. Damn log. I gave it an impatient kick.

I should have hurt my toe with that kick. I should have been limping around, nursing my foot. But this felt like kicking a soccer ball gone flat. Curious, I stooped down, then reeled back.

It wasn't a log. It was a body, or what was left of one after the fire. Its knees were drawn up into the fetal position, its elbows bent, hands clenched. The skin was charred, like a burned marshmallow, and where the intense heat had caused the skin to split open, it had peeled back, revealing ugly patches of red, roasted flesh. There wasn't much left of the face to recognize – no nose, no ears. When caught by the fire, the man had been wearing jeans. What remained of his shirt was fused to the skin on his chest. One twisted foot still wore a tennis shoe; the remains of the other shoe lay on the ground nearby.

This could have been me.

I had to get out of there.

I ran back the way I had come, back to the truck, where I staggered around to the back and with one hand holding on to the tailgate, I quietly parted company with my Goombay Punch.

Six o'clock had come and gone by the time the ferry dropped us off on the dock at *Windswept*.

Heavy footed, we trudged up the dock together, with Paul's arm draped loosely over my shoulder. I dragged myself up the steps to the porch and collapsed on a lounge chair. 'I'm so tired!'

'Move over,' my husband said.

'And I stink.'

He ignored me and sat down, then nuzzled my neck. 'Not really. You smell woodsy, like a campfire with a bit of eau de creosote thrown in.'

I snuggled against him, trying vainly to disassociate myself from the horror in the woods. I shivered and buried my face in his chest. Overwhelmed by heat, smoke, soot and stress, I began to cry. 'I'm sorry,' I said after a while, swiping at my streaming nose with the back of my hand.

Paul cupped my chin, turned my face to his and wiped the tears away from my cheeks with his thumb. 'No need to apologize, Hannah. It's not your fault.'

'That poor fellow.' I stopped and looked at my husband, fresh tears cooling on my cheeks. 'Oh, God, Paul. I couldn't even tell if it was a man or a woman!'

After my embarrassing performance with the Goombay punch, I had been grateful when Mimi took charge. From the back of her truck, she produced a blue tarp which Paul and Jeff helped spread over the body, anchoring the corners with rocks.

'Don't get involved,' Mimi warned when I started to call the police on my radio. She plucked the radio from my fingers. 'Let me handle it.'

So I did. Gladly.

It's like a TV show, I told myself. Think about that. How many seasons of *CSI* have gone by? How many episodes of *Law and Order* – regular, *SVU* and *CI*? Hundreds of bodies? Thousands? Shot, stabbed, beaten, burned, dismembered – in a home, on the street, on a slab in the medical examiner's office. Tamara Tunie looking up from a Y-cut – *this girl was six weeks pregnant when he shot her.*

It's a prop. It's a rental body from Dapper Cadaver. It's *CSI, Law and Order, Dexter, Bones.*

It was also no good. Better to think about the horses.

'Are the horses safe, really safe?' I asked my husband as he headed for the shower.

'They are for now.'

'I'm wondering why they can't put the horses in trailers and drive them to safety. There's only eight of them.'

We'd reached the shower enclosure by then, and Paul began stripping off his shirt. 'They're *wild* horses, Hannah. You've seen what it's like out there. First you'd have to find them. Then you'd have to use a tranquilizer gun to get them into a trailer.' He returned my sheepish grin with a grin of his own, then unzipped and stepped out of his filthy trousers, hooked them on his toes and tossed them into the bushes. 'But I'm betting Mimi's a dab hand with a tranquilizer gun, too.'

Paul began soaping up in the shower, so I nipped inside to fetch us both some clean underwear. When I got back, he was singing an off-key version of 'I got the horse right here, the name is Paul Revere,' from the musical *Guys and Dolls*.

I waited outside the enclosure, leaning against the siding. 'Don't try to cheer me up. It won't work.'

'Can do, can do, this guy says the horse can do,' Paul sang, ignoring me. Sudsy water from his vigorous shampooing began running out of the shower stall and along the concrete apron at my feet.

'Even the curly tails are running for cover,' I added.

The water stopped running. My husband emerged from the shower, squeaky clean and smelling of Suave Cucumber Melon Splash. 'I can tell you one thing, Hannah, you're not going to cook tonight.' He relieved me of the clean underwear and hung it on the hook outside the shower. Then he began to unbutton my shirt.

'You know what they say?' I asked as the first two buttons came undone.

'No, what?'

'"Save water, shower with a friend?"'

And he drew me under the healing stream where we stood, locked together, until the hot water ran out.

Nine

THERE ARE STORIES ABOUT CORRUPT COPS WHO ACCEPT BRIBES, PURPOSELY FAIL TO SHOW UP FOR COMPLAINTS OR CRIME SCENES, OR FILE REPORTS ON CASES INVOLVING FRIENDS, FAMILY OR SOMEONE WILLING TO PAY FOR THEIR SILENCE, INTENTIONALLY CHOOSING TO PREVENT JUSTICE RATHER THAN ADHERING TO THEIR SWORN OATH.

The Nassau Tribune, July 25 2008

After my baptism, quite literally by fire, moderating the Cruisers' Net the rest of the week seemed like a tropical breeze.

There were the usual weather reports, arrivals and departures, a lost wallet, a found passport – 'Don't panic, Terri Ryburn, your passport has been found at Café Florance. Call me on seven-three after the Net and we'll get you reunited.'

Paul had followed through on his 'no cooking' promise, and then some. We'd lunched at Wally's, the Golden Grouper and Cracker P's – but the one invitation I didn't want to pass up was the Sunday pig roast at Nippers Beach Bar and Grill on Great Guana Cay.

142

Paul took my advice.

Perched high on a forty-foot dune overlooking the Atlantic, Nippers has to be experienced to be appreciated. Imagine: raffia umbrellas stirring in a gentle island breeze; picnic tables painted every color of the tropical rainbow; a double-decker pool connected by a waterfall where you can swim right up to the bar; a hat rack labeled *Hang Bikini Tops Here*; and sipping frozen Nippers in plastic cups while grooving to the music of a two-piece reggae band.

Self-medication never felt so good.

I remember stopping at Milo's stand to purchase some tomatoes, and the long walk up the hill past the cemetery where a sign reminds all visitors that 'the wages of sin is death' – thanks for sharing! – but after enjoying my first frozen Nippers, a pink fruit juice and rum Slushee, smooth and sneaky, everything gets a bit hazy.

One drink was so yummy that I had to have two, and I may even have split a third one with Paul ... hard to say. Weaving down the dunes, wading in the surf, lying down in the sand for a nice long nap, face *up*, no matter what Paul tells you.

Everyone says I had a good time.

All week I had been hoping for news about the body I'd found in the Wild Horses of Abaco preserve. If that had happened in Annapolis, WBAL would have been all over it. CNN, too. But, we were in the i'lans, mon. Nobody was

143

sayin' nuffin.

The Marsh Harbour authorities had claimed the body, and everyone assumed it would be shipped down to Nassau for an autopsy, but other than that, there was no news, no ID.

Molly Weston said that Winnie Albury told her that Forbes Albury had mentioned that one of his boatyard workers hadn't showed up for a week. Everyone assumed he'd gone back to Haiti, to visit an ill mother someone said, but nobody knew for sure.

I'd wondered if my status as Net anchor would give me a leg up in the information department, but I was wrong. I made a few phone calls, but ended up none the wiser. Maybe it was because I didn't have Pattie's connections.

When the next edition of *The Abaconian* hit the stands, I snagged a copy, but the article didn't tell me much I didn't already know:

Police retrieved the body, which had been severely burned, and had it transported to the Marsh Harbour Community Clinic, where it was officially pronounced dead.

While police do not suspect foul play at this time, the body will be flown to New Providence, where an autopsy will be performed in order to determine the exact cause of death.

Central Detective Unit officers from Grand Bahama are presently on the island assisting officers there with the investigation.

'Officially pronounced dead.' I shuddered. As if

144

there ever had been any question of that.

After the Net, I puttered over to Hawksbill in *Pro Bono* and went looking for Gator Crockett, dive shopowner, unofficial constable, island point man for reckless teens, Mr Knock-a-Few-Heads-Together. I found him in the shack he laughingly called his office, patching a wetsuit with DAP contact cement. Justice, the potcake, lay snoozing at his feet.

I watched Gator work for a while before he noticed me.

'Morning.' He waved a glue brush. 'Sit.'

I parked my buns in a plastic lawn chair that see-sawed alarmingly on the uneven dirt floor. 'Can you talk for a minute?'

He nodded, pressing the edges of the patch together with his fingers.

'I was the one who tripped over the body after the wildfire.'

'Uh huh.'

'I've been waiting to hear that the body's been identified, but nothing's been reported so far. I was wondering if you'd heard anything.'

Gator tossed the glue brush into a tin can, considered me with pale-blue eyes, saying nothing.

I tried again. 'Who can I call?'

The corner of his mouth twitched in what might have been the beginning of a smile. 'You don't call. You don't want to get involved. If the police find out you're the one who stumbled over the body, and it turns out that there was foul play...' The smile vanished. 'Best case,

145

you're tied up in the court system for years. Worst case, they'll turn you into a suspect.'

Don't get involved. The same advice I'd received from Mimi, but still I said, 'You're kidding me.'

Gator shrugged. 'It's happened.'

'So what do I do?'

'You keep your mouth shut.'

Hannah Ives keeping her mouth shut. If Paul had been there, he'd have been laughing hysterically.

Perhaps it was the Anglophile in me, but I tended to trust organizations with the word 'royal' in their titles, organizations like 'The Royal Bahamian Police Force'. That said, I hadn't exactly been dazzled by the notices I'd read about the outfit on the Abaco tourist blogs. Consider this: *Police have few emergency vehicles, streets and houses are unmarked, so the best thing to do when you are a crime victim is go to the police station nearest you and provide transportation to the crime scene. CSI* it wasn't.

'If I knew anything, I'd certainly tell you,' Gator had concluded before powering off with Justice and some tourists for an all-day, two-tank dive on Fowl Cay.

And I had to be satisfied with that.

As if to compensate, it had been happy days on the Net. No email emergencies except the good kind – a baby granddaughter for the couple anchored behind Scotland Cay on *Always Something* – and lost-and-founds with happy endings.

A boat cat answering to Marmalade had gone missing after an altercation with a local potcake, but had turned up the following day snacking happily on conch bits behind George's conch salad stand next door to the Harbour View Marina on Bay Street. It's a troubling thought, but more people were worried and out searching for that cat than cared about whoever it was who had burned to a crisp on the preserve.

Happily, the wildfires were out.

The weather continued happily, too. Sunny, highs in the eighties, chance of widely scattered thunderstorms.

And, ugly as it was, every cruiser seemed to share a we're-all-in-this-together camaraderie as we watched our stock portfolios go up and down like an Episcopalian in church.

Like I said, it was Same-Old-Same-Old on the Net, until the morning Tony Sands called in on open mike.

I was taking calls as usual.

'*Sea's the Day*, I hear you. Stand by. Anyone else?

'*Reel Time* I hear you, too. Stand by. Anyone else?' When no one else spoke up, I continued. 'Nothing heard. Go ahead *Sea's the Day*.'

Brian Jones on *Sea's the Day* was a new arrival to the Abacos and needed to know where to get a haircut (Lanie's Cuts and Curls in Memorial Plaza), and where to find an ATM that dispenses US dollars. (As if!) With Brian

147

half satisfied, I moved on to Tony.

'*Reel Time*, go ahead Tony.'

We knew Tony fairly well. A charter fishing boat captain operating out of Man-O-War Cay, he'd taken Paul deep-sea fishing, but the only fish Paul ever landed was a thirty-pound barracuda. Not particularly edible, but it made a great picture. At least his colleagues back at the Academy were impressed.

'I'm looking for the sailing vessel *Wanderer*,' Tony broadcast, 'a Reliant 41, green hull, three days overdue from Lake Worth, Florida. *Wanderer* is skippered by Frank Parker. His wife, Sally, is also aboard.'

My head swam. We knew Frank and Sally Parker! I took a deep, steadying breath and tried to remember what, as Net anchor, I was supposed to say next. I tried to keep my voice neutral as I pressed the talk button and repeated Tony's announcement in case anyone missed it. Meanwhile, I was gesturing frantically to Paul with my free hand. As I spoke, I watched Paul's expression change from surprise to worry.

'Anyone seen the vessel *Wanderer*, a Reliant 41, come now,' I said. The airwaves were heavy with silence as I waited hopefully for someone to call in with a positive sighting. I hated having to say, 'Nothing heard.'

'Is there anybody in range of Green Turtle Cay who can relay for the Net?' I asked.

Knot Hers volunteered, and I listened again as the message about *Wanderer* was repeated, but again, the only response was a disappointing

148

silence.

I tried not to worry as I hurried through a recap of the weather, completely skipped the trivia question (trivial, under the circumstances) and wound up the Net.

'If there's nothing further...' I took my thumb off the talk button and waited. 'Then the Net is clear.'

I slotted the mike into its cradle, leaned back in my chair and sighed. 'Frank and Sally. Dear God, I hope they're OK.'

While I had been wrapping up the Net, Paul had powered up his laptop. Now he looked up from the screen. 'I've got Frank's cellphone number here somewhere.' He tapped a few keys. 'After Frank retired, he and Sally were supposed to be cruising the Intracoastal. Why is Tony looking for them, I wonder?'

Paul crossed to the radio and picked up the mike, still hot and sweaty from where I'd been clutching it for almost an hour. *'Reel Time, Reel Time*, this is *Windswept.* Come back.'

The airwaves crackled. *'Reel Time* here, Paul. Switch and answer seven three?'

'Seven three.'

'Tony, what's up?' Paul asked after the connection was made. 'I know Frank Parker. He used to teach oceanography at the Naval Academy, went on to consult for the Smithsonian's environmental research center south of Annapolis. What's he doing in the Abacos?'

'You know the meeting in Hope Town on Wednesday?'

'Right?'

'Parker was going to testify on behalf of Save Hawksbill Cay.'

'If the government didn't believe Jean Michael Cousteau, what would make them believe Frank Parker?'

'Parker has contacts at the University of Florida. They were refuting the claims of the environmental impact statement made by Mueller's so-called experts. Parker's not being paid – the scientists who wrote that report are on Mueller's payroll – so he's got no personal interest in the project.'

'Do you know what Parker was going to say?'

'That the project is an environmental catastrophe.'

'Ouch.'

'Well, it's true.'

'When did you hear from Parker last?'

'Tuesday. He'd made the crossing and had put down his hook in Great Sale.'

The crossing. I knew that meant Frank and Sally Parker had successfully crossed the Gulf Stream from Florida, a voyage not to be taken lightly if the weather isn't favorable. While Paul talked, I consulted the map we had taped to the side of the refrigerator. With my finger, I followed the chain of islands west from Hawksbill Cay. I found Great Sale Cay easily, almost due north from Grand Bahama. From the air, it looked like an anchor.

I knew you could sail from Great Sale to Allens-Pensacola in a day. From there to Green

Turtle was another day, and if the weather was right – and it'd been nothing but fine, wind speed and direction-wise, for the past week – the trip from Green Turtle through the Whale Passage to Hawksbill couldn't have taken more than a day. So, according to my calculations, for the whole trip I'd say three, four days, max.

When I turned back to the radio, Paul was saying, 'Maybe they're just taking their time?'

'I don't think so,' Tony replied. 'Last time Parker telephoned, he said he'd see me on Thursday and pop a Kalik. It's not like him not to call if he ran into any trouble or changed his plans.'

'I have to agree. Not like him at all. At the Academy he was always the first to turn his grades in. Not like Sally, either. She's a friend of my wife's going way back.'

That was the truth. Sally was the organizer's organizer, the woman who was living proof of the saying, 'If you want something done, find the busiest person you know.' It was Sally who engineered my post-surgery, post-chemo dinner brigade. Every day for six weeks, someone from the Naval Academy Women's Club had showed up on my doorstep at five thirty sharp, holding a hot casserole in her oven-mitted hands.

A thought occurred to me, and I scribbled it down on one of the Post-it notes that still littered the table. I slid it in front of Paul.

Paul picked up my note and squinted at it. 'Was their dog with them, too?'

151

'Duffy? Yeah. I even asked Winnie to order a supply of special dog food for the little yapper.'

Frank, Sally and their Scottish terrier, Duffy. Overdue. I refused to use the term 'missing.'

It was easy, I knew all too well, to lose track of time while in paradise. Frank wasn't scheduled to speak until Wednesday. They were probably dawdling along, anchored in an idyllic lagoon, swimming, laughing, with Duffy barking at them playfully from the bow as they splashed in the water below him.

We knew *Wanderer*, too, a Reliant 41 yawl built by Cheoy Lee. We'd often sailed with the Parkers on the Chesapeake before Frank's retirement had taken them away. They had sailed, quite literally, into the sunset, following a lifelong dream. Postcards had come from Norfolk, Charleston, Savannah, Hilton Head, Fernandina Beach, St Augustine and Cape Canaveral as they made their way south along the inland waterway.

'I wish I had known they were coming,' I complained to Paul when he'd finished his conversation with Tony and had cradled the mike. 'We've got plenty of room on the dock. They could have tied up there. Slept in the snore box.'

'We'll tell them when we see them.' Paul laid his hand on mine and gave it a reassuring squeeze. 'Don't worry.'

Ten

MR THEODORE R. ZICKES ... CAME HERE AND ORDERED A THIRTY-FOOT AUXILIARY SLOOP. UNCLE WILL COMPLETED THE BOAT ... AND IT WAS NAMED *SWEET-HEART*. THE *SWEET-HEART* WAS LEFT HERE YEAR ROUND IN UNCLE WILL'S CARE. I WET THE DECKS EACH MORNING WHEN IT DID NOT RAIN AND THERE WAS NO DEW. FOR THIS JOB I RECEIV-ED TWO SHILLINGS (28 CENTS) PER MONTH. EACH YEAR THE *SWEET-HEART* WAS GIVEN A COMPLETE PAINT JOB BY SOME OF UNCLE WILL'S WORKMEN.

Haziel L. Albury,
Man-O-War My Island Home, p. 55

I stuck my head into the bedroom where Paul had been hiding out all morning with his laptop, manipulating geometrical shapes with his Sketchpad software. A cube was spinning crazily around the screen.

'The barge is just in, so I'm off to the grocery.'

'Apples,' he said without looking up. 'And English muffins if they have them.'

His fingers only paused; they were still glued to the keys.

'Dreamer,' I muttered. The last time the Pink Store had English muffins, they had been three weeks past their sell-by date, but I bought them anyway. A shout out for calcium propionate, sorbic acid and monoglycerides.

I added 'apples' to my list and an optimistic 'Eng muff,' slipped the list into my pocket and my feet into my Crocs. As I emerged into the sunlight from the shade of the porch, I checked the sky. A malevolent black cloud had settled over Abaco. I wondered if I had time to get to the grocery and back before it reached Bonefish Cay and gave me and my purchases a good drenching.

I made a quick detour to haul the clothes off the line, toss them into the laundry basket without folding and slide it on to the bunkhouse porch under the shelter of the roof. They would need ironing, but since we didn't have an iron – such a pity! – what did it matter?

Ten minutes later, I tied *Pro Bono* up at the government dock in Hawksbill Harbour and went ashore. The barge was still unloading cardboard crates of produce and dairy products at the Pink Store, so I walked on, stopping for a minute or two at Hawksbill Marina to enjoy the view. Fishing boats and luxury yachts that Paul and I could never afford in a million years were tied up to finger piers, gently rocking. I wondered if any of their owners would be moving to Mueller's Tamarand Tree Marina when it opened in six months' time, and what effect their desertion would have on the locals.

Next door, at Tropical Treats, I placed an order for lunch – two conch burgers and fries to go. Service at Tropical Treats is glacial – you pay extra for that – so I knew I could dilly-dally around town for as long as an hour before my order would be ready. But the food was always worth the wait.

At Pinder's Boat Yard, I loitered outside the shed to observe while workers put the finishing touches on one of their custom-made launches. As I peered through the open doors, they lowered the helm into place on a twenty-five foot beauty and began fastening it to the deck. Nearby sat a fiberglass hull still in the mold; the next boat that would come off their modest, low-tech assembly line. I would have stayed longer, but I was starting to hallucinate on fiberglass resin fumes, so I decided to see what was going on in the yard outside.

Behind the shed, two other workers had manoeuvered a yacht on to a sled and were hauling it out of the water on a marine railroad. The sled was attached by a steel cable to an electric winch, which cranked the vessel along the rails, across the road and up a slight incline where another winch and pair of rails moved the boat sideways. The whole operation took less than ten minutes, and when it was done, the boat was tucked neatly into a slot between two other boats at least fifty feet up on dry land. Impressive. Back home, that task would have taken three guys, one supervisor and a hundred ton, half-million dollar Marine Travelift the size of a town house.

Because it was hurricane season, the yard was full of yachts propped up on jack stands, packed together like proverbial canned sardines, awaiting the return of their owners in November when the threat of hurricanes would be over. Some were covered with shrink wrap, others with tarps. Still others were being cleaned, repaired and repainted, like the sailboat someone I recognized was working on now.

'Bonjou, Daniel.'

Daniel stood on the top rung of a ladder propped up on the side of the vessel's hull. He was brushing varnish on the wooden toe rail with deft, fluid strokes. When I spoke, he balanced his paintbrush on the rim of the varnish can and looked down. 'Bonjou!'

'Bel bato, n'est-ce que pas!'

Ah, I should own such a boat. A cobalt-blue hull, color so pure and deep I felt I could dive right into it. Woodwork varnished to a high gloss, glowing in the sun. Someone was very lucky.

'Ki-moun posede sa bato?' I asked Daniel.

Daniel grinned. 'Mister Jaime.' With his paintbrush, Daniel gestured toward the stern of the vessel, which I took as an invitation to check it out for myself.

At the stern I found another worker up on a ladder lettering A-L-I-C-E I-N W-O-N-D-E-R-L-A-N-D on the transom. That figured. The jerk probably thought that naming a boat after his wife would make up for the black eye.

As I admired the boat, though, I grew increasingly uncomfortable. Like luggage on airport baggage carousels, many boats look alike – their fiberglass bodies are laid out one after another in identical molds, after all – yet this one seemed familiar.

I stepped back for a broader view. The *Alice in Wonderland* had two masts, the smaller of the two mounted in the stern, behind the helm. So it was a yawl. An unusual rig for a boat these days. I could count on the fingers of one hand the number of yawls we'd seen in the Abacos since our arrival.

Trying to act casual, I paced off the distance from bow to stern. Forty feet, more or less.

My heart did a quick rat-a-tat-tat in my chest. Frank and Sally's *Wanderer* was a forty-one foot yawl.

I couldn't count the number of times we'd sailed the Chesapeake Bay with the Parkers on *Wanderer*. I remembered one long day on the bay when Frank, trying to beat a squall, plowed *Wanderer* into a piling, gouging her bow. I walked around to the bow of *Alice in Wonderland* and reached up as high as I could, running my fingers along the rounded seam, feeling for any sign of damage. But if there'd been any, it had been repaired.

Paul would tell me that I was letting my imagination run away with me.

And yet as I stared at the boat, at its distinc-

157

tive keel, I flashed back to a Sunday afternoon at the Naval Academy marina where Paul and I had helped Frank and Sally roll anti-fouling paint on *Wanderer's* hull. I'd painted around that propeller shaft myself, or one exactly like it.

If I were to prove that this vessel was Frank and Sally's boat, I'd have to get inside. But I couldn't do that while Daniel and his co-workers were on the job.

I thought about the problem as I walked to the grocery where I picked out the supplies I needed – alas for Paul, no English muffins – and set them down on the checkout counter. I visited with Winnie for a while, killing time until noon when I hoped the boat-yard workers would break for lunch.

'How's Lisa?' I asked as I packed my purchases into the Trader Joe's bag I'd brought with me. There'd been a benefit supper for the seven-year-old, Winnie's granddaughter, at one of the local churches. Hand-printed signs announcing the event had been tacked up on every telephone pole in town.

'She's in good spirits,' Winnie told me. 'Ted took her to Nassau yesterday. They may have to do surgery.'

'That's too bad,' I said, meaning it. I'd rather straddle a log and dog-paddle to a hospital in Florida than have surgery for anything more serious than a hangnail in Nassau. 'Do you mind if I ask what kind of surgery?'

'It's a heart valve defect. Congenital.'

Yikes, I thought. That's one for the Mayo Clinic, not Princess Margaret in Nassau.

We chatted until the clock over Winnie's head read eleven fifty-five, then I picked up my groceries, wished her goodbye, good luck and God speed, and made my way back to the boatyard.

As I had hoped, Daniel and his co-workers were at lunch, most of the men sitting on upturned buckets in the shade of a tree, playing cards, using the top of a cable spool as a table. Daniel sat with his back against an upturned dinghy, eating a sandwich and reading his Bible.

I waved casually, nodded, smiled and walked on, but as soon as I was out of their sight, I ducked around the corner of a utility shed and into the boatyard.

Alice in Wonderland appeared deserted, Daniel's ladder still propped against her hull.

After a quick look around, I stashed my groceries next to an empty trash can and scampered up the ladder. I threw my leg over the lifelines, hopped into the cockpit and crouched down, hardly breathing, feeling about as inconspicuous as a fly on a wedding cake. Tools lay on the cockpit bench where they'd been neatly arranged by one of the workers who had apparently been in the process of installing an autopilot when he broke for lunch. The instrument itself hung half in and half out of the control panel on the steering pedestal, dangling by its wires.

No sirens, no alarms, no shouts of 'Hey you!' so I got slowly to my feet and sat down behind the wheel. I remembered my sister-in-law Connie's sailboat, *Sea Song*, had its hull identification number stamped into the fiberglass on the stern. Taking a chance I'd not be spotted, I peered over the stern, searching the transom. But if there had ever been any numbers inscribed there, they were gone now.

I needed to look inside.

I hustled down the companionway ladder and found myself standing in a rich, teak-paneled cabin as familiar to me as my own living room: a dinette to port, a galley to starboard, a navigation station to the rear. Many boats were laid out that way, however, even Connie's.

Where Frank and Sally had a liquor cabinet, there was a microwave, and although our friends had never had a TV, a flat screen hung on the bulkhead of the V-berth in the master cabin.

A stainless-steel cover was drawn over the stove. I checked under it quickly. Three burners. Just like *Wanderer*, but thousands of other boats, too.

It was the upholstery on the cushions throughout the boat that really got my attention: a distinctive red, green, blue and black tartan. Sally's maiden name was McDuff. Their dog was named Duffy. Sally'd picked that fabric out herself, the tartan of Clan McDuff. That was proof enough for me.

Jaime Mueller might have been able to hire a

crew of Haitians to strip, clean and repaint a boat within a matter of days, I thought, but re-upholstering was another matter. I knew from Pattie's Net bible that there was only one guy in Marsh Harbour who reupholstered boat cush-ions, and his waiting list was a mile long. He ordered all his fabric from the States, which took forever. Even all of Jaime's daddy's money couldn't turn boat cushions around that fast in the Abacos.

Think, Hannah. If you go to the Marsh Harbour police with your suspicions, they'll listen politely, then show you the door. *Plaid, madam?* I could hear the laughter now.

I checked my watch. Daniel and his co-work-ers would still be at lunch. By my calculations I had twelve minutes, no more, before they came back. Sweat rolled down my cheeks and between my breasts.

There had to be something to prove that this was the Parkers' boat!

I checked the medicine cabinet. Empty.

I opened the door under the sink where Sally had kept her cleaning supplies. Spotless.

I peeked into the fridge. Not a speck of food.

Someone had scrubbed the stove, too, polish-ing its stainless-steel surface to a high gloss. Even the oven gleamed. It could have been new.

I leaned back on the stove, and it moved, reminding me of one of my less stellar cruising maneuvers.

Nautical stoves are gimballed. They swing

with the motion of the boat, so that pots and pans stay level while you're cooking under way. I got down on my hands and knees in front of the oven and pushed the stove back, squinting under it into the narrow space between the bottom of the oven and the floor.

On the white fiberglass surface near the back of the stove there was a dark, reddish-brown stain the size of my fist.

I sat back on my heels. Jesus! It had been my fault, that stain. Sally had spaghetti sauce simmering. We girls had been down below, making salad when *Wanderer* hit a wake and I'd crashed into the stove, sending the pot flying and the sauce splashing over the cook top and dribbling down the side. Apparently, my clean-up had been less than thorough.

Well you see, officer, there was this dried-up spaghetti sauce. Right. That would convince them.

Keep looking.

I pawed through the contents of the navigation station, searching for registration papers, anything that would identify this vessel as Frank and Sally Parker's boat, *Wanderer*, but the only contents of the nav station were a 2008 edition of Steve Dodge's *A Cruising Guide to the Abacos*, a brand-new logbook, a pair of binoculars and two pens.

I got down on my hands and knees, crawled around the floor, looking for clues, peeping into nooks and crannies not normally peeped into – unless one is falling down drunk – like under the companionway stairs. Nothing, not a scrap. I lifted the seat cushions and looked under them. Nada. I even pulled up the floorboards and peered into the bilge.

When I sat down on a settee to think, I noticed a drawer in the settee opposite. I pulled the drawer open and when I saw it was empty, pulled it out completely to examine the space behind. Disappointed again, I started to slide the drawer back, but as I did I noticed something written in pencil on the bottom. '2304.' I checked the bottom of the drawer under the settee I had just been sitting on. It also had '2304' penciled on the raw wood. Was it a part number of some sort? Hoping somebody could tell me, I pulled my iPhone out of my fanny pack and took a picture.

I was still puzzled why this boat didn't seem to have a builder's plaque. On Connie's boat, it was nailed to the hatch cover. Where would it be on a Cheoy Lee?

There had been nothing of a plaque-like description in the cockpit. I didn't find it in my crawl around the interior of *Alice in Wonderland*. The only objects hanging on the bulkhead were a barometer and a clock, and one of Andy Albury's smaller half-boat models. From the slightly pitted brass, I could tell that the barometer and the clock had been there forever, but the boat model looked new.

I popped up to the cockpit, grabbed a screwdriver from the array on the bench and quickly backed out one of the screws that held the ship model in place. I loosened the second screw and moved the model to one side.

The model had been hiding two screw holes, about six inches apart, but whatever had been mounted there was gone.

I had to give Jaime Mueller credit. When he stole a boat, he was thorough.

I snapped a picture of the screw holes with my iPhone, reattached the model and got the hell out.

Paul raised both hands. 'Stop babbling, Hannah.'

I had been going on and on about *Wanderer*, starting from when I first spotted the vessel in the boatyard, followed by a blow-by-blow description of what led up to my discovery of the spaghetti-sauce spill.

'Don't build me a watch, Hannah. Just tell me what time it is.'

'*Alice in Wonderland* is *Wanderer*,' I sputtered. 'And I think we can prove it.'

'Ah.' Paul laced his fingers together and rested his hands on his chest. 'The spaghetti-sauce clue.'

'Don't be impossible!' I pawed in my fanny pack for my iPhone, launched the camera icon, and showed Paul the picture of the number written on the bottom of the drawer.

'2304. What does that mean?' he asked.

'I don't know. I was hoping you'd tell me.' I flicked forward to the picture of the pair of screw holes I'd discovered in the wall behind the ship model. 'And here's where something was removed from the wall. Could have been the builder's plaque.'

Paul slipped the iPhone out of my fingers and studied the picture closely. 'Hard to tell from this. Could have been anything mounted up there. "The Captain's Word is Law" or "Don't Flush Anything You Haven't Eaten First."'

'Ha ha ha.' I pinched his ear lobe, hard, then sat down on the sofa. 'I looked all over the boat for its hull identification number, but couldn't find one.'

'I hate to tell you this, Hannah, but boats built in the sixties weren't required to have hull identification numbers. *Wanderer*, and this boat, might not even have one.'

'Bummer,' I said. Then I brightened as a thought occurred to me. 'Do you think *Wanderer* might have been documented? Can we look it up on the Internet?' I stood up. 'Where's your laptop?'

With Paul's help, I located the NOAA website where one could search the vessel documentation database by name. I typed in *'Wanderer,'* pressed Enter, and waited for the results. I sat back, disappointed. 'Oh, damn. There's a hundred and seventy-two of them!'

'It's a popular name, Hannah. Eric Hiscock sailed three or four *Wanderers* around the world and wrote books about it. He's every blue-water dreamer's hero.'

'Help me to narrow it down, then. What's *Wanderer*'s port of call?'

165

'If it's not Annapolis, I don't have a clue.'

Only one vessel hailed from Annapolis, and it wasn't a Cheoy Lee Reliant, but as I scrolled through the display, I realized I could also narrow the search by boat length. Five minutes later I cried, 'I found it!' and then, 'Dammit!' when I clicked on the record and found that, as Paul had predicted, the space for the hull identification number was blank.

'Jot down the Coast Guard documentation number,' Paul suggested. 'Sometimes owners engrave them on the hull.'

I did as Paul suggested, but didn't hold out much hope of that. I'd been all over that boat, and if there had been a Coast Guard number anywhere on board, I should have found it.

I stared at the computer screen, chewing my lower lip. 'What now?'

'Let's ask the pro.' Paul rose from his chair, crossed into the living room and picked up the radio. 'Dive Gator, Dive Gator, this is *Windswept*.' There was no response. After a couple of minutes, he tried again, but Gator was either busy or out of radio range.

'Sit down and eat your lunch,' Paul suggested. 'It's getting cold.'

'I'm too upset to eat.' I tucked my conch burger back into its Styrofoam clamshell and stuck it into the fridge. 'If Jaime Mueller has Frank and Sally's boat, then where are Frank and Sally?'

I washed my hands, tried to reach Gator again. This time he replied. 'What can I do for you, Hannah?'

Since I didn't want to broadcast my suspicions to everyone who might have been listening in on that channel, I made arrangements to drop by Gator's office when he returned from his dive.

The afternoon dragged.

I spent some time Googling Cheoy Lee. The company was still in business, but hadn't made the Reliant since 1976. They built large power yachts now. There appeared to be an active owners' association, however. I bookmarked both.

Just as I was about to email the Rhodes Reliant and Offshore Forty website, the power failed. I telephoned the Bahamas Electric Company to report the outage. The worker who answered the phone assured me the power would be back in an hour, but with the BEC, that didn't mean a damn thing. Could be an hour, could be days, depending upon how long it took workers to find and repair the break in the underwater cable. Molly swears they do it with duct tape.

No power, no backup generator, no Internet. Bummer.

Nothing to do but wait.

Eleven

THE NATIONAL VESSEL DOCUMENTATION CENTER FACILITATES MARITIME COMMERCE AND THE AVAILABILITY OF FINANCING WHILE PROTECTING ECONOMIC PRIVILEGES OF UNITED STATES CITIZENS THROUGH THE ENFORCEMENT OF REGULATIONS, AND PROVIDES A REGISTER OF VESSELS AVAILABLE IN TIME OF WAR OR EMERGENCY TO DEFEND AND PROTECT THE UNITED STATES OF AMERICA.

Mission Statement, United States Coast Guard, National Vessel Documentation Center

I found Gator in the cockpit of *Deep Magic*, slinging empty air tanks on to the dock. I stopped to help.

'You know that missing sailboat, the *Wanderer*?'

Gator stopped in mid-swing. 'Yup.'

'I think I found it.'

He lowered the tank to the deck and squinted up at me. 'You're shitting me. Where?'

'It's in Pinder's boatyard. It's been stripped and repainted, but I'm pretty sure it's the same vessel.' I explained how I knew the Parkers and had sailed on their boat. I told him about the tartan upholstery, the penciled numbers, the telltale screw holes, and even about the spaghetti sauce.

'Come on. Let's have a look.'

Faster than I would have thought possible, Gator stepped from *Deep Magic* to the dock, leaving his boat rocking. He double-timed it up the pier in the direction of his golf cart. By the time I caught up to him, he was already turning the key in the ignition. 'Hop in.'

The engine sputtered and caught. Gator reached behind his right leg to shove the gear into forward, and we were off. At the boatyard, he brought the cart to a jarring halt in front of the utility shed, hopped out, and motioned for me to follow.

We found Daniel and another Haitian on board the *Alice in Wonderland*, busily brushing teak oil on the decking.

Gator knocked on the hull until he got Daniel's attention. 'Morning, Daniel. Fine boat. Mind if I take a look?'

Daniel beamed down on us. 'Go ahead, mon.'

The direct approach. Why hadn't I thought of that?

Gator clambered up the ladder, now propped against the stern of the vessel, and hopped into the cockpit. I followed. While Daniel and his co-worker went on with their task, Gator and I went inside.

If anything, the boat was cleaner than it had

been earlier that morning. When I bent over to show Gator the spaghetti-sauce spill, there wasn't a trace of it, either.

'Damn.'

The only concrete 'evidence' I had left to show him were the numbers penciled on the bottoms of the drawers, and the two screw holes behind the half model where I suspected the builder's plaque might have been.

While I watched, Gator unscrewed the model and studied the bulkhead behind it, touching a finger to each of the holes, looking thoughtful. He swept his ball cap off his head, and while still holding it, scratched his head. 'Boat's so clean you could perform open-heart surgery in here.'

I dredged up a smile. 'You don't believe me, do you?'

'Oh, I believe you,' he said. 'That number you found is probably the boat's yard number. They'd write it on the various components of the boat as they were being built to tell the installer which boat the part was destined for.'

'Maybe Cheoy Lee kept records?'

'Maybe.' He returned the model to its original position and screwed it back down. 'And Reliants are supposed to have a builder's plaque right here.' He tapped the wall with the knuckle of his index finger.

Gator stuck his head out of the hatch and called into the cockpit where one of the Haitians had started polishing up the bright work on the helm. 'Michael!'

170

'Wi?'

'Kisa bagay vou...' Gator cast his eyes heavenward, as if expecting God to write an English to Creole translation in the clouds. He shifted from one foot to the other uncomfortably. 'Uh, what thing you take off that wall down there? Konprann?'

At first I thought Michael didn't 'konprann,' but after processing Gator's question for a few seconds, he shaped his thumbs and fingers into an oval about the size of a saucer.

Gator beamed, and plopped his hat back on his head. 'Mesi.'

I beamed at Michael, too. 'Nou ap chache...' Now it was my turn to run out of Creole. I raised both hands, palms up and added, 'Kote?' *Where?*

'Bokit fatra.'

I looked at Gator. 'Bokit I get. Bucket. But what's fatra?'

'Rubbish, I think.'

'Trash bin!' I shouted.

Gator and I practically tripped over one another in our race for the ladder, but only one of us could go down at a time. I descended quickly, backwards, rung by rung, with Gator several rungs behind, trying (vainly) not to step on my fingers.

Once on level ground, Gator pointed toward the stern of *Alice in Wonderland*. 'You go that way, and I'll check the shed area.'

I walked around the boat, looking in every container. I turned up wooden blocks, sand-

171

paper, oily rags, bits of fiberglass, but nothing remotely resembling a plaque. I worked my way along the dock, kicking up debris as I went, following the track of the marine railroad down to the water where a school of yellow jacks was nosing about, angling for a handout. In the water I could see lumps of metal, sacrificial leads that had done their duty and disintegrated instead of the propeller shafts to which they had been attached. A few lost screws flashed brightly in the sun.

At the end of the pier, in deeper water, I identified a five-gallon gasoline can, a water-logged seat cushion green with algae, and what looked like several hatch covers – four-by-four squares of corrugated steel, each tethered to the dock by a rope. As I straightened and opened my mouth to call Gator, he appeared behind me. 'What are those?' I asked, pointing to the hatch covers.

'Lobster condos,' he replied.

'Condos? For lobsters?'

'Traps, actually,' Gator explained. 'Those are being seasoned. In a week or two we'll haul them out to the reef.'

'How do you catch a lobster with that?' I wondered aloud. 'It's just a flat piece of metal nailed to a couple of two-by-fours.'

'Lobsters are nocturnal. They hide out in dens during the day. We used to use discarded bathtubs, car hoods, hurricane shutters and the like to make artificial dens for them. As you can see, we've gone high-tech.'

I laughed at the concept. 'So what do you do? Send a diver down, lift up the condo and start grabbing?'

'Something like that. Lobsters used to be taken by breath-hold divers using spear-guns. Sometimes they'd squirt bleach into the reef to force the lobsters out into the open.'

Thinking about what that would do to the reef, I gasped.

'Exactly. That's why it's now illegal. This method is the least damaging to the reef.'

Gator bent down, picked up one of the ropes and tugged it, raising a corner of the condo so I could see underneath. No lobsters, but I'd hardly expect any in a busy harbor.

'So,' I said. 'If I come across one of those condos out there, I can pick up a quick lobster dinner?'

Gator began to play out the rope. 'I wouldn't if I were you. Local fishermen take their traps very seriously. I wouldn't want to be caught between a lobsterman and his catch.'

As the condo came to rest again against the bottom, a roundish object about the size of a coffee can half buried in the sand caught my eye. I swallowed hard, croaked, then managed to find my voice. 'Gator!'

Gator dropped the rope and stared at me as if I'd lost my marbles.

I pointed. 'Down there! Next to the condo.'

Gator peered into the water. 'I'll be damned.' He took off his hat, handed it to me, then grabbed the hem of his T-shirt and pulled it off over his head, baring a fine set of pecs covered with sun-bleached fuzz. 'Let's have a look.'

Before I could say, 'But you're not wearing a bathing suit,' he had dived into the water. He reached the bottom in two easy strokes, picked up the disk, rotated it, then stuck it into the waistband of his pants and shot to the surface. He swam along the railway tracks until he could stand, then waded ashore.

I ran up the dock to meet him as he emerged from the water. 'Well?'

Gator flicked water out of his buzz cut with the flat of his hand. He reached into his waistband, pulled out the disk, and handed it to me. 'See for yourself.'

I was holding a polished steel oval, neatly framed in teak. The varnish had peeled off the frame in spots, but the engraving on the metal was plain as day: Cheoy Lee Boat Yard. Yard #2304. And the date, 1969.

All it would take was an email to Ben Stavis, keeper of the Rhodes Reliant Owners website or a phone call to the Cheoy Lee Boat Yard, still doing business in Hong Kong to prove what I knew for sure. There could be only one Cheoy Lee Reliant, yard number 2304. *Alice in Wonderland* was *Wanderer.*

'So what do we do now?'

'I think we need to have a little chat with Jaime.'

Twelve

AFTER A SHORT WALK UP THE HILL, I WAS SITTING AT THE BAR AT THE BLUFF HOUSE CHATTING WITH MY NEW FRIENDS WHEN A MAYDAY CAME ACROSS THE RADIO. 'MAY-DAY, MAYDAY, THIS IS OCEAN 55 ON A REEF OFF ELBOW CAY TAKING ON LOADS OF WATER.' LATER DURING A VISIT TO HOPE TOWN, I FOUND THE BOAT COMPLETELY SUNK, AND KEEPING WITH ISLAND TRADI-TION THE SALVAGERS WERE OUT THERE THE NEXT MORNING STRIPPING THE BOAT OF ANYTHING USABLE, LIKE PROPS, RAILS ETC.

Log of the *Motu Iti*, May 2000

Early the next morning, at my insistence, Paul took the ferry over to Marsh Harbour to see about buying a portable generator. Fine steaks were hard to come by in the islands, and watching helpless as they thawed ... well, let's say I know how the cavewoman felt when the gazelle she speared for dinner got up and ran away.

So that's how it happened that the first time I set foot on the grounds of the Tamarind Tree Resort and Marina, it was in the company of a sun-bleached son of the islands, not my husband.

As we bumped along in Gator's golf cart, the Queen's Highway changed from a narrow strip of pavement to an even narrower one, then to a rutted dirt track, finally to hard-packed sand as it curved away from the settlement toward the sea. On the Atlantic side of the island it doubled back, crested a hill, then – fwap! – a spectacular view of the Sea of Abaco nearly knocked me out of my Crocs. 'They should have *this* in their brochures,' I raved as we coasted down the other side.

Near the resort, the track widened to a less teeth-rattling strip of concrete wide enough for two golf carts to pass, although we didn't meet anyone coming from the opposite direction. The lane was bordered by sea grape, hibiscus and patches of flame-red poinsettias from which life-size animal sculptures peeked; clearly a landscape designer had been at work.

Before long we arrived at a crimson gate-house designed like an old-style British telephone booth. A gate decorated with driftwood painted like barracuda barred our way.

Gator mashed his foot down on the brake pedal and the cart slowed silently to a stop. A guard dressed in the Tamarind Tree uniform stepped out of the booth to check us out. I recognized the young man as being among the volunteers at the wildfire the other day, but couldn't remember his name. His shirt saved me the trouble. When he got close enough, I could read the writing on the pocket: Lou.

Gator seemed to recognize the guy, too. 'Hey, Lou. We need to see Jaime Mueller. Is he in?'

'Do you have an appointment?' Lou sounded more like a receptionist at a law firm than a security guard in paradise.

'Since when do *I* need an appointment?' Gator grumbled.

'Just following orders, sir.' Lou slipped a hand-held out of his belt and pressed the call button. 'Jenny, Jenny, this is Gate One. Come in.'

The radio crackled to life. 'Jenny here. Go ahead, Lou.'

'Got some people here to see Jaime. He around? Over.'

'Tennis courts, I think. Over.'

'Thanks. Gate One out.'

'Out.'

Still holding his radio and giving me the hairy eyeball, Lou asked, 'Can I tell him who's looking?'

'Gator Crockett, from the dive shop. And this is Hannah Ives.'

'Oh, sorry, Mr Crockett. I should have known.' He pushed a button on a remote he carried on his belt and the gate swung slowly open.

As we drove through, I muttered, 'Darn right, he should have known. Your dive-shop logo is plastered all over the hood of your cart.'

Gator snorted.

'Hey!' Lou called after us. 'Follow the path

177

around to the left. There'll be signs directing you to the tennis courts. I'll let Mr Mueller know you're coming.'

I watched in the mirror as the gate swung shut behind us.

Gator guided his cart along paved, gently curving lanes lined with tropical plantings and tiki lights on six-foot poles. The same artist who'd painted the fish on the main gate had also designed the whimsical directional signs we saw throughout the resort. We came to a fork in the road where a turtle directed us to the right for 'tennis courts,' but Gator sailed right past.

'Tennis courts are that way,' I said, pointing behind me and to the right.

'I know.' Gator spun the steering wheel to the left, gunned the accelerator and grinned. 'Now that we're here, I thought we might take a little tour.'

We passed a grouper, a pelican and a frigate bird directing us to the kitchen, laundry room, and crew's quarters, respectively, before rounding a bend that skirted an ornamental pond and appeared to dead end at a greenhouse. I was squinting at the greenhouse windows, trying to see the orchids that Rudy Mueller had told me about, but everything blurred as Gator steered hard left and we shot through a gap in the casuarinas.

Long before we got to the dolphin that said 'Generator' we heard the drone of its engine, progressively increasing to a mind-numbing whine as we drew closer. Immediately behind the generator enclosure the water-treatment plant loomed into view, a state-of-the-art facility that supposedly used a reverse osmosis process to convert sea water to drinking water. Clearly, Mueller's Tamarind Tree Resort and Marina had no intention of falling to its knees at the mercy of either the BEC or Mother Nature.

Gator's tour had taken us in a wide circle to the western end of the island. When we reached the Atlantic beach, Gator killed the engine and climbed out of the cart. With both hands in his pockets he stood quietly on the dune, surveying the reef. 'We're standing on the fifth hole.'

I got out of the cart and joined him, appreciating the view while I could. 'It's criminal, isn't it?'

'How many golf courses does a small group of islands need?' he wondered aloud. 'Baker's Bay, Treasure Cay, Abaco Beach Resort ... they're all just a stone's throw from Hawksbill.'

I stole a look at him. His profile was set, grim. I wanted to hug the man and tell him everything would be all right even when I knew it probably wouldn't. 'It's not over 'til it's over,' I said.

Gator adjusted his cap, pulling the bill down over his forehead to better shade his eyes against the glare of the sun slanting off the water. 'It's like trying to stop an avalanche.'

The man was in mourning. How do you console someone for the death of an island, a way of life?

I returned to the golf cart, climbed in and sat

there quietly, leaving Gator alone with his thoughts. After a few minutes, he hopped in next to me, turned the key, floored the accelerator and sent the cart hurtling down the ocean path at breakneck speed, or what passes for breakneck speed in a golf cart, which is to say about fifteen miles per hour. He steered the vehicle around a curve and up a steep incline. The near-silent whine of the battery-powered engine changed to a rude putt-putt-putt as the gasoline booster kicked in to give us the extra oomph we needed to get up and over the hill.

At the bottom of the hill, we rounded a curve and sailed past the spa which was built up on stilts, South Pacific-style, before coming to a dolphin with 'Tennis Court' carved into its tail.

There was not one court, however, but three. Jaime Mueller was doing a stationary prance on one of them, looking very GQ in white tennis shorts and a blue polo shirt. A matching sweatband encircled his forehead. He was lobbing balls back and forth across the net with another one of the uniformed college boys.

Gator slotted his golf cart next to a cart emblazoned with the familiar TTR logo and we watched as Jaime missed a few easy ones. Gator chuckled. 'Hole in the boy's racquet.'

'Maybe he's letting the other guy win?'

'Jaime? What are you smoking?'

Jaime's opponent was poised with his racquet aloft and a tennis ball in his left hand when he noticed us. He lowered the racquet. 'Mr Mueller?'

Jaime noticed us, too, and waved his racquet, halting the game. He ambled over to the sideline, snatched a towel off a chair and approached us, mopping his face and neck. 'Hey, Gator. And it's Hannah, isn't it?' He flashed a grin so white and toothy that I could have played chopsticks on his teeth. He flipped the towel over a silver buttonwood bush. 'I never forget a pretty face.'

I bit my tongue.

'So, what can I do for you?'

'Some place we can talk?'

'Iced tea?'

'Yeah.'

'Meet you up at the lodge, then.'

A few minutes later, Gator and I had parked the cart and were meandering up the well-maintained, beautifully landscaped path that led to the Tamarind Tree restaurant. 'A bit more upmarket than the Cruise Inn and Conch Out, isn't it?' I commented.

The short path that led from the Queen's Highway to our favorite local establishment was neatly bordered with polished conch shells, its yellow elder and one small gumbo-limbo tree festooned with flotsam and jetsam – considered good luck in the islands – like a Christmas tree on Gilligan's Island. At the Cruise Inn and Conch Out, one ate inside.

At the Tamarind Tree, on the other hand, one dined on the veranda in green wicker chairs – plastic-coated but expensive – while fans with blades like palm branches rotated slowly overhead. White cloths covered tables decorated with fresh hibiscus in tall, oriental-style vases. We sat down at one of them and talked about the weather while awaiting the arrival of our iced tea, delivered after a few minutes by a beautiful Bahamian girl who couldn't have been more than sixteen.

Jaime leered. 'Thanks, sweetheart.'

She ducked her head modestly and scurried away. Smart girl. Looked to me like Jaime'd been fixing to pat her tush.

Jaime ripped open a packet of Sweet'N Low and dumped it into his tea. 'So, what can I do for you?' He tore the wrapper off a straw, plopped the straw into his tea and stirred vigorously. 'Have you reconsidered my offer to operate out of the dive shop here at Tamarind Tree?'

Gator skewered Jaime with ice-cold eyes and got straight to the point. 'The *Alice in Wonderland*. Tell me about it.'

I watched Jaime's face as a full range of emotions played across it – a self-satisfied smile, puzzlement, worry, and finally a straight-lipped, raised-eyebrow glare that I could describe only as arrogant. Jaime put the straw to his lips and sipped, making a production out of drawing the liquid up slowly, swallowing, and setting his glass back on the table. Buying time, I decided. Making up his cover story as he went along.

Gator and I waited patiently while Jaime got his act together.

'Found it,' he said at last.

'You *found* it?' I blurted.

'Had to take some prospects back to Harbour Island the other day. As I came back across the Devil's Backbone, I found it grounded on the rocks off Spanish Wells, sails still up and flapping. Pulled alongside, as anyone would, to see if there was anything I could do to help.' He spread his hands, palms up, and shrugged. 'But nobody was aboard.'

'Nobody?'

'Not a soul. Like they'd evaporated or something. I tied up alongside, climbed aboard and looked around. It was fucking spooky, like that ghost ship, the Marie Something.'

'Mary,' I corrected. 'The *Mary Celeste*.'

'Right.'

'What was the name of the boat you boarded?'

'*Wanderer*.' Jaime yawned.

I wanted to slap him. 'Did you know that there is a bulletin out for that vessel? It belongs to Frank Parker, a scientist from the Smithsonian Institution in Washington DC.'

'No shit!'

We waited, saying nothing. Jaime stared at us until he felt compelled to fill the silence with the sound of his own voice. 'I figured pirates.'

Gator snorted. 'Pirates? In the Abacos? There haven't been any pirates in the Bahamas since the eighteenth century.'

'Haitians, then.' Jaime raised his hands in mock surrender. 'Look, man, when I got on board, there wasn't nobody there. No ... who'd

183

you say? Frank Parker? No papers. Nada. I reported it to the police. What more do you want?'

'I've been asking about *Wanderer* and the Parkers on the Cruisers' Net every day for a week now.'

'I don't listen to the Cruisers' Net, do I? So how was I to know? Maybe you should have printed up a "lost" notice and tacked it to all the telephone poles around the island.' His eyes narrowed. 'Besides, how do I know it's the same boat? Lots of boats have the same name.'

That, at least, was true. 'It won't take long to trace the numbers on the boat's builder's plaque,' I said. 'Which brings up an interesting point. Why did you have the plaque removed?'

'I figured it didn't matter.'

I took a deep breath, counted silently to three and let it out. 'Didn't matter? I'm sure it mattered to the boat's owner.'

'*I'm* the owner.'

I opened my mouth to protest, but Gator laid a cautionary hand on my arm. 'He's right. If the boat was abandoned, and he salvaged it, then it's his.'

Across the table Jaime nodded like a bobble-head doll. 'The boat was a derelict, thrown up on the rocks, jagged hole in her hull. I'd say that qualified as being deserted by those in charge of it, without hope of recovery, and with no intention of returning, don't you? Bahamian Law. Chapter 274, Title 7.' He pressed on in that vein, peppering his dissertation with legal-

184

speak and words like flotsam, jetsam and ligan. The S.O.B. had memorized the law. I wanted to wipe the smirk off the supercilious bastard's face.

'Whatever happened to the Parkers,' I said, turning to Gator, 'it happened on that boat. Frank and Sally *never* would have left *Wanderer* voluntarily. It was their *home*!'

'You're free to search it if you want,' Jaime said.

I looked hopefully at Gator. 'We should contact the police. Have them look the boat over for signs of...'

Jaime leaned back in his chair and laughed. 'Foul play? Oh, right. *CSI* Marsh Harbour.'

'Don't they...' I began.

Gator leaned toward me, forearms resting on his knees. 'I'll talk to them, Hannah. Since US citizens are involved, they may send out the crime scene unit from Grand Bahama.'

'How about the US Coast Guard?' As I talked I skimmed through my mental Roledex of contacts in Washington DC. 'The FBI? Or Interpol?'

Gator touched my arm. 'One step at a time.'

Nothing about what Jaime said made any sense. Frank and Sally had last been sighted in Great Sale, heading toward Hawksbill Cay. Eleuthera, where Jaime insisted *Wanderer* had been found, was an island chain way to the south and east of the Abacos. *Wanderer* would have had to sail *past* Hawksbill Cay, down the eastern shore of Great Abaco and out into the

185

Atlantic Ocean before reaching Eleuthera. A two-day sail, at least.

'Do you have any witnesses to back up what you're telling us,' I blurted.

Jaime sucked in his lower lip and shook his head. 'Yes and no.'

We waited. If the jerk didn't start telling the truth soon, I was going to rip a tiki torch out of its holder and club him to death with it.

Jaime took a deep breath. 'The guy who was with me? Craig Meeks?' A sigh. 'Thought you might have heard.' A long pause while Jaime arranged his face into a fairly good imitation of sadness and concern. 'He's the one who died in the wildfire.'

A vision of Craig Meeks as I had last seen him swam into my brain, taking dark possession of it. The tiny sips of tea I had consumed threatened to make an encore. I pressed a napkin to my mouth. 'Excuse me,' I mumbled. I sprang to my feet and dashed madly in the direction of the ladies room, hoping I'd make it into a cubicle before disgracing myself in the frangipani.

When I returned to the veranda five minutes later, Jamie was nowhere to be seen, and Gator was waiting for me in the golf cart. As the main gate swung shut behind us, Gator said, 'Died in the fire, huh? How very convenient.'

Still fighting back waves of nausea I said, 'Jaime's a lying sack of shit.'

'He's also a bit fuzzy on maritime law, Hannah. A salvor can take possession of an

186

abandoned boat, but technically it's still the property of the owner. If the owner wants it back, he's obliged to come to some sort of agreement with the salvor. Money usually, but the owner can say, screw it, keep the boat.'

'If you can find the owners,' I added grimly.

I hung on to the canopy to keep from being dumped into the casuarinas when Gator made a hard right. He center-lined the wheel and turned his head to look at me. 'I *know* the bastard stole that boat, but what I can't figure out is why. He's got more money than God. Or at least his Papa has.'

'Guys like Jaime learn early on that rules apply only to other people,' I said. I thought about the special treatment recruited athletes get, even at the Naval Academy where sports weren't supposed to be as big a deal as they were in the Big Ten. Cocky jocks whose performance on the field was so important to mankind that it couldn't be interrupted by anything so mundane as class work or exams. Or, if one really got into trouble, jail time. 'Maybe Papa keeps his little boy on a short leash,' I added.

Suddenly, the wheels on my side of the cart wobbled off the pavement and dipped into the sand. I made a grab for the wheel, shouting, 'Eyes on the road!'

Seconds before we might have gone crashing ignominiously into a poisonwood tree, Gator regained control.

When we were safely on the road again, I said, *Wanderer* might have been abandoned for some reason I don't even want to contemplate, but barring some dramatic shift in the tectonic plates of the time-space continuum, there's no way in hell she was all the way down in Eleuthera, not if that cruiser who reported seeing her up in Great Sale a few days ago was right.'

'Bermuda Triangle?' Gator snorted at his own joke and gunned the accelerator.

Back in Hawksbill settlement, Gator eased his golf cart into a vacant parking spot near the Pink Grocery and walked back with me to the dock where I'd tied *Pro Bono*. As I climbed down the ladder and jumped into my boat, he said, 'I'll contact the Marsh Harbour police and make sure they know that the *Wanderer*'s been found.'

'Thanks, Gator.'

He untied the painter and after I'd started the motor, dropped the rope down to me. 'Meanwhile, see if you can rustle up anyone on the Net who actually saw *Wanderer* with the Parkers aboard between Great Sale and here.'

'Will do.'

'And, Hannah?'

I looked up, way up, into Gator's worried, suntanned face. 'Yes?'

'Remember what I told you. This is the Bahamas, not Maryland USA. Leave it to the locals. Don't get involved.'

I pushed *Pro Bono* away from the piling and pointed her out into the harbor. 'I'll try, Gator,' I shouted to his diminishing figure. 'It's not in my nature, but I'll honestly try.'

Thirteen

I'N'I BUILD A CABIN, I'N'I PLANT THE CORN;
DIDN'T MY PEOPLE BEFORE ME SLAVE FOR
THIS COUNTRY?
NOW YOU LOOK ME WITH THAT SCORN, THEN
YOU EAT UP ALL MY CORN.

WE GONNA CHASE THOSE CRAZY, CHASE
THEM CRAZY, CHASE THOSE CRAZY BALD-
HEADS OUT OF TOWN!

Bob Marley, *Crazy Baldheads*

The next morning on open mike, I asked listeners if anyone had seen *Wanderer*. My question was met with depressing silence.

The next day it was much the same. *Breaking Wind* called in to report seeing a vessel named *Wanderer* anchored in Black Sound up Green Turtle Cay way, but it turned out to be a Hunter, not a Reliant.

On Friday, my last official day as moderator of the Net, my open mike call was returned by an Ericson 38 just returning to radio range after a cruise to Allen's Pensacola, an uninhabited island to the north and west of us.

'*Windswept, Windswept,* this is *Northern Star.*'

'Come in, *Northern Star.*'

'You're looking for a boat called *Wanderer?* A Reliant for...?'

I was so excited that I stepped on his transmission, depressing the talk button before he had finished. 'That sounds like the boat, Captain. Over.'

'About ten days ago, *Wanderer* was anchored in Poinciana Cove behind Hawksbill Cay. My wife and I dinghied over to invite the owners for cocktails.'

'Frank and Sally Parker?'

'Roger. They joined us on *Northern Star,* stayed for dinner. Frank told me about the work he was doing on behalf of Save Hawksbill Cay. Said he was going to do a couple of night dives. You can't get a full picture of the health of a reef unless you can see it at night. What fish are out. What they're eating. Yada yada.'

'Anyone else in the cove with you?'

'Nope. Just the two boats. Even for hurricane season, it was pretty empty.'

'When did they leave?' I asked with growing dread.

'They were still there the next morning when we weighed anchor. I don't think they had any intention of leaving. Frank told me he was planning to testify at a meeting over in Hope...'

'*Sea Wolf, Sea Wolf, Sea Wolf.* Come back to *Happy Hooker.*'

Some fisherman with a more powerful radio

190

and no sense of netiquette was overriding our signal. I waited for *Happy Hooker* to finish impressing *Sea Wolf* with the sixty-pound amberjack he'd wrestled aboard his Hatteras, then hailed *Northern Star* again.

But, *Northern Star* couldn't add anything to what he'd already told me. Frank and Sally had been anchored in Poinciana Cove off Hawksbill Cay at the end of July. By the beginning of August they had vanished. It was looking very bleak for my friends.

Had Frank stumbled on something during his dive, something that Jaime Mueller, or someone else in the Mueller family wanted to keep secret?

I thought about all the laws the government of the Bahamas had put in place to control fishing and boating as well as the construction industry, regulations that were sometimes just for show, that could be bypassed if the right amount of money reached the right bank account of the right government official at the right time.

El Mirador Land Corporation had dotted all their I's and crossed all their T's. They'd been given a clean bill of health by the big shots in Nassau. As long as they didn't deviate from their plans and permits, they would be untouchable.

Was El Mirador up to something else, then? Something worth killing for?

It was clear to everyone involved in the meeting that Frank M. Parker, BS, PhD, SERC Senior

Scientist (Retired), cruising sailor, husband and friend, would not be testifying for Save Hawksbill Cay in Hope Town on Wednesday evening. Callers to the Net that morning had wondered if the meeting was still on. Henry Allen, Warden of the Abaco Land and Sea Park, representing himself as well as the Bahamas National Trust, assured everyone that it was. Five thirty. St James Methodist Church. Be there or be square.

The day of the meeting dawned hot, humid and virtually windless, the only breeze ruffling our hair being generated by *Pro Bono* itself as Paul, Molly and I skimmed along the Sea of Abaco from Bonefish to Elbow Cay.

By day, Hope Town's signature candy-striped lighthouse served as a landmark, welcoming boaters in; by night, its beacon (which can be seen for seventeen miles) warned them away from a dangerous reef where eighteenth-century locals had supplemented their income by 'wrecking.' The village probably looked a lot then as it does today – a quaint, pastel-colored New England fishing village.

Paul successfully negotiated the busy channel at the harbor's narrow entrance, and managed to snag a prime 'parking spot' at the Hope Town dinghy dock well inside the snug, protected harbor.

While Paul made *Pro Bono* secure, I rooted through my fanny pack. 'Who has the shopping list?'

'I do,' he said. 'First stop, Lighthouse Liquors. Seems we've been running through the Sauvignon Blanc at a fairly fast clip.'

'Guilty,' I said. I stole a glance at Molly. 'Not making any excuses for the bottle I drank last night, practically single-handed, but it seemed like a good idea at the time.'

Molly wrapped an arm around my waist, hugged me close. 'I know you're worried about the Parkers, sugar, but you shouldn't let it get to you. Worrying yourself to death isn't going to help anyone, least of all the Parkers.'

Angry tears pricked my eyes. 'If Jaime Mueller is at the meeting, you might have to hold me back, Molly.'

'Come on.' She looped her arm through mine as we turned left and walked 'Down Along,' one of only two principal streets on the island, both so narrow that not even golf carts were allowed to drive on them. Where 'Down Along' split we took the right fork and headed up the hill, carefully negotiating the cracks in the concrete. We left Paul at Lighthouse Liquors to restock our modest liquor cabinet as he saw fit, and continued on to Vernon's Grocery, a concrete, practically windowless building on Back Street. Its owner, Vernon Malone – Mr Vernon to you – was an island institution. His seven-times great grandmother, Wyannie Malone, had founded Hope Town settlement in 1785.

We were still downwind from the store when I stopped, breathing deeply. 'Ohmahgawd, do you smell that?'

Molly grinned. 'Coconut bread, I think.'

'I hope we haven't missed the key lime pie.'

193

We followed our noses to Vernon's bakery, the Upper Crust, which was tacked to the side of his grocery almost like an afterthought. The door to the bakery stood open so we stuck our heads in, inhaling appreciatively. Key lime pies topped with mountains of golden-peaked meringue sat out on the table. Coconut pies, fresh from the oven, cooled on the windowsill.

I pressed my hand to my chest. 'I think I'm hallucinating.'

The door to the grocery was behind us. Molly grabbed my hand and pulled me through it. 'Quick, before you OD.'

Just inside, Vernon himself was ringing up a purchase on an elderly cash register. He glared at us over the tops of his eyeglasses. 'In door's over there. That's the out.'

Since we were already inside the store, it seemed silly to leave, but I figured Vernon himself would stare us down forever until we did it his way. 'Sorry.' I bowed my head and backed out the way I'd come.

Giggling, Molly and I scuttled around the bag ice machine, past a stack of boxes and empty water jugs and pulled open a front door that reflected our bemused faces back at us, like a mirror.

Vernon, a wiry man somewhere in his mid-sixties, was bagging groceries for another customer. 'Afternoon, ladies.'

All was right with the world now that we'd mended our ways.

A sign hung at eye-level caught my eye as we

194

entered the store: *If you're looking for Wal-Mart, it's 200 miles to the right.*

More witticisms hand-written on pages torn from legal pads, four-by-five index cards, and even computer printouts labeled 'Off the wall ... at Vernon's,' kept us chuckling as we poked along the narrow aisles making our selections. Mr Vernon stocked more than groceries, apparently. He also stocked a wry sense of humor.

The weather is here. Wish you were beautiful! as I reached for the M&Ms on the candy and mixed-nuts rack.

Dyslexics, Untie! under the Hearth Club Custard Powder and next to a lone box of star anise.

If you're smoking in here, you'd better be on fire over the cash register as Vernon totted up our purchases. I reintroduced myself and said, 'Are you going to the Save Hawksbill Cay meeting tonight?'

'Yup.'

The answer didn't surprise me. Grocer, baker, Justice of the Peace, lay preacher – Vernon Malone was deeply involved in the life of his community. It was probably genetic. From Wyannie Malone it was passed down the generations to Vernon, and from Vernon to his children. His daughter not only owned the liquor store, but coordinated weddings out of Da Finer Tings, and was a volunteer firefighter, too.

'I'm just a second-home owner,' Molly added, 'but I'm hoping I can make some small contribution.'

195

Vernon boxed our pies and eased them into plastic sacks. 'Second-home owners are the bread and butter of this place, Ms Molly. Most of you've been breaking your butts for thirty years to afford to come here. We need to make sure the island stays worth coming to.'

Clearly, an ally. 'Thanks, Vernon. See you tonight, then.'

The three of us decided on an early dinner at Cap'n Jack's, sitting on the deck overlooking Hope Town harbor where we munched on conch fritters washed down with Kalik. While Paul splurged on grilled grouper with macaroni and cheese – a spicy island version, light years away from Kraft in a box – Molly and I shared a Greek salad.

At five fifteen, we wandered up the road past the clinic and the post office to St James Methodist Church, a simple white, one-story structure built on a dune overlooking the Atlantic Ocean. The branches of a voluptuous cherry-red bougainvillea cascaded over the gate. We climbed the steps and went through the double doors into a cool sanctuary.

While Paul and Molly wandered off on errands of their own, I slipped into one of the dark wooden pews.

St Katherine's needs this view, I thought, feeling a twinge of homesickness, suddenly missing my friend, Pastor Eva, and her little Episcopal church in West Annapolis. With the exception of the altar hanging, the entire eastern wall of St James consisted of sliding glass doors that framed a spectacular view of the Atlantic Ocean. Who needs stained glass when you've got swaying palms, cottony clouds and the gently rolling sea? The sermons here could be boring as dirt, but the congregation would sit rapt. Guaranteed.

My eyes strayed to the cross, and as people began to fill the pews in front and behind me, I said a prayer for Frank and Sally Parker, wherever they might be.

I had gone in search of Paul, when Henry Allen barged through the swinging doors at the rear of the church struggling with a notebook, a pile of printouts, and a canvas bag containing an LCD projector and a laptop computer. Cables dangled from the mouth of the bag like a tangle of black and white spaghetti.

I met him halfway down the aisle, relieving him of the notebook and printouts. 'I'm sorry we didn't get over to see your video, Henry, but with the wildfire on the preserve, things have been a little hectic.'

'That's OK. I'm showing it tonight anyway.' He glanced around the sanctuary. 'There's supposed to be a screen here, somewhere. Oh, there it is!'

'Need help getting set up?'

'That'd be great. Thanks.'

A table had been centered about halfway up the aisle, so I set Henry's LCD projector down on it while he went off in search of an extension cord. When everything was plugged in, we aimed the projector at the screen, hooked up his laptop and powered on all the equipment.

Henry watched the screen apprehensively, worry changing to relief when the familiar Windows icons finally appeared. He launched his PowerPoint program and soon the screen was filled with the title page of his presentation, 'Hawksbill Cay Development: a Case Study of a Coastal Ecosystem' superimposed over a swirly blue background that I recognized as the 'Calm Sea' theme.

'Appropriate template,' I said.

Henry smiled. 'It's the one I always use. Some of the other templates sound appropriate, like "Starfish," but they make my eyes hurt.'

Henry clicked through the first few slides of his presentation, grunted in approval, then clicked back to his title page which included the URL for his website. I was reminded that I'd forgotten to ask him about the imposter website that linked to teen porn.

When I mentioned it, he scowled darkly. 'Know who did it, but can't prove it. Got an attorney trying to get the Internet provider to pull the plug, but nobody's breaking any laws. Should have registered all variations of that domain name ourselves, of course, but...' He shrugged. 'Frustrating.'

'Who do you think is responsible?'

Henry's eyebrows shot up in surprise. 'Mueller, of course, or that free-loading son of his.' He picked up the packet of handouts I'd set aside at the end of a pew and held them out to me. 'Can't think about it too much or it makes me crazy. Would you mind passing these out for me?'

I saw that the handout was a PowerPoint summary of his presentation, nine slides per page. In my experience with the corporate world it was best to save the handouts until after your talk, otherwise you'd be distracted by rattling pages all the while you were speaking, but this was Henry's show, not mine, so I said, 'Sure,' and went to look for Molly.

I found her at the refreshments table near the entrance to the sanctuary arranging sugar cookies on paper plates. An orange and white Thermos the size of a barrel sat at one end of the table, surrounded by stacks of paper cups. 'What's in the Thermos?' I asked.

'Ice water. Want some?'

'Maybe later. I've got these handouts. Want to help?'

Molly worked the right side of the aisle and I the left, the job taking longer than anticipated because we had to greet and chat with everyone along the way. I handed one to Gator Crockett personally. He had spruced up for the occasion, digging deep into his closet for olive-green Dockers and a pale-yellow polo shirt. 'Hey, Gator. I nearly didn't recognize you without your hat.'

'Wouldn't miss this meeting for all the world.' He accepted the printout and scanned the top sheet quickly. 'It's a pity Frank Parker can't be here. He didn't turn up, did he?'

'No,' I said simply.

'Is anybody filling in?'

'Not that I know of.'

I met other people I recognized from the settlement, including Winnie looking extraordinarily pretty in pink, and her husband, Ted. The postmistress, a well-rounded woman of sturdy island stock, sat in the front row clutching an oversized tote bag to her bosom. From the way she stared straight ahead and scowled at the pulpit, I thought she might be carrying rotten tomatoes, in case the discussion turned ugly.

Troy Albury, freshly shaved and with his mustache neatly trimmed, hurried in, glanced around, then sat down next to Pattie Toler. The two had their heads together, talking earnestly. A few minutes later, Vernon Malone slipped into the end of the pew.

I didn't see any Muellers until five minutes before show time when Gabriele wafted in, smiling and looking confident, dressed for success in a yellow and white sundress and high-heeled sandals. Her dark hair hung loose; tendrils caressing her collarbone. Without stopping to talk to anyone, she made a beeline for Henry Allen who stood behind the pulpit, arranging his papers. She extended her hand. 'My father sends his regrets, Mr Allen, but he's tied up in San Antonio.'

Swivel, turn, a dazzling smile for me. 'One of the twins has appendicitis, Mrs Ives. I'm sure you understand.'

Step, turn, a hair flip for Henry. 'But I'm here to represent the family, and I'll be happy to address any of your concerns.'

'Is your brother here?' I asked. I was impervious to hair flips.

'No. Just me.'

That was a relief. I watched as she coasted back down the aisle, taking a seat in the rear.

Henry, too, seemed relieved at the news that his meeting would proceed Jaime-less. He stood taller, straighter. Cool eyes appraising the audience. Acknowledging individuals with a nod, or a wave.

Paul had been saving a place for me, so I eased myself into the second row between him and Molly.

'Good evening, ladies and gentlemen,' Henry began. 'Most of you know me. I'm Henry Allen, warden at Out Island Land and Sea Park. As you know, ever since we learned of El Mirador Land Corporation's purchase of the old Island Fantasy property, we've been concerned about the impact their planned development will have on our island, our reef and our livelihoods.'

Henry aimed a remote at the laptop and clicked over to his first slide, a picture of two men climbing into an airplane, a bright-yellow, two-seater Savage Cub. 'First, I want to show you how Hawksbill Cay looked two years ago, prior to the commencement of construction.'

I wasn't surprised by the slides, which had been taken about the same time as the aerial photographs Paul and I had seen at the art show in Marsh Harbour. As Henry paged through the slides, Hawksbill's small settlement stood out clearly over the wing of the airplane: a simple grid of narrow streets beaded with cottages, its marina and shipyard piers delicately fringing the water, with a scattering of pleasure boats moored like sequins in the harbor.

The northwestern end of the island stood out in jewel-like perfection, too, like a brooch of emerald green, trimmed with a brilliant strip of sand, all set in the translucent turquoise of the sea.

'Before,' Henry said simply. He aimed his remote and pressed the button. 'Now we come to the "After."'

As one slide transitioned to the next, there was a collective gasp as the audience gradually came to realize what they were seeing. I was prepared for the gash of the runway, of course; I'd seen it from *Windswept*. But the extent of the damage that construction had brought to the interior of Hawksbill Cay was astonishing.

From the raw end of the runway a long tongue of silt curled into the sea. 'Where are the silt containment curtains we were assured would be used during all phases of construction?' Henry asked. 'Only in the El Mirador brochures, apparently.'

The next slide was even more alarming. The mangroves that had formerly grown thick along Tom's Creek had been bulldozed and burned, the gently curving shoreline turned into mud flats, desolate as a moonscape. To one side of the photo a backhoe crouched, its bucket resting on the ground, looking almost apologetic for the damage it had caused.

'I come from Kentucky,' someone in the audience behind me shouted. 'Our strip mines look better than that!'

Henry acknowledged the interruption with a nod, then clicked to the next slide. 'This is where the condos are going to be built,' he continued.

I realized I was staring at an aerial shot of what had once been a hillside leading down to a pristine creek. El Mirador's hungry backhoes had scraped the earth bare, literally wounding the island, leaving ugly brown scabs. 'This is not hard land,' Henry continued, highlighting the hillside area with a wavering beam of a red laser pointer. 'It is porous limestone directly connected to the wetlands. Destruction of our mangrove and sea grass nurseries will have a hugely negative impact on the reef communities that support our local populations of commercially important fish as well as our lobster and conch.'

'I suppose this is what El Mirador meant when they advertised that all the bungalows will be nestled within a lovely mangrove forest,' Molly grumbled.

Gabriele was on her feet. 'Naturally we have to clear land if we are going to build houses,' she said as she glided toward the front of the sanctuary, addressing the audience to the right and to the left of her as she made her way up the aisle. 'But the impact on the ecosystem has been shown to be minimal. Our environmental impact statement is already on record and has been approved by BEST. As you may recall, we hired an independent researcher led by Adam Hardin, a top marine scientist.'

'What's BEST?' I whispered to Molly.

'Bahamian Environment, Science and Technology Commission,' she whispered. 'They're supposed to review environmental impact statements and coordinate between developers and the government. They're supposed to be on our side.'

'That's a crock!' someone wearing a red ball cap shouted. 'Your so-called scientist is the son-in-law of one of El Mirador's major investors!'

'Is this true, Henry?' someone else asked in a more reasonable tone.

Gabriele answered for him. 'Yes, but Hardin's credentials are impeccable, and so is his report.'

The guy in the red ball cap wasn't buying it. 'Ha!'

Henry raised both hands. 'Calm down a minute. No need to shout.'

From the back of the sanctuary, Vernon spoke up. 'What I want to know is what happened to that fellow from the Smithsonian Environmental Research Center. Wasn't he supposed to testify tonight?'

'Thanks for asking, Vernon. Yes, he was, but I'm afraid Frank Parker's been delayed.'

'If he can't be here, why don't we have a copy

of his report?' Vernon wondered.

I elbowed Paul. 'That's a good question. Do you think Frank sent a copy of his report to anybody?'

'Regrettably, we don't have a copy of his report,' Henry continued. 'As some of you may know, we were expecting Mr Parker to speak here tonight, but his vessel is overdue. He and his wife are missing.'

Lots of murmuring agreement from the audience, many of whom had probably been following our efforts to locate *Wanderer* on the Cruisers' Net each morning. Some had probably overheard when *Northern Star* reported a sighting of *Wanderer* in Poinciana Cove. But there was only a handful of people who knew that *Wanderer*, the sailboat, had been found without her captain and first mate aboard, and that she was now rechristened the *Alice in Wonderland* and in Jaime Mueller's possession.

Winnie stood, shoulders back, arms to her sides. 'One thing that the El Mirador environmental impact study doesn't adequately address is the impact that their desalinization plant will have on our island. Have there been any studies on that?'

'Nothing on the federal level,' Gabriele admitted. 'Most of the studies of desalinization have been funded by private business.'

'Well, we all know how unbiased *that* would be!' Winnie's eyes went on scan, making contact with everyone in the room, who nodded in agreement.

'We have a state-of-the-art facility,' Gabriele assured the audience. 'Please, tell me. What are your specific concerns?'

'You have to get the water from our sea,' Gator boomed from the back row. 'I'm worried about the impact your water-intake pipes will have on the fish, particularly with such a large-scale plant.'

Gabriele managed a straight-lipped response. 'We have been assured that that isn't a concern.'

Gator pressed on. 'In what way isn't it a concern? Fish will be sucked in through the pipes, isn't that so?'

'The pipes will be screened.'

Gator looked up, rolled his eyes, as if seeking patience from the cross. 'Then organisms will collide with the screen, Ms Mueller. Fish, and smaller organisms, like zooplankton will go right on through.'

'Wait a minute!' A suntanned arm attached to a petite islander was waving for attention. 'Once you take the salt out of the water, Ms Mueller, what are you going to do with it? You can't tell me that pumping that stuff back into the ocean wouldn't have an impact on our reefs.'

Gabriele sighed. She'd obviously fielded this question before, and was boring even herself with the answer. 'The salty sludge will be combined with post-treatment sewage plant effluence and injected into deep wells.'

'Wait a minute!' The girl jumped to her feet,

bouncing on tiptoes to see over taller heads. 'Doesn't the plant run on electricity? And how do you plan to generate that electricity, Ms Mueller?'

'I'm sure you know that at Tamarind Tree we have our own power generator.'

'Doesn't it run on diesel?' the girl pressed. 'Doesn't diesel generate greenhouse gasses?'

'I'll tell you what I think,' the postmistress chimed in without budging from her seat. 'You just need to use less water! You rich people are spoiled rotten. Can't live without your bathtubs and your dishwashers. Bet you still run the tap for five minutes while you stand in front of the bathroom sink brushing your teeth.'

'Well, I'm all in favor of the resort,' another woman announced from one of the side aisles. 'I think they've been nothing but environmentally responsible and upfront about it from Day One. And my house is adjacent to the Tamarind Tree restaurant.'

A guy wearing a red tropical shirt shot to his feet. 'Well, of course you're in favor of it, Arlene. You're so much in favor of it that you've put your house on the market. Isn't that right?'

To a chorus of *that's rights* and *uh huhs*, Arlene sucked in her lips and sat down.

'Your father promised he'd hire Bahamians,' Mr Red Shirt continued, addressing Gabriele. 'All I've ever seen around the place is foreigners. Damn Haitians and those boys from that fancy college in Florida.'

'He is hiring Bahamians, Alvin,' Arlene grumbled from her seat. 'My son is working as a *supervisor* for one of the contractors.'

'OK, Arlene. You just ask your boy how many of his workers are Bahamian. Go on, I dare you. I hear there's nothing but Mexicans over there.'

'We work exclusively with Bahamian contractors,' Gabriele assured him using her best anything-to-appease-the-natives tone. 'But to be perfectly honest, we have little control over the people that our contractors hire, including the various subcontractors, so if you have any issues with the make-up of our contract workforce, you'll have to take them up with the individual contractors.'

I thought about the lovely waitress who had brought me my iced tea the other day. That's one Bahamian. I was trying to come up with a second Bahamian when Winnie shouted in exasperation, 'And another thing! Who has been stealing our signs?'

For the first time that evening, Gabriele Mueller wrinkled her flawless brow. 'What signs?'

'Our protest signs.'

'I don't know anything about that, but surely you aren't suggesting...'

'That's exactly what I'm suggesting!'

'I'll look into it.' Gabriele raised her hands in an attitude of surrender. 'Look, we're not hiding anything. If any of you are still skeptical, please, come see us. I'm issuing an open invitation to all of you. Come visit, tour the facilities. I am speaking for my father when I say we are committed to keeping the Tamarind Tree Resort and Marina as environmentally safe as possible. You have my promise on that.'

'They think that if they promise to take our garbage away, we'll fall all over ourselves to welcome them,' Molly muttered to the guy sitting on her right.

'Money talks, and we have no money,' he grumbled back.

While Troy Albury gave an update on the legal efforts of Save Guana Cay Reef to halt the Baker's Bay Development on his tiny island, I stared at the aerial photo that remained on the screen following the conclusion of Henry's presentation. Troy was giddy with the news that the Privy Council had agreed to hear the case they had filed against both the developer and the government of the Bahamas, but I was more interested in Henry's slide. It showed the pier at Tamarind Tree Resort as it was now, undergoing repair. Something was bothering me about it. When the meeting broke up and everyone was gathering on the church steps to analyze and dissect it, I pulled Henry aside.

'Henry, do you mind if I look at a couple of your slides again?'

'Not a problem.'

'Can you page back to an earlier slide for me?' Henry picked up the remote and moved backwards through his presentation.

'No, not that one. Uh, uh. Stop!' It was another picture of the pier, taken just before the repairs had begun. 'When was this picture taken, Henry?'

'That would be two weeks ago, I think.'

'Can you put that slide next to the last one?'

'Sure.' I watched while Henry copied the photograph, paged forward to the final slide, and pasted it next to it. 'There.'

'What's this?' I said, pointing to an odd discoloration in the water, a blue oblong just to the left of the pier.

Henry squinted at the screen, took a few steps back and looked again. 'I don't know. Didn't notice it before. Some sort of fish trap?'

'How big do you think it is?'

'Hard to say. Compared to the pilings, I'd say twenty, twenty-five feet.'

'What's curious to me, Henry, is that whatever this thing is, it was in the water two weeks ago.' I tapped the screen where the later photo was projected. 'Now it's gone.'

Henry pointed out, quite correctly, that a golf cart and a dune buggy appeared in the earlier photo, but weren't present in the later one. 'Could be related to the construction, or to the pier repairs, I suppose.' He rubbed his chin where a five o'clock shadow was just beginning to make an appearance. 'Could be junk, too.' He tapped the more recent of the two slides. 'And they cleaned it up.'

I thought about all the discarded refrigerators, sinks and water heaters I'd seen at the bottom of the Sea of Abaco and thought, maybe he's right. Tube-shaped. Could be a water heater.

If hot-water heaters are blue.

210

Fourteen

DO YOU LIKE FISH? WELL, HE LIKES YOU TOO...

Jaws (1975)

After seeing Henry's photographs, I knew what I had to do.

Conditions had to be perfect: high sun, calm sea, gentle wind, and the tide as near to low as possible. That these conditions coincided with lunch hour at the Tamarind Tree Resort and Marina was a welcome plus. Jaime and Gabriele would be busy at the restaurant, and their workers would have abandoned their backhoes for lunch somewhere in the shade.

Wearing my bathing suit and a long-sleeved T-shirt, I waved to my husband from the living room doorway. He was thoroughly occupied on a marathon Skyping session with Brent.

'I'm off for a swim. Want to come?'

I waited for Paul to look up from his laptop, holding my breath, hoping he'd be too busy consulting with Brent to say 'yes.'

Paul put Brent on mute for a moment and said, 'Where to?'

'I'm going to collect more sand dollars.' In way of illustration, I raised my bucket. 'I'm thinking of turning them into Christmas tree ornaments.'

That part of it, at least, was true. I wasn't much of a do-it-yourselfer, but even I could thread a red ribbon through one of the five holes on the sand dollar's shell and tie the two ends of the ribbon into a decorative knot.

Paul waggled his fingers. 'Have fun!'

I blew him a kiss and headed off.

Frank and Sally had last been seen in Poinciana Cove, so that's where *Pro Bono* and I headed. Poinciana Cove was very like the cove Molly and I had explored earlier, but a bit more was going on ashore. The runway was still under construction to the left, marked by the addition of a windsock. To the right, a construction crane was poised over an extension to the Tamarind Tree Marina. I'd heard they planned to add thirty slips.

There were no condos on shore – yet – but three cottages had been built for the Mueller family on Poinciana Point, a bluff overlooking the cove.

I throttled down and pulled as close to shore as I dared, skirting the edge of an extensive reef a mere fifty feet from the beach. To my left, run-off from runway construction was obvious. To my right, where the marina extension would soon be, mangroves were already being ripped from the shore. A backhoe was parked there, and from the look of it, his job was only half done.

Repair had begun on a section of the old Island Fantasy pier. A barge carrying a pile-driver was lashed to the middle of the pier at a spot where the row of new pilings ended. Each had been capped with white plastic dunce caps. The clean white of the new planks stood out in sharp contrast to the gray of the seasoned wood.

A sign posted at the end of the pier said, 'Private Property. Keep Off. Unauthorized Vessels Will Be Towed,' so I guided *Pro Bono* to the edge of the reef and dropped the anchor in about ten feet of water.

I eased my feet into my swim fins, put my mask over my face, and slipped overboard.

It was immediately clear that the reef off Poinciana Point was in distress. Beneath me grew a brain coral the size of a Volkswagen. Normally a mustardy brown, large sections of the coral had died, leaving behind a bleached white skeleton. Elkhorn showed evidence of white band disease, working its way up from the base of the coral in ever-widening stripes. Everywhere, algae flourished. The only creatures that seemed happy about it were the parrot fish, scraping the algae off the skeletons with their teeth.

Broken twigs of acropora.

Purple sea fans brown with fungus.

I wanted to weep.

Half buried in the sand, a cable the thickness of my wrist extended from shore and disappeared into the infinite blue of the Sea of Abaco. I decided to follow it ashore. I swam over an oil drum, abandoned and rusted out, empty except for a squirrelfish pecking away, and a bathroom sink, ugly, but not a particular threat to sea life.

A sea turtle swam by, checked me out, then continued on its way, surfacing for a moment to gulp air, then dive again.

The cable dead ended at the pier. Mueller's crew had done a piss-poor job of clean up. As I snorkeled along the length of the structure, I could distinctly see ruins not all that obvious from above. Ragged netting, rotten and sunken pilings, the upside-down hull of a wooden boat, that might have been casualties of a hurricane. Clearly there was a lot of work still to be done. No wonder Mueller brought visitors into the resort on the marina side of the development.

A small, eco-friendly marina for twenty boats up to 200 feet in length. I smiled grimly. Everything about that phrase was an oxymoron.

I surfaced for a moment, clutching the tatty remains of an old fishing net to keep the tide from carrying me sideways. I heard the growl of an engine starting up – a chainsaw? – then continued working my way along the pier, looking for something, anything even remotely suspicious.

The pipe I had been following appeared not to have been used in some time; parts of it lay in pieces, like elbow macaroni. Sea grass flourished on the sand bottom. Nearer shore, I noticed rectangular patterns in the grass, each roughly the size of a carry-on suitcase. Something had lain there long enough to smother the sea grass, and recently, too.

I surfaced under the dock, breathing fast. Is that what Frank had seen? What he'd died for? I held on to a piling, thinking furiously. The first thing that came to mind was drugs, but I'd never seen a package of drugs that hadn't come from a pharmacy. Were they small as a brick? Large as a footlocker? And could they be water-proofed?

I had taken a breath to go down for a second look when I felt it. Vibrations. Somebody was heavy-footing it along the pier.

Hugging the piling, I eased around under the pier just as his shadow passed overhead. Through gaps in the planking I could see the zigzag tread of a boat shoe, a bit of bare ankle. I hoped he couldn't see me.

My visitor began whistling tunelessly. 'Here you go,' he said. There was a whoosh followed by a red-tinged splash as a bucketful of mahi-mahi heads, backbones and tails hit the water not eight feet away from where I hung, still clinging to the rotting net.

Gross. I had picked a bad time to explore. I loved eating fish, but getting so up close and personal to their remains made me want to barf. One particularly large fish head stared at me reproachfully, as if chastising me for all the seafood meals I'd enjoyed both now and in the future, as it floated on the surface for a moment,

215

then spiraled slowly to the bottom.

Drawn by some underwater radar, schools of yellow jacks and smallmouth grunts flashed in out of nowhere to chow down. A nurse shark, brownish-grey and about eight feet long, moseyed over from where he'd been dozing in the mangrove, joined by another one, slightly smaller. Then a third joined the banquet. Instinctively, I moved away. Nurse sharks are relatively harmless – they prefer to suck down their prey rather than bite it – but the mouths on these fellows looked as big as aircraft carriers from where I was hanging, and I wasn't sure how keen their eyesight was.

The whistling stopped.

Something was wrong. The nurse sharks sensed it, too. Ignoring the free lunch, the trio shied away. Had they spotted me?

It's a common misconception that shark attacks are preceded by 'dah-da, dah-da, dah-da, dah-da,' grating strings and blaring horns, accelerating rapidly as the shark gets closer.

Not true. It's silent, eerily so.

A fish I recognized immediately sleeked into view – a reef shark, his skin flashing silver in the sun. There are several varieties of reef shark – white tip, black tip, gray and silver – but when they're swimming in your direction at five hundred miles per hour, you don't stop to check your Fish Watcher's Field Guide to find out which kind. As I hung there, frozen in fear, he circled the pier, coming so close to me at one point that I could have touched his fin.

I had no intention of sticking around and becoming the main course among the sea of floating hors d'oeuvres, but I didn't want to call attention to myself.

What had I read in the survivor's guide?

One. Remain calm. (Easier said than done.)

Two. Don't splash around like an injured or dying fish. (Noted.)

Three. If a shark approaches, strike it repeatedly with a balled-up fist on its most sensitive parts, the eyes and the gills. Uh, right. The eye in question was passing me again, black as wet coal, round as a silver dollar.

I'd seen sharks in aquariums, but they never looked so big. The shark made another circuit, looming bigger, ever bigger. Blood pounded in my ears. I balled up my fist, holding it close to my chest, getting ready.

The shark shot by, so close I felt the backwash. Its tail touched my leg, scraping along my thigh like sandpaper. His jaw yawned open, his black eye closed, and two yellow jacks that had been wrangling over a mahi-mahi head disappeared in a single snap. Last time they'd scrap over a meal.

While the shark was busy swallowing the jacks, I took the fourth piece of advice from the handbook – I turned and slowly swam away.

I didn't look back until I reached *Pro Bono*, hoisted myself up on the rope ladder and threw myself in.

When I dared to look back at the pier, the water was churning as the shark finished off what was left of his feast.

The man still stood at the end of the dock. It was Jaime Mueller.

And I could hear him laughing.

Fifteen

LOBSTERS USUALLY MOVE AROUND AND
HUNT FOR FOOD AT NIGHT. IT WAS ONCE
THOUGHT THAT LOBSTERS WERE SCAVEN-
GERS AND ATE PRIMARILY DEAD THINGS.
HOWEVER, RESEARCHERS HAVE DISCOVER-
ED THAT LOBSTERS CATCH MAINLY FRESH
FOOD (EXCEPT FOR BAIT), WHICH INCLUDES
FISH, CRABS, CLAMS, MUSSELS, SEA URCH-
INS, AND SOMETIMES EVEN OTHER LOB-
STERS!

Lobster FAQ, NOAA's
National Marine Fisheries Service,
Northeast Fisheries Science Center

It wasn't until I got back to *Windswept* and had
sprawled on the bench at the end of our dock
that I was able to think, let alone catch my
breath.

Did Jaime know I was under the pier? Did he
churn the water on purpose, or was it simply a
case of my being in the wrong place at the
wrong time? I didn't have an answer.

When I thought I would be able to talk about
what had just happened, I slogged up the dock

to the house.

Paul stood at the kitchen counter holding a fork like a weapon, stabbing the life out of some meat. As I dragged myself into the room he looked up. 'Thought we'd barbecue some steaks tonight.'

I frowned. When Paul volunteered for cooking duty, it was usually because he wanted something.

'Hey, Hannah, what's wrong?'

I plopped down in a kitchen chair. 'I could really use some iced tea.'

While Paul assembled a glass, ice, tea and some lemon slices, I decided that nothing was wrong. The last thing that I needed just then was a lecture.

'How was your expedition?' he asked, handing me the glass. 'Successful?'

'Yes,' I lied, hoping that he wouldn't ask to inspect my haul of sand dollars.

'Good.' He turned his attention back to the meat, drowning it in salad oil, red wine and vinegar. 'I hope you're in a good mood because I need to talk to you about something.'

'Yes?'

He unscrewed the cap from a jar of lemon pepper and started sprinkling it over the steaks. 'It all started with Euclid.'

I closed my eyes, pressed the cool side of the glass to my temple. 'Doesn't it always?'

'He wrote "Elements of Geometry" way back in 300 BC. It was so good that no other texts from that period even survive. Euclid wiped out the competition.'

I opened one eye. 'To quote someone I know, don't build me a clock, Paul. Just tell me what time it is.'

'I need to go to Baltimore.'

I sat up straight in my chair, slopping iced tea down the front of my shirt. 'You *what*?'

Paul grabbed the back of the chair opposite me, pushed it so close that our knees touched when he sat down on it, and took my hand. 'Just for a few days. I need to consult a copy of the first English translation of Euclid's *Elements*, the one Sir Henry Billingsley wrote in 1570.'

Marsh Harbour had a library, a small one, but I doubted they kept ancient Greeks on their shelves. 'What's wrong with the copy you've got?' I asked. The book with the familiar green cover had been sitting on Paul's bedside table ever since our arrival in the islands.

'Brent Morris has an original copy, and I need to see it. Billingsley illustrates the theorems in book eleven with three-dimensional pop-ups that are glued to the pages.'

'Can't you use your imagination?' I pouted.

He squeezed my hand. 'I need to *see* the book, Hannah. Brent's also trying to arrange a meeting with Andy Gleason for me. If that pans out, we'll take the train up to Cambridge for a day. Andy's done for calculus what I plan to do for geometry, and talking to him will be enormously valuable.'

'When do you leave?'

'Tomorrow?'

221

'Fine.' There was no point in arguing. Paul had to work, I understood that. I was simply along for the ride.

'It's charming,' Paul said a few minutes later, coming up behind me and laying a kiss on my neck.

I backed away, still steaming. 'What's charming?'

' "If therefore a folide angle be contayned under three playne fuperficiall angles euery two of thofe three angles..." '

I pinched his lips together, cutting him off. 'Do shut up.'

He enveloped me in a bear hug and rested his chin on the top of my head. 'You're not angry with me, are you?'

'Yes.'

'I won't be away long.'

'That's what you always say.'

He tipped my chin up until he was looking directly into my eyes. 'I mean it. This sabbatical has been the closest thing to paradise...' He paused. 'Well, except for the fire.'

'Yes. Except for that.'

And except for Frank, and Sally, and their little dog, Duffy.

And whoever thought it was a good idea to frighten me away from Poinciana Cove.

The next morning I waved Paul off on the eleven thirty ferry just as Molly was pulling *Good Golly* up to her dock.

'Where have you been so early?' I shouted

222

across the stretch of water that separated our two docks.

'Teaching a class at the school,' she called back. 'Poetry, if you can believe it!'

'Where's Paul off to this morning?' Molly asked a few minutes later as she joined me in my front yard.

'Baltimore,' I said. 'For work.'

'So it's just you and me, then?'

I hadn't thought about it, but Molly was right. Unless someone had come in overnight, *Windswept* and *Southern Exposure* were the only homes presently occupied on all of Bonefish Cay.

Molly patted my arm. 'I vote we have lunch in town. I found another sheet of plywood under the house, so I was going to ask you to join me anyway. Thought we'd take it to Winnie. Game?'

'You bet.'

As we pulled *Good Golly* up to the government dock we saw Gator standing at a wooden counter, cleaning a large snapper. The tide was out and Molly's Zodiac sat so low in the water that I had to crane my neck to see him. 'Hey, Gator,' I yelled.

Fine spray misted my face as Gator used a hose to rinse fish guts off the counter. I shivered, thinking about my last encounter with fish parts.

Apparently he hadn't heard us.

'Gay-tor!' This from Molly, using her outside voice. It apparently worked because water

223

stopped trickling through the gaps in the plank-ing.

Gator leaned over, holding on to a piling with one hand. 'Mornin' Hannah, Miz Molly.'

Molly pointed to the bow of her boat. 'Got another sign for you, Gator.'

I helped Molly untie the plywood and hand it up to Gator, who promptly manhandled it down the dock and parked it temporarily against the trunk of a tree.

'I'm heading over to Tom's Creek,' he said when he rejoined us on the deck, standing near the stern of *Deep Magic*. 'Got a few lobster traps out that way. Going over to check.'

'For lobsters?'

Gator picked up a blue plastic case about the size of a lunchbox that had been sitting on the fish-cleaning counter. 'Hear that Mueller's started running his desalinization plant. Low-impact, ha ha ha. Want to see what it's doing to the creek.'

'Is that a testing kit?' I asked as we watched Gator climb into his boat. We'd used something similar to test the ancient pipes in our Anna-polis home for lead.

'Yup.'

Molly looked at me and I knew what she was thinking. An adventure. 'Can we come along?' I asked.

'Sure. Hop in.'

While Gator manned the helm and Justice rode on the bow like a figurehead, his ears flap-ping, Molly and I shared a bench in the stern, our heads just inches away from a honking big Yamaha 225 outboard. If we'd wanted to talk, we'd have had to use sign language. I knew a little bit, but I wasn't sure about Molly.

Gator throttled down as he guided the boat through the harbor, skirting the Tamarind Tree Marina and its mooring field, but once he nosed out of the cut, he gunned it. Before *Deep Magic* had even reached twenty miles per hour, she popped up on a plane, dancing over the waves as if they didn't exist.

We flew past Poinciana Point heading northwest. We passed Kelchner's Cove, where the family's locked up cottage lay, rounded the tip of the island and headed into the open sea.

'How do you know where the traps are?' Molly screamed over the thunder of the engine.

'GPS!' he shouted back. A few minutes later I heard a faint *peep-peep-peep* as Gator throttled down, cut the engine and dropped anchor in about ten feet of water.

I looked overboard. Bingo! *Deep Magic* floated almost directly over a lobster trap. A cinder block weighted it down.

Gator donned his mask, strapped on a weight belt, and gathered up his tools – a narrow rod about three feet long called a tickle stick, and a net.

Molly and I knelt on the white vinyl seats, our elbows resting on the gunwale, watching Gator as he slipped over the side. He floated over the trap for a moment, took a deep breath, then dived. We watched him circle the trap, the tickle stick in one hand, the net in the other.

After two circumnavigations, Gator surfaced, spit out his snorkel to say, 'It'd be easier if you helped, Hannah.'

'I'd be glad to.' It was a hot day; the water would feel good.

'Got a bathing suit?' he asked.

I tugged on my tank top. 'Underneath.' I turned to Molly. 'Want to come?'

Eyes wide in mock panic, she pressed a hand to her chest and said, '*Moi*? No thanks. I think I'll just watch.'

It took only half a minute for me to strip to my bathing suit and join Gator overboard.

What appeared from the deck of *Deep Magic* as an undulating square of metal, I could see clearly now. A forest of long, whip-like feelers and the smaller, spiny limbs that gave the lobster its name, waved at me from the perimeter of the trap. Using his hands, Gator showed me how to plant the net. Meanwhile, he used his tickle stick to entice one of the lobsters out of his hiding place. As I watched, keeping the net firmly pressed against the bottom as instructed, he tapped smartly on the lobster's white-spotted shell, annoying the creature until it scooted backwards into the net I was holding.

Gator collected the net from me, and we bobbed to the surface. 'Easy to see if the bug's legal size,' he burbled as he popped his snorkel, 'but we need to make sure it's not female.' He turned the brownish-green lobster over while still in the net, examined the shape of the fins,

226

checked for telltale eggs.

'Good to go! How many you want?'

Looking up into the boat, shielding my eyes from the sun, I had a silent consultation with Molly.

'Dinner at my place tonight, then,' Molly said. 'So four? Five?'

'You can freeze them,' Gator suggested.

'Six, then.'

Gator transferred his catch from the net into a lobster bag hanging from a rope tied to one of *Deep Magic's* cleats. 'Your turn.' He handed me the tickle stick.

I examined it like some skinny alien being, then handed it back. 'I'd like to see you do it one more time.'

Gator nodded, dragged his mask down over his eyes and nose, and ducked once again under the surface. I took a deep breath and followed.

Once again, I placed the net and held it steady while Gator used the tickle stick to walk a lobster backwards into it. We shot to the surface to check the legal status of our catch and transferred it to the bag. This time, Gator handed me the tickle stick and we headed back down.

Back at the trap, I picked an unlucky lobster and tried to tease it out from under the trap. It was harder than it looked. Instead of coming out, the creature backed away. I used the tickle stick to probe for it, but he'd disappeared under the siding.

Using a scooping motion that was probably not quite kosher, I swept the stick under the

227

trap, trying to coax the lobster from its hiding place, but it must have scuttled out of range.

I shot to the surface, took a deep breath of air, then headed back down to try again. When I withdrew the stick this time, I'd caught something on it, but it wasn't a lobster. It was a bit of white knit fabric.

I extended the tickle stick in Gator's direction, shrugged. He picked the fabric off, and we bobbed to the surface, where Gator slid his mask to the top of his head and examined the object in the sun. 'Looks like a bit of sock.'

'You use socks in your traps?'

'Nope.' He looked puzzled.

'Do lobsters drag objects into their dens with them?'

'Never known it to happen, Hannah. Let's have a look.'

We repositioned our masks and sank to the bottom again. Gator pushed the cinder block off the trap, and with me standing on one side and he on the other, we lifted the platform.

There were lobsters under it all right. Dozens of them. Startled by the sudden blast of sunlight, they scampered in every direction.

But what they were feeding on made me gag. I spit out my snorkel, shot to the surface, and held on to the swim ladder at the stern of the boat with both hands while I quietly parted company with my breakfast.

'Hannah! What's wrong?' Molly peered at me over the side, her hands white knuckled, gripping the rail. 'Is Gator OK?'

'Oh, my God.' I felt dizzy. I tried to take deep breaths, but ended up retching instead. Molly leaned over me solicitously, patting my hand.

In the meantime, Gator had surfaced nearby, his snorkel dangling. He laid a hand on my shoulder. 'Take it easy, Hannah.'

'Seasick?' Molly asked.

When I didn't answer, Gator said, 'She's had a shock. Bodies down there. Two of 'em.'

Two bodies, fully clothed, staring up into nothingness with wide, sightless eyes. One was a woman, I had no doubt of that. As I struggled to make sense of what I was seeing, her dark hair had drifted, swayed in the current like seaweed around her ruined face.

Gator coughed. 'Never seen anything like that before.'

Molly's gaze was fixed on the hideous spot in the water. 'Can you tell who they are?'

Gator rubbed his eyes. 'Lobsters did quite a job on the soft tissues of their faces.' He paused, glanced from Molly to me and back again, seeming to flush under his tan. 'Sorry.'

'I set the trap back down to keep the bodies from floating away,' he continued, 'but before I did, I found this.' He uncurled his fingers. In his palm lay a broad gold wedding band. 'It might mean something to you, Hannah.'

With my free hand, I picked the ring out of Gator's palm and examined it in the sunlight. Engraving inside the band read, FP+SA 9/5/62.

Frank and Sally Parker.

Gator waited until I was safely up the swim

ladder before climbing back into the boat himself. Using strong hands on each of my shoulders, he practically forced me down on a bench, then wrapped me in a foul-weather jacket. In spite of the warmth of the sun, I began to shiver. I drew the jacket more tightly around my shoulders. 'Were they...?' I stuttered. 'Could you tell...?' I swallowed the words.

Without answering, Gator crossed to the console and reached for his microphone. 'Didn't crawl under there themselves.' He pressed the talk button. 'Dive Guana, Dive Guana. This is *Deep Magic*. Come in, Troy.'

'Things like this simply don't happen here,' Molly said while we waited for Troy to show up with the rescue boat from Guana Cay, although there was precious little to rescue. For Frank and Sally Parker it was way too late.

'Only seventy-some murders in all the islands last year,' Gator told us. He sat bent over, hands dangling between his knees. 'Fifty of them in Nassau. Drug-related, of course.'

I scratched Nassau off my list of one thousand and one places to see before I died and asked, 'What do we do now?'

'Wait for Troy.'

'And after that?'

'As I said before. Nothing. Getting involved with the Bahamian police can take years off your life.'

I felt like screaming, but managed a croak. 'Gator! You can't *not* report this! Those people

230

were my friends!'

'You mistook my meaning, Hannah. I'm just asking you to let Troy and me handle it.'

I folded my arms across my chest, hugging myself for warmth. Tears pooled in my eyes, spilled over and ran hotly down my cheeks. 'What I want to know is what Frank and Sally are doing here, dead, when the last time they were seen was miles away in Eleuthera.'

'We only have Jaime's word for that. And Jaime's word is worth, what? Next to nothing?'

Molly blinked rapidly, fighting tears, too. 'Ain't worth shee-it! He killed them, didn't he?'

'Somebody sure did,' Gator said.

'Who else could have done it? Frank and Sally go missing, then Jaime shows up sailing their boat.' I shrugged out of the jacket, picked up my shorts and top. 'Why else was he having *Wanderer* repainted? Idiot thought nobody would notice.' I shivered. 'How did he think he was going to get away with it, Gator?'

'It's early in the lobster season. He probably thought that by the time I got around to checking the traps, the lobsters would have done their work.'

As *Deep Magic* rocked gently at anchor on the undulating sea, I staggered to the stern where I untied the lobster bag from the cleat and dumped our catch over the side.

No one protested.

Exhausted, I sat down and rested my forehead on the gunwale, as soothing as a cool washcloth. While Molly rubbed my back, I thought about Jaime's victims, *all* of Jaime's victims. Frank and Sally Parker, the mangroves, the reef, the sea turtles and even poor Alice Madonna Robinson. 'The man is evil, pure evil.'

Molly wrapped an arm around me and squeezed. 'The question is, what are we going to do about it?'

Later, much later, Molly and I sat on her porch, a dinner of leftover spaghetti glistening under candlelight. The power had gone out again. Adding insult to injury, Paul had left for Baltimore with the generator he'd purchased still packed in its box, so I'd collected my frozen food from the freezer and taken it over to Molly's where lights were on in her kitchen, her generator humming.

Molly's contribution to dinner had been a salad, a delicious mix of spinach and romaine, but I only nibbled on mine.

'You have to eat sometime, Hannah.'

'But not now.' I bit my lower lip, lost in thought. 'I can't get it out of my mind, Molly. Frank and Sally ... God!'

She laid down her fork. 'It's the body bags that got me, Hannah. Hefty Cinch Saks! Mah gawd. I kept reading the side of that box – *new, unscented odor block technology.* I swear I'll never be able to use a Hefty bag again.'

The three strands of noodle and two slices of tomato that I'd managed to choke down threatened to make a reappearance, but I pressed my

232

fingernails into my palms and took deep breaths until the feeling passed.

'Gator called,' Molly told me. 'Said Troy would take the bodies to Marsh Harbour. Apparently they have some sort of make-do morgue over there. After a doctor declares them dead...' Her voice trailed off into the darkness beyond the candlelight.

'As if there's any doubt.' I cringed. 'Then they'll be taken to Nassau for autopsy, like that poor fellow who died in the wildfire.'

Molly sipped her wine, then set the glass down. 'I practically live here, but I don't have much experience with this sort of thing, as you can well imagine. But the Parkers are American citizens. Won't US authorities be involved?'

'Only if invited by the Bahamians, Gator told me. Otherwise the Royal Bahamas Police handle all investigations themselves.'

'And we're sure they're not going to mess up the investigation, how?'

I studied my friend in the candlelight, her eyes bright with tears. 'I'm going to make some phone calls, Molly. First to Paul...'

'FBI?' she interrupted.

I nodded. 'Interpol, too, if necessary.'

'Good.' Molly stood, dinner plate in hand. 'Tell me, Hannah. What did you say to Gator when he dropped us off?'

'I suggested that if we wanted a proper investigation, we should take Frank and Sally to the waters off Fort Lauderdale and set their bodies afloat off the beach.' I snorted, then cackled. Even to myself, I sounded hysterical. 'And you know what?'

'What?'

'He half agreed with me.'

'But the police say they found no trace of foul play aboard *Wanderer*! They even gave custody of the boat back to Jaime Mueller until he can contact the Parkers ... well, I guess now it'd be their heirs. Makes me sick.' Using her fork, she scraped the scraps from her plate over the porch rail. Snack time for the hermit crabs who lived under the oleander.

'The Parkers didn't have any children,' I said.

'Oh. In that case, Jaime Mueller's probably the proud owner of a used boat.'

'Maybe Jaime didn't kill them on their boat, Molly. Maybe he murdered them on shore. Their dinghy's never been found, you know.'

A theory took shape in my mind. I imagined *Wanderer* bobbing peacefully at anchor in Poinciana Cove. Frank and Sally, after dark, motoring their dinghy ashore. Dragging it up on the sand and hiding it in the mangroves. Creeping up the beach, into the woods, looking around and checking for ... what? Something that was polluting the reef?

'What's Jaime's motive, Hannah? Surely not possession of the sailboat. He could buy ten sailboats like *Wanderer* easy, cold cash in a suitcase.'

I discarded my first theory and went with the obvious. 'I think Frank and Sally anchored in the cove, and Frank went down for a night dive, like he told the captain of *Northern Lights* he was going to. Then he saw something that Jaime or somebody else didn't want him to see.'

'Like what?'

I picked a crescent of celery out of my salad, popped it into my mouth and chewed it thoughtfully. 'Something illegal, of course.'

'Like what?'

'Smuggling leaps to mind,' I said, thinking about the little cottage in Kelchner's Cove all locked up nice and tight. 'Maybe he brought in stuff for his resort that he didn't want to pay thirty percent duty on. Computers, for example. Or air conditioners. Booze?'

'Interesting theory, Hannah, but El Mirador Land Corporation has deep pockets. Hard to imagine any of those fat cats risking life in prison to save a couple of thousand bucks on air conditioners.'

'Hard to say what rich folks will do to save a few bucks,' I mused aloud. 'Think about Martha Stewart.' Another thought occurred to me. 'Could be drugs.'

'Yikes! That *would* be dangerous.'

'I can tell you one thing, Molly. If the Bahamian cops don't nail Jaime's ass to the wall, I swear to God, I will.'

For the first time that evening, Molly looked at me and smiled. 'And I kin help,' she drawled.

235

Sixteen

DRUGS ARE AN ABSOLUTE NO-NO IN THE BAHAMAS. THE PENALTIES FOR POSSESSION AND USE OF ILLEGAL DRUGS ARE SEVERE. IT WILL MAKE NO DIFFERENCE THAT YOU ARE A FOREIGN CITIZEN, AND PRISON SENTENCES CAN BE LONG.

Dold, Vaitilingam and Folster,
Bahamas: Includes Turks and Caicos,
Rough Guides, 2003, p. 41

'Do I have to go home?' I lay in Molly's hammock, swaying gently. The evening breeze had freshened, but I found it a welcome relief from the heat of the day.

Molly sat nearby, leaning back in her chair with her feet propped against the porch rail. 'Stay as long as you want, sugar.'

We watched in companionable silence as the lights of Hawksbill settlement twinkled out one by one. Nine o'clock was bedtime across the channel, and it usually was at our house, too, unless a good DVD was on the agenda. 'I'm not very sleepy,' I confessed.

'Probably the chocolate,' Molly said. I heard

paper rustling, then a snap. 'Here, have another one.'

There are no finer comfort foods than Vosges exotic candy bars. I accepted the square of Oaxaca that Molly handed me and popped it into my mouth, savoring the intoxicating blend of dark chocolate and chilies that set my tongue a-tingling. 'What do we do when these are gone?'

'I've got a Goji and a Bacon Bar,' she mumbled around a mouth full of chocolate. 'After that, it's Cadbury.'

'How we suffer.'

'Pitiful.'

After the chocolate was gone, I got up to go. 'Thanks for everything, Molly. I don't know why these things always happen to me when Paul is away.'

'Finding bodies?'

'Uh huh.'

'It's happened before?'

'I'm the Jessica Fletcher of Annapolis. It's a curse.'

Molly snorted. 'You'll have to tell me about it sometime.' She handed me my flashlight. 'But it's late. Have you reached Paul?'

'No. He's still in transit, but I left a message.' I gave her a hug. 'Honestly, I don't know what I would have done without you today.'

'Walk me to the generator, then. The noise is driving me crazy.'

Illuminating the path with my flashlight, I accompanied Molly to the generator shed

237

where she shut off the engine for the evening. 'Well, goodnight.'

'Goodnight, Hannah. I hope you sleep well. And if you feel like it, come over for coffee during the Cruisers' Net in the morning. I'll crank up the generator at eight if the power doesn't come back on its own.'

I smiled into the dark, thinking about my coffee pot, no better than a doorstop without electricity. 'Count on it.'

My flashlight barely penetrated the darkness beyond the path as I stumbled along the rocks going home. I hadn't left a candle burning, so *Windswept* was dark as pitch against an even darker sky strewn with bright, cold stars. There was no moon.

Once in my bedroom, I found a candle and lit it, filling the room with a shimmering, golden light. I put on my nightshirt, brushed the taste of chocolate out of my mouth, and lay down in bed. But I couldn't sleep. I tried to read, but the light from the guttering candle made my eyes ache.

'Screw it!' I said out loud. I hauled the blanket off the bed, wrapped it around my shoulders, and stomped outside to sit on the porch.

Night sounds surrounded me. The *clack-clack-clack* of hermit crabs scrabbling through the bushes, the *wheep-wheep* of a nighthawk, the *ooh-wah-hoo-o-o* of a mourning dove who apparently couldn't sleep either.

Something startled a bird, and he flapped his way out of the trees. I squinted into the dark trying to see where it'd gone, when a moving light caught my eye. Hawksbill settlement was unusually dark, its generators, like ours, silenced for the night. Yet someone was moving around over there.

As I stared at the light, it divided, became two. Two became three, flittering like fireflies in the vicinity of the pier at the Tamarind Tree Resort. I wondered if the boys were skinny dipping and I shuddered. *Don't go swimming at night. That's when the big fish come in to feed.* A grizzled live-aboard had given me that advice one languid afternoon at Pete's Pub in Little Harbour. But the big fish come by day, too, especially if you churn the water.

Still wearing the blanket, I went in search of the binoculars. Where had I put the damn things? Clutching the doorframe with one hand, I bumbled into the kitchen, ran my hands along the counter, the refrigerator, the table, another counter. I found the binoculars where I'd left them, next to the radio.

Thinking I should have laid a trail of breadcrumbs, it took me a minute or two to retrace my steps. When I got back to the porch, I put the binoculars to my eyes and stared across the harbor. There were more lights now. With magnification I could see three distinct lights that I figured were flashlights, and two other bright beams that could have been the headlights on a golf cart.

A light flashed, went out, flashed again. This time, it was near the end of the pier. Somebody *was* going swimming tonight. I squinted and diddled with the focus dial on the binoculars. No, two somebodies. An individual standing on the pier shone a light on the ladder as two swimmers, first one and then the other, climbed into the water. Meanwhile, lights wavered and jiggled as people moved up and down the beach.

Some sort of party? If so, where was the music?

With the binoculars trained on one line of lights, I ended up looking at the runway again. More lights on, then off, as the golf cart turned and drove away.

A chilling thought: Was I witnessing what Frank and Sally had observed on another moonless night?

I wondered if the view would be better from Molly's porch, and whether she was still awake.

I fumbled my way into the bedroom, picked my shorts up off the floor, and pulled them on under my nightshirt. I slipped into my Crocs and collected my flashlight. I crashed around the bedroom until I found my iPhone where I'd left it on the bedside table, hoping for a call from Paul, and stuck it in my pocket.

I could have awakened the dead with all the noise I made thrashing through the underbrush, but since Molly and I were the only residents at present, it didn't seem to matter.

At Molly's cottage, a single light still burned in her bedroom window. I stood on the sand under it, a hand of thatch palm tickling my chin.

'Molly!'

Molly's worried face appeared like a Halloween mask in the window. 'Hannah! What the heck are you doing out there?'

'Come out on your porch. There's something going on at the Tamarind Tree Resort that I think you need to see.'

While Molly slipped into a bathrobe, I walked around her house and climbed the steps on to her porch. By the time her glass doors slid open, I was already checking out the activity across the way. 'There's more lights, now,' I whispered. 'I think they're lining them up along the runway.' I turned to my friend in the dark. 'Crazy bastards are going to land a plane! I'd bet my IRA on it!'

Molly carried binoculars, too. 'Something similar was going on a couple of weeks ago, but it wasn't as clear an evening then. The only thing I was sure of was the plane landing. That was hard to miss.'

'A couple of weeks ago? When was that exactly?'

'About the time...' she gasped. 'Oh, Hannah, how can I have been so dense? This must have been what Frank Parker saw!' She laid the binoculars in her lap. 'It's *got* to be drugs. Why else would you try to land an airplane in the middle of nowhere in the dead of night. Like dropping an elephant on a postage stamp.

'And why tonight?' she continued, raising the binoculars to her eyes for another look.

'I think that's easy.' I picked up my iPhone,

brought up the screen, and flicked open the moon phase web application. I tapped in the date. The crescent moon would appear to-morrow. And twenty-eight days ago, on August 1...

I rotated the display so Molly could see it. 'No moon. A good night to be out if you're up to mischief. You can't see Poinciana Cove from Hawksbill settlement, and they probably think nobody's at home over here. The power being out is a bonus. You can count on most people sticking close to home, at least until the power comes back on.'

I set my iPhone down on the table where the display eerily illuminated a polished conch shell. 'Do you have pencil and paper?'

Molly rose from her chair. 'I'll go get it.'

'My inclination is to hop in *Pro Bono* and toot on over there,' I said, only half in jest.

'Oh, *that* would be a grand idea!' Molly scolded. 'They'd hear us coming the minute we left your dock!' She returned a few minutes later with a candlestick, balanced it carefully on the porch rail and settled into her chair, the notebook on her lap. 'When did you first notice the lights?'

'Ten fifteen, or thereabouts.'

Molly's pencil moved across the page. 'How many lights, and what did they seem to be doing?'

As Molly wrote, I tried to recall everything I'd seen from the porch of *Windswept* before coming over to wake her up. Between the two

242

of us, we recorded a timeline all the way up to 11:08 p.m. at which point my cellphone battery died and the digital clock on its face winked out.

So I'm not exactly sure what time it was when we first heard the drone of an engine.

I picked up my binoculars, ready for action. 'Here comes the plane!'

The hum of the engine became a thrum. From the volume and direction of the sound, I figured the pilot was navigating along the island chain, aided by lights in the settlements below. I wondered if he depended on those lights, or if he had a GPS. If not, his job would be tricky, as large portions of the islands would be darker than usual tonight.

To be on the safe side, I blew out the candle just as the airplane buzzed the tops of Molly's trees, aiming for the makeshift runway less than half a mile away.

'Damn! I wish these things would stop wiggling.' Molly leaned forward, elbows propped up on the porch rail, trying to stabilize the binoculars. 'What are they doing now?'

'The plane's on the ground. Wait a minute! They've started up some sort of portable generator light. I can almost make out...'

'I got it now. What are those people doing?'

We watched, transfixed, as six or seven men swarmed over the runway removing packages from the airplane, loading them on a dune buggy, and driving them down to the beach.

'It *is* drugs,' I said. 'Gotta be. Cocaine, most

likely. Hell! I wish I had a night-vision camera!'

'Shouldn't we call somebody?'

'Even if the power were on, we couldn't use the radio, or we'd tip them off.' I reached for my iPhone. 'Oh, damn. Not much use without a charger.'

'What are they doing with the packages?'

'They're stashing them underwater.' I told Molly about my visit to the pier, and about the rectangular impressions I'd seen in the sea grass.

'How on earth do they keep the drugs dry?'

'I'm certainly not an expert in that department, Molly. Wrap them up good in plastic, I guess.'

'What happens next?'

'I don't know. You'd think they'd fly the cocaine straight into the States without stopping here first.'

'Maybe it's easier to fly a plane into the Bahamas than it is into the States. DEA and the Coast Guard have really been cracking down if what I see on CNN is true.'

'Maybe they're putting drugs *on* the plane!'

We watched all the to-ings and fro-ings, taking careful notes.

By midnight, whatever they'd been doing was finished. The dune buggy disappeared, the lights were extinguished, and everything was as it had been before. Dark and quiet.

'Let's go over in the morning. Check out the pier.'

'We can take my boat,' Molly said.

'I don't mind driving.'

'My outboard is quieter than yours,' she said, sealing the deal. 'When do you want to leave?'

'Can you be ready at dawn? I'd like to get over there just as the sun is coming up. There'll be less chance of being spotted.' I grinned. 'Especially since everyone seems to have been up partying so late.'

'We need to tell Gator what we're doing.'

'We'll tell Gator after we check it out.'

I was awake before the sun, stunned into consciousness at five thirty a.m. by the squeal of my wind-up alarm clock. The power was still out, but at least I could see in the gray light of dawn.

I got dressed, fed Dickie, then went over to wake up Molly. She was already up. When I entered her kitchen the aroma of fresh coffee nearly made me swoon. The woman was a magician. 'How did you *do* that?' I asked.

'Gas stove.'

She handed me a paper cup. 'So you can take it with you,' and poured a cup for herself. She opened the refrigerator, grabbed the milk and closed the door quickly, so that as little of the cool air would escape as possible. 'I'll run the generator when I get back. It'll be fine,' she said, and repeated the procedure to put the milk back in.

She pushed a box across the counter. 'Cinnamon bun?'

'Where did you get them?'

'Lola's. Made a trip over to Man-O-War the other day.'

Lola's cinnamon buns – and her bread and her rolls – are on everyone's Best Of list. Heaven is Lola's buns and coffee. We walked down the dock, sipping coffee and munching.

Good Golly's white rubber hull glistened with dew. Molly grabbed a towel and dried our seats, then I hopped down and joined her. She started the engine, backed slowly out of her slip, and soon we were on our way toward Hawksbill Cay.

Molly didn't approach Poinciana Cove directly. We aimed for the settlement, then slowed the engine almost to an idle as we eased around the point, cutting as close to shore as possible.

Although the beach was deserted, we could see the plane still sitting on the runway. 'It's a Haviland, I think. A six seater.'

'How do you know so much about airplanes, Molly?'

'My late husband flew a Piper Cherokee.'

We passed the end of the runway, approaching the dock. The Zodiac drew only a few inches of water, so we could get up as close as the propeller of the outboard would allow. At the dock, Molly killed the engine, and we worked our way silently towards shore, using the oars.

'What's that?'

Intent on paddling, Molly said, 'Where?'

'Under the water. Looks like a torpedo from here.' I told Molly about the object I'd noticed in Henry Allen's slides.

Raising her oar out of the water, Molly peered down. 'Could be some sort of water-sampling device.'

I shook my head. 'I think it's a submarine.' I leaned way over until my face was almost in the water. 'A real do-it-yourself job, too, like they put it together out of a plan in *Popular Mechanics*.'

Although my iPhone was dead, I'd remembered to bring my camera along. I snapped a picture of the object. Molly sculled, edging the dinghy a few feet closer and I shot another one, hoping the pictures would turn out in the flat, early-morning light.

'Hey!' someone shouted. 'Private property! Get away from here!'

I snapped a few more pictures before turning around. 'Is that the same guard that tried to run us off the other day?'

Molly squinted toward the beach. 'I think so. Just ignore him. We're *not* on private...'

Bloof-phoom! The side of the Zodiac I was sitting on exploded. A split second later, I heard a gunshot. 'My God! He's shooting at us.'

Molly and I dropped to the floor of the inflatable trying to put the tube between our bodies and the shooter. *Foomp!* Another bullet zinged into the section of the tube nearest the outboard engine. Air didn't hiss out of the tube compartments, it exploded with a *foosht* like a balloon being let go, propelling poor *Good Golly* sideways.

Molly had been flung to the hard floor of the inflatable. I leaned over her. 'Are you all right?'

'I think I broke my butt bone.'

'Can you start the engine?'

It was impossible to keep her head completely down, but Molly eeled her way into the driver's seat and turned the key. The engine cranked, caught, and Molly began to back us away from the dock.

This seemed to be the desired result, because the shooting stopped. When I dared to look toward the beach, the guard still stood there, holding his gun sideways like Brad Pitt in *Seven*. 'We're looking for sand dollars, you asshole! Are you trying to kill us?'

He lowered his weapon. 'If I were, you'd be dead.'

That was probably true. In spite of his gangsta-style shooting posture, he'd been remarkably accurate. With a silent apology to Molly I yelled, 'I've got an elderly lady with me here. We're sinking! Call somebody!'

The guard turned, holstering his gun at the small of his back. 'Sorry, don't think I can hear you.' And he disappeared over a dune.

As *Good Golly* limped toward Hawksbill settlement, I noticed that one of the guard's bullets had passed completely though the starboard side tube, missing my leg by inches, and plowed into the port-side tube, deflating it, too. Only one of the four 'air-tight' compartments in the Zodiac was holding air. In less than five minutes, *Good Golly* had been transformed from a perky little wave-dancer into a flaccid cushion of uncooperative rubberized fabric.

Baling was useless. So was calling nine-one-one. We were in no danger of drowning in only four feet of water.

'Keep her near the shore, Molly. Let's try to make it to the beach this side of the marina. If we have to abandon ship, at least we'll be able to walk.'

Molly managed to coax another ten yards out of *Good Golly* before the weight of the wooden floor and the outboard motor defeated her. We rolled out of the boat and dug our feet into the sand. Using the ropes that were looped on each side of the boat, we started hauling her ashore.

'I hope my camera isn't ruined.' I huffed, tugging on the rope. *Good Golly*'s propeller was dragging, making our job even harder.

'Your camera? Boo hoo. How about my *boat*?'

'Sorry.' We were standing in water up to our ankles. A few more yards, and *Good Golly* would be beached.

'Hannah?'

While Molly tilted the outboard up and out of the way of the bottom, I gave the boat a final tug. 'Ooph!'

'If that submarine thingy is related to the activity we saw last night, and if someone *is* running drugs out of Tamarind Tree Resort, why *aren't* we dead?'

249

'Maybe that guard wasn't involved with anything that went on last night. I don't have a lot of experience in running a drug cartel, but I imagine it's pretty much "need to know." All he needed to know was "Hey, Joe, keep everyone off that beach."'

'He could have killed us.'

'I know. And he's not going to get away with it.'

Although it would have taken a team of X-Men to steal *Good Golly* at that point, we tied her carefully to a poisonwood tree, nevertheless. While Molly shook sand out of her tennis shoes, I tucked my soaking-wet T-shirt into my shorts and tried to look halfway presentable.

'Where to?' Molly asked.

'First we're going to see Gator. Then, I'm going to make sure you get your boat back.'

Seventeen

ANY PERSON WHO PURCHASES, ACQUIRES OR HAS IN HIS POSSESSION, USES OR CARRIES A GUN WITHOUT A LICENCE THEREFOR SHALL BE LIABLE ... TO IMPRISONMENT FOR A TERM OF TEN YEARS AND TO A FINE OF TEN THOUSAND DOLLARS.

Commonwealth Of The Bahamas, Statute Law,
Chapter 213, Part IV, Section 15(2)(a)

CONDITIONS AT FOX HILL PRISON, THE COUNTRY'S ONLY PRISON, REMAINED HARSH. THE PRISON REMAND AREA, BUILT TO HOLD 300 PRISONERS, WAS INSUFFICIENT TO HOLD THE 650 PRISONERS AWAITING TRIAL, LEAVING MANY PRE-TRIAL DETAINEES CONFINED IN CELLS WITH CONVICTED PRISONERS [WHERE THEY] WERE CROWDED INTO POORLY VENTILATED CELLS THAT GENERALLY LACKED REGULAR RUNNING WATER, TOILETS, AND LAUNDRY FACILITIES. MOST PRISONERS LACKED BEDS, SLEPT ON CONCRETE FLOORS, AND WERE LOCKED IN SMALL CELLS 23 HOURS PER DAY, OFTEN WITH HUMAN WASTE.

Bahamas, US Department of State, *Country Reports on Human Rights Practices,* 2006

It wasn't even eight o'clock, but I felt like I'd lived a whole lifetime since dawn. Leaving the ruined Zodiac behind us on the beach, Molly and I trudged over the dune and on to the Queen's Highway. Wet, disheveled, my hair and clothing stiff with salt, I hoped we wouldn't run into anyone we knew. On Hawksbill Cay, that simply wasn't possible.

At the Pink Store, the generator was working overtime, keeping the lights and refrigeration running. Winnie had just opened her doors, so we bought bottled apple juice out of the cold case and had to explain to Winnie why we looked like objects the cat dragged in – 'damn dinghy overturned' – before being allowed to sit outside on the bench to drink it.

I was relieved to find Gator in his shack, getting his equipment ready for the day. 'Morning, ladies.' It took a moment for our appearance to register. 'Jesus, what happened to you?'

I was in no mood to mince words. 'We took Molly's boat over to Poinciana Point this morning where one of Rudy Mueller's goons pulled a gun and shot Molly's Zodiac out from under us.'

From the look of astonishment on Gator's face, I knew there were a lot of things about that statement that didn't exactly fit with laid-back island life. 'He pulled a *gun*?'

Molly, her hands primly folded in front of her,

252

said, 'An automatic.'

'Mueller's people aren't licensed for guns. Were you on Mueller's property?'

She shook her head. 'We were on the water.'

'Unbelievable!'

'That's what we thought, too, as we were paddling for our lives.'

Gator put down the swim fin he was adjusting. 'Which guard was it, do you know?'

'He wasn't one of the college kids. He's older, in his thirties maybe. Blond hair. Wears one of those ridiculous soul patches on his chin, so he's either a sloppy shaver, or going for a retro Frank Zappa look. Poinciana Cove must be his beat because we'd run into him there before.'

'Before. What's this *before* business?'

I bit my thumbnail and tried to look demure. 'We were collecting sand dollars. There are a lot of really nice ones over there.'

'Sand dollars! Give me a break. So you were trespassing?'

'When that man accosted us,' Molly insisted, 'we were well below the high-water mark.'

'And today,' I hastened to add, 'we were on the water. On public property, so to speak. That's what we want to talk to you about.'

'I think we better sit down.'

Gator retrieved a couple of plastic lawn chairs from underneath a tarp, unfolded them, and placed them side by side on the concrete apron that surrounded his shack. He pulled up an empty barrel, turned it over and sat down facing us. 'OK. Shoot.'

'Last night after dinner, Molly and I were sitting on her porch and saw some unusual activity going on over at the Tamarind Tree Resort. Near the runway.' I went on to explain about the lights, the plane, and the mysterious packages. 'Molly tells me that she observed similar activity approximately a month ago, around the time that Frank and Sally Parker went missing.'

Gator opened his mouth to say something, then snapped it shut.

Molly shot me a glance. 'I think we've stunned him into silence.'

'That's why we went over there this morning,' I went on. 'The plane is still parked on the runway, at least it was about an hour ago, but it's what we saw tied up at the end of the dock that was interesting.' I stood and rooted in the pocket of my cargo shorts until I found my camera. 'I took some pictures of it, but I'm afraid my camera got a good dunking.'

I pressed the ON/OFF switch on the camera but, as I had feared, nothing happened. 'Damn! Must be the battery. I'll dry it out, then see if it'll hold a charge.'

I opened a compartment on the side of the camera and pulled out the tiny memory chip. 'But there shouldn't be anything wrong with this.' I held it out. 'Do you have something you can read it on?'

'Have you seen my office?'

'All right, then. I'll take it back to the house, dry everything out, and see what we have.' I tucked the chip back into the camera for safe-keeping. 'I can email it to you as an attach-ment.'

Gator raised both hands, palms out. 'So, let's cut to the chase. Tell me what you think you have on that chip.'

'Frankly, Gator, I'm not sure. It looks like a World War II torpedo, except it's painted blue. Rusty in spots, pretty banged up. It's got this propeller thing on the tail.' I demonstrated by rotating my finger rapidly in the air.

'How long?'

I shrugged. 'Hard to say. Thirty feet maybe?'

'Could it have been a submarine?'

'It didn't have a conning tower, if that's what you mean.'

'Kind of small for a submarine,' Molly inter-jected. 'You could squeeze a couple of people into it, but there wouldn't be room enough to swing a cat.'

Gator stood up, tugged at the waistband of his shorts. 'I think I'd better have a look. Have you called the police to report the shooting?'

'I would have, but we don't have a generator, so my cellphone ran out of juice last night.'

'That's all right. We can use mine. Then, I'm going to get you ladies back to your cottages.'

For the first time since we set off on our morning adventure, Molly smiled. 'Thanks. I'd forgotten for a moment that my boat is out of commission.'

Gator dropped me at my dock, then ferried Molly to hers. I dragged myself along the

255

planking, the vision of a long, hot soapy shower shimmering like a mirage at the end of the sidewalk. I'd actually taken my clothes off and climbed into the shower enclosure before I remembered – no power, no water pump, no water. Stark naked, I leaned back against the wall and bawled.

I was taking a shower at Molly's when the power came back on. After Molly cut off her generator, I did a little happy dance around her garden.

Once we were sure it wasn't a fluke, I removed my meat from Molly's freezer and carried it back to *Windswept* where my refrigerator was humming away. Never came so close to hugging a major appliance.

I'd asked Molly what she wanted to do about repairing her dinghy. Pleading exhaustion, she went down for a nap. She'd call the insurance company when she woke up.

I reset all the clocks, stunned to discover that it was not yet noon.

When I finally plugged my iPhone in to its cradle, there were three voice messages from Paul, each increasingly more frantic. He'd heard about the Parkers on the news and was home in Annapolis, awaiting my call.

But he wasn't. When I called, I got the machine. He wasn't at Emily's either, but I had a nice chat with my daughter and her family – skipping all the scary bits – then called Paul back, leaving a message that I was fine, and not to worry.

Then I brewed myself a cup of hot tea, and thought about what I would do next.

If it hadn't been for Molly's ruined boat, I could half convince myself that the previous night had been a dream. As I sipped my tea, a phantom Paul perched on my shoulder asking for a rational explanation, so I tried to give him one.

First, the airplane. Could be Rudy Mueller, running late, returning to his resort.

How about the packages we'd seen? Nothing more than luggage. Or supplies in bulk.

I still didn't know what to make of the mini-sub. It looked old, decrepit. I knew they sank old ships to make artificial reefs. Maybe that's what Mueller had planned for the sub.

There was one way to find out, though. Ask.

I changed into white jeans and a flowered top, found my boat shoes under the bed, and drove *Pro Bono* over to the settlement. I had to eat lunch somewhere, I reasoned, and it might as well be at the Tamarind Tree. Even though I didn't own a golf cart, it was an easy, half-mile stroll down a paved path to the entrance of the resort where Lou was on duty at the gate. Amazingly, he recognized me. Maybe my picture was posted inside the gatehouse: BOLO, Hannah Ives, Troublemaker.

'Good to see you again, Mrs Ives.'

'You, too, Lou. Are they serving lunch to-day?'

'They are. Go on in.'

I skirted the gate and ambled up the path.

At the Tamarind Tree restaurant, I stood at the wooden podium. My fingers traced the intricately carved decorations – geckos chasing each other's tails – while I waited for the hostess to seat me. To my surprise, the woman who crossed the room to greet me like her best friend from college was Gabriele Mueller.

'How lovely to see you, Hannah. I was wondering when we'd have the pleasure of entertaining you and your husband.' Her eyes flicked right and left, checking the empty air behind me. 'Is Paul with you today?'

Mind like a steel trap, our Gabriele. Met us only once and had our names down pat. My brain, on the other hand, remained largely untrained in spite of taking Kevin Trudeau's Mega Memory course. If I remembered a name for more than five minutes, it was a miracle.

'Sadly, he's gone back to Baltimore on business. So it's just me!' I chirped.

I was starving, and the aroma of fresh seafood wafting my way from the direction of the outdoor grill was making me swoon. But I knew I'd not enjoy a single bite if some questions weren't answered to my satisfaction. 'Is your father here, Gabriele?'

'He is. He came in late last night. I absolutely hate it when he flies in after dark. One day he's going to kill himself, and then where will we be?'

Answer to question number one. Onward and upward. 'Is he here now? I'd like to talk to him.'

'Sorry, no. He took the launch to Marsh Harbour on business. Is there something I can help you with?'

'Do you expect him soon?'

'Later this afternoon, perhaps. It's always hard to say with Papa.'

'Perhaps you *can* help me, then, Gabriele. I hate to interrupt you while you're working, but is there someplace private we can talk?'

'Oh, that's not a problem! I just play at being hostess from time to time, remind everyone who's boss.' She waved her arm to attract the attention of a lovely young Bahamian dressed in the ladies' version of the TTR uniform: a polo shirt identical to the men, but with a khaki skirt instead of pants.

'Thanks, Lucy.' Gabriele handed the girl the stack of menus she was carrying, then motioned for me to follow her.

'We can use my father's office. I'm sure he won't mind.'

Gabriele led me down a long hallway, open to the outside world at both ends. Grass cloth covered the walls above a dark wooden chair rail, and small parsons tables had been placed here and there along the way. On each table, an oriental vase held arrangements of tropical flowers. I touched one of the hibiscus as I went by. It was real.

Rudy Mueller's desk was huge, a block of walnut the size of a Volkswagen, with carvings of pineapples and palm leaves snaking along its sides. Gabriele showed me to one of two chintz-

259

covered armchairs that flanked a gas fireplace, then sat down in the one opposite.

'Can I get you anything, Mrs Ives. Coffee, tea? It's no trouble, really.'

'No thank you. I'm here to lodge a serious complaint, actually, one that you'll probably hear about in due course as I had no alternative but to report the incident to the police.'

Cool as a cucumber, Gabriele sat at attention, hands folded, eyes locked on mine as if every word that fell from my mouth was a tiny, polished diamond. When she didn't respond, I went on. 'This morning, my neighbor and I, an elderly woman who lives on Bonefish Cay, Molly Weston, perhaps you know her?'

Gabriele shook her head.

'Molly and I had heard that Poinciana Point was a fabulous place for collecting sand dollars,' I continued, 'so we came over in Molly's Zodiac and...'

Gabriele's hand shot out across the fireplace screen and grabbed mine. '*You* were on that Zodiac? Oh, Mrs Ives, I'm so incredibly sorry. I had no idea. When Kyle reported what had happened, I sent someone after you. When we found the boat ... well, we knew you'd made it safely to shore. Since then, I've been trying to find the Zodiac's owner. That's one of the things Papa's looking into right now.

'I don't know what got into Kyle!' she babbled on. 'He's only worked for us a couple of months, but we'd never had any reason to question his reliability.' Gabriele blinked, massaged her temples with her fingers. 'The man was drunk, I'm afraid. I could smell the booze on him. A *gun*!' She pressed a perfectly manicured hand to her chest. 'We don't permit our people to carry weapons. How he even got it into the country, what with Nine-Eleven and all the airline restrictions, I'll never know.'

'He tried to kill us, Gabriele.'

'Kyle claims he was simply trying to scare you off. Papa's instructions were to keep people off that beach. Kyle was a bit over-zealous, I'm afraid.' She crossed one beautifully tanned leg over the other and rested a wrist on her knee. 'But he won't trouble you any more. The man's been sacked. Papa took care of that.

'And *please*,' she rushed on, 'tell Mrs Weston we will replace her Zodiac with a brand-new boat of exactly the same model. It will take a few days to get here – Papa will have to order it from Florida. In the meantime, we'll arrange a rental from Water Ways in Man-O-War, so hopefully Mrs Weston won't be inconvenienced any further.'

I didn't know what to say.

We'd been shot at, but nobody died.

Molly's dinghy was totaled, but it was being replaced.

The man responsible had been fired.

Gabriele Mueller had clearly aced her course in Hospitality Management 101.

I'd filed a complaint with the Bahamian authorities, so I'd just have to let them worry about nailing Kyle's ass to the wall for posses-

261

sion and use of a handgun. I personally wanted to tie him to a plank and set him adrift off Antarctica, but he could get ten years in a Bahamian prison. From what I'd read about Fox Hill, he'd probably prefer the Antarctic.

'Thank you, that's very generous,' I said. 'I'll tell Molly to get in touch with you, then?'

'Now that we know the boat's owner, and where she lives, I'm sure my father will be calling on her personally.'

Gabriele rose from her chair. Crisis averted. Things to do. People to see. 'Now, may I treat you to lunch?'

'That's very kind.'

Side by side, we walked down the hall. At the entrance to the dining room, I paused. 'I have a question, Gabriele. While Molly and I were hunting for sand dollars, we noticed this big blue object tied up at the end of the pier. What on earth is it?'

'That? It's a little submarine. Another one of Papa's projects. He bought it from a salvage dealer in Florida. Thought he'd install a glass window in the side so the children could ride around and look at fish. Can you imagine? My stepmother put a stop to that, I can tell you.'

Gabriele giggled, making it seem sultry rather than feather-brained. She picked up a menu from the podium and escorted me to a table. 'Here by the window is nice, don't you agree?'

I did. 'It's like dining in a rain forest.'

She pulled out my chair.

'The grilled grouper is especially good today,'

she recommended as I sat down. 'And Benicio is a magician with crème brûlée.' She raised her arm and snapped her fingers to attract the attention of one of the young servers. 'Ice water please for Mrs Ives!' Still holding the menu, she bent at the waist and whispered, as if she were divulging a secret recipe, 'Today's special is crème brûlée à l'orange. He uses heavy cream and Grand Marnier.'

I moaned. She'd used the C.B. word. My diet was doomed.

I accepted the menu from Gabriele and opened it to the first page. While pretending to read the specials of the day I asked, 'Is your brother here today, Gabriele?'

'Jaime's on the island somewhere, Hannah, but I really don't have the time to keep up with him. He has his own projects. I'm too busy to get involved.'

I'll bet. Gabriele was a smart cookie. If Jaime was up to what I think he was up to, she'd keep as much distance between herself and her brother as possible.

'How about Alice?' I glanced up from the menu to judge Gabriele's reaction. 'We had a chance to chat at the art show. She's lovely.'

A cloud passed over her face. Was that a smirk? 'Alice and Jaime share one of the cottages on Poinciana Point. She's been a bit under the weather lately, sticking close to home. If I see her, I'll tell her you asked.'

'Please do.'

The Mueller family. All present and accounted for.

I closed the menu and handed it back to her with a smile that didn't go beyond my face. 'The grilled grouper will be fine.'

While I waited for my entrée I played with my banana bread, tearing off bite-size pieces with my fingers, putting them in my mouth and chewing thoughtfully. Gabriele had given me plausible answers to all my questions, except one.

No matter how you cut it, Jaime Mueller had lied about where he'd found *Wanderer*. *Wanderer* had never left Hawksbill Cay. And sadly, neither had Frank and Sally Parker.

Eighteen

WHILE A HURRICANE IS IN TROPICAL WATERS, IT IS INFLUENCED BY THE NORTH EAST TRADE WINDS AND MOVES TOWARD THE WEST OR WEST-NORTH WEST AT A SPEED OF ABOUT 10 TO 15 KNOTS, BUT IT IS DIFFICULT TO MAKE ACCURATE PREDICTIONS CONCERNING THE PATHS OF HURRICANES.
  Sallie Townsend, *Boating Weather: How To Predict It And What To Do About It*, p. 21

Sometime during the first week of August, 2008, Frank and Sally Parker had died of ligature strangulation. This information didn't come to me from the authorities in Nassau, nor from the Marsh Harbour police. I found it out from Paul who had it from FBI Special Agent Amanda Crisp, whose supervisor contacted the office of the Bahamian Minister of Health, Hubert Minnis, and pressured a nervous office assistant, dazzled by being singled out for attention by the FBI, into divulging the results of the autopsy. On condition of anonymity, of course.

Due to the high-profile nature of the case, two

pathologists had performed the procedure, Paul reported, a Bahamian doctor and one especially flown in from Florida. In a follow-up email to my iPhone, Paul wrote that the cause of death was listed as asphyxiation by a cord-like object partially circumferencing the victims' necks, the pattern and dimensions of which were consistent with a three-strand twisted polyester rope, approximately five-eighths of an inch in diameter, commonly available.

Commonly available. Jeesh. Boat lines, dock lines, anchor lines, mooring lines, tow lines, halyards, sheets for main and jib. A properly rigged sailboat used dozens of lines. But presuming you could identify the specific rope that killed our friends among all that spaghetti, even Super Glue fuming couldn't bring up fingerprints on it.

I rode across the harbor in *Pro Bono* to share what I knew about the autopsy with Gator.

'Nice of them to let me know,' Gator grumbled.

'Paul tells me there'll be an inquest. Will I have to testify?'

'I will for sure.' He picked up an air tank and strapped it into a rolling carrier. 'Probably you and Molly, too, having been there when we found them.' He grunted, hefted another tank into the carrier. 'It's the law. Once they set a date, you'll get a summons.'

'Are you telling me, don't leave town?'

'Something like that.' Gator started up the dock toward his dive shack, dragging the air

266

tanks, and motioned for me to follow. 'Been meaning to tell you. You know that mini-sub you were talking about?'

'Yeah?'

'It's gone. Towed out to sea and scuttled, according to Jaime Mueller.'

I glared, head cocked, fists on hips. 'And you believe him, Gator?'

'It's not like I could check it out, Hannah. The bank drops off to twenty-five hundred meters out there.' He waved vaguely in the direction of the Atlantic Ocean as if he thought I didn't know where it was.

I watched Gator thread a dock line through an eye bolt screwed into the roof of his dive shack and secure it to a cleat set in the concrete. 'Just as well it's gone. Wouldn't want something like that banging up against your dock with a hurricane coming.'

'Hurricane? You're kidding.' Without Paul home to noodge me awake, I'd overslept and missed the Cruisers' Net that morning, so this was news to me.

'Tropical storm Helen for now, but they may upgrade her shortly. They're predicting she'll reach us Friday. Winds eighty to a hundred, they say.'

'Is that bad?'

'Seen worse.' He stepped over Justice, picked up a dock line and threaded it through another eye bolt.

Gator's strange activities had suddenly become clear. 'So you're tying stuff down.'

'Lots to do.' He bent down, picked up a coil of rope and tossed it to me. 'Give me a hand?'

Our landlords used the side of the refrigerator like a bulletin board. Who to call if the propane tank runs out (Earl Sands). Where to report a power outage (BEC). What to do in the unlikely event of a hurricane (Pray). The first thing I did when I got home was consult it.

Bring porch furniture in, secure doors and windows ... on and on and on I read. Dozens of bullet points about how to secure their property, but nothing about what I should do personally other than getting myself to the airport and flying the hell out. I'd have to talk to Molly.

My talk with Molly was delayed temporarily by a visit from a representative of the Royal Bahamas Police Force, Marsh Harbour Division. I had been fixing to go to Molly's, when someone pulled up to the dock. I watched curiously from the living room window as he alighted from his Boston Whaler, ambled up the dock, tall and straight and proud, all decked out in his uniform – a light-blue short-sleeved, open-necked shirt tucked into navy-blue trousers with a wide, red stripe running up the side. His military-style hat, also navy-blue with a red stripe, was perched on his head at a rakish angle. He carried a clipboard, the pages flapping as he climbed the steps to the porch and rang our bell.

I came out, all smiles. 'How can I help you,

officer?'

He consulted his clipboard. 'Good morning, ma'am. I'm Sergeant Wilbur. Are you Hannah Miles?'

'It's Ives, officer. I-V-E-S. Ives. Would you care to sit down?' I indicated one of the wicker chairs. He sat in one and I took the other. I folded my hands primly and waited.

Sergeant Wilbur eased a pen from his breast pocket, scribbled something on his papers – presumably changing 'Miles' to 'Ives,' ascertained that I was, indeed, one of the people aboard *Deep Magic* when the bodies of Frank and Sally Parker were discovered, and asked me to tell him about it.

While I was talking, he took notes.

When I wound down, he asked, 'I understand that you knew the deceased.'

I explained the Naval Academy connection. 'But I hadn't seen the Parkers for several years,' I added quickly, 'and I certainly didn't know Frank had been invited to Hawksbill Cay. I wish I had. Things might have turned out differently.'

Suspicion flashed in his dark eyes.

'What I mean,' I blathered on, 'is if we had known they were coming, they might have stayed with us here at *Windswept* and not been in Poinciana Cove at all.'

'Why do you think they were in Poinciana Cove?'

'I heard it from someone on the Cruisers' Net,' I said, tap-dancing as fast as I could.

His eyes began a slow roll, which he checked almost at once. It was abundantly clear that Sergeant Wilbur considered the Cruisers' Net a bunch of unreliable nosey-parkers. 'We have credible information that their boat was found near Eleuthera.'

I didn't comment. What was the point? From that single statement, I knew he'd talked to Jaime Mueller and had taken what the creep told him seriously. I'd believe the word of a cruising sailor over that of a spoiled-rotten daddy's boy any day.

'We theorize that the Parkers were attacked somewhere near where their bodies were discovered,' he continued. 'Then their boat was taken to Eleuthera where it was stripped and abandoned by the thieves.'

It's *my* personal theory that if enough money is involved, certain Bahamian authorities can be convinced that the Gulf Stream flows from north to south and the sun rises in the west.

'Pirates?' I said. What bullshit, I thought. Pirates, drug-runners, desperate Haitians, teenagers partying late who need a ride home ... they'd steal a go-fast or a cabin cruiser, or even a peppy little runabout before they'd saddle themselves with a sailboat that could make only seven knots per hour even with a twenty-five knot wind pushing on its sails.

'Yes, ma'am,' he nodded sagely.

Wilbur opened the clip on his clipboard, released a sheet of paper and handed it to me. 'There's going to be an inquest on September

10 at the courtroom in Marsh Harbour. This is a summons requesting that you appear.'

I must have looked worried because he added, 'Don't worry. You'll just tell the coroner and the jury what you told me today. There'll be other witnesses, too. Then the jury will bring in a verdict.' He stood, rearranged his papers under the clip, and extended his hand for me to shake.

'But what about the storm? I hear there's a big one coming.'

'We cross that bridge when we come to it, ma'am. If the inquest is cancelled, we'll be sure to let you know.'

'Can you tell me how the Parkers died?' I asked even though I already knew the answer.

'No ma'am. Sorry. That's for the pathologists to say.' He checked his clipboard again. 'Which dock belongs to a Mrs Molly Weston?'

I pointed to the path through the bushes. 'You can leave your boat tied up here, Sergeant Wilbur. Her house is just through the trees.'

When the last blue speck of Wilbur's uniform disappeared into the foliage, I powered up my laptop and Googled the police website. Little seemed to have been updated since 2006. Many of the links were 'under construction,' amateur clip art warred with text blocks sometimes overwriting them, and a click on 'Abaco' produced a *404 file not found* error. I suspected that the link to 'Police Most Wanted' would return mug shots of thugs who had long ago escaped the short arm of the law, but decided not to test my theory.

I knew ten-year-olds who could build better websites. Didn't do much to inspire confidence in the Royal Bahamian Police Force.

When I heard the *rrrhumm* of Wilbur's departing Whaler, I popped next door.

I had to laugh. Molly had received Officer Wilbur wearing a 1950s-style cotton house dress and fuzzy-pink bunny slippers. Her hair stood out in erratic spikes like a victim of The Mad Mousser.

'You get a summons, Molly?' I asked.

'Same as you.'

'Did you hear we've got a tropical storm coming?'

'Oh yes,' she said wearily, pointing to her television where CNN was tracking the storm. 'Believe it when I see it.'

'I was thinking of evacuating, especially since Paul's back in Maryland. But with this summons, I'm kind of stuck.'

'I'm not leaving,' she said. 'This old place has survived every hurricane for the past fifty years, and that includes some humdingers like Floyd, Frances and Jeanne. The biggest danger is storm surge, and we're high enough above sea level never to be bothered by that.' Her eyes widened. 'Tell me you're not really leaving, Hannah?'

I paused to consider her question. Paul would have a fit and fall in it if I stayed. But he'd be worrying unnecessarily. I'd been through hurricanes before. Eloise, Floyd, even Isabel scored direct hits on Annapolis, but other than a foot of water in the basement, a few lost shingles and a twisted gutter, we'd lived to tell the tale. As long as I could hold out inside a sturdy, well-built house, I wasn't particularly concerned. *Windswept*, like *Southern Exposure*, had been built by shipbuilders, men who knew how to confront, exploit and tame both wind and sea. We'd be just fine.

But I didn't fancy riding out the storm alone, so I smiled at my friend and said, 'Not if you aren't.'

Nineteen

TROPICAL AND GLOBAL FORECAST MODELS
ARE IN GOOD AGREEMENT ON NEWLY FORM-
ED TROPICAL STORM HELEN'S MOVEMENT.
SHE'LL LIKELY APPROACH THE BAHAMAS,
PROBABLY THE ABACOS FRIDAY SEPT 5.
INTENSITY MODELS SUGGEST HELEN WILL
BE A POTENT CATEGORY 2 OR 3 HURRICANE
WITH WIND 80 KNOTS TO 100 KNOTS.
Chris Parker, *Wx Update*, Bahamas, Tue 2, 10a

Paul called on my iPhone, fully expecting that
I'd have closed down the house by then, and be
well on my way home. In Ft Lauderdale, perhaps, or West Palm. 'Where are you?'

'I'm standing in the Pink Store, buying
supplies.'

'I thought you were coming home!'

'It's a tropical storm, Paul, not a hurricane.'

'I beg to differ. It's a hurricane, Hannah. CNN
just said so. And I want you to come home.
Now.'

Milk and bread had long since disappeared
from the Pink Store's shelves, as well as toilet
paper. As I tried to calm my husband down, I

274

pushed the cart around the narrow aisles, dropping in napkins as a substitute for toilet paper, a
package of Fig Newtons, a box of Ritz crackers
and two jars of Skippy Super Chunk peanut
butter.

'I can't, Paul. I've been summoned to the
inquest in Marsh Harbour next week. If I don't
show up, they can arrest me.' I glommed on to
the last package of McVitie's Hobnobs and
tucked them into my basket, along with a four-
ounce jar of instant coffee, although I really
hated the stuff. 'I don't think I want to spend
time in a Bahamian prison.'

'I can make some phone calls.'

'Please don't muddy the water, Paul. As far as
I know, they plan to go on with the inquest as
scheduled. If the Bahamians aren't too concerned about the weather, you shouldn't be
either.'

'I don't like what I see on CNN. They say
Helen's heading directly for the Abacos.'

'Hurricanes can be very unpredictable. Look
what happened with Jeanne.' Molly had mentioned to us earlier that Jeanne had meandered
around the Caribbean for ten days before
steaming out into the empty Atlantic. Then she
surprised everyone by making a two hundred
and seventy degree turn and heading back
toward land. Just like a woman. Unpredictable.

On the other end of the line Paul snorted.
'May I remind you that Jeanne devastated the
Abacos.'

'Bad example,' I said, picking up an apple and

checking it for brown spots.

'You must always assume a storm is going to turn in your direction and act accordingly, Hannah.'

'That's why the house is battened down and I'm in the Pink Store, buying groceries.'

By the time I reached Winnie and the check-out counter, I had promised Paul that if it looked like the hurricane was going to be a doozey, I'd hie myself to the airport and nip out of there, pronto.

Over the next two days, resorts emptied. An unbroken procession of golf carts, ferries and taxis transported grumbling guests and their belongings to the airport where they waited in long lines – sitting on their bags, sleeping at uncomfortable angles on plastic chairs – for the privilege of being packed into tiny planes and flown to safety on the mainland.

Safety. I had to smile. When Hurricane Helen finished with Abaco, she'd no doubt head straight for Florida, then where'd they be?

Rudolph Mueller joined the stream of evacuees, too, flying himself back to San Antonio where his young family awaited. He left his son, Jaime, in charge. Jaime, who nobody'd laid eyes on for weeks. Maybe he'd evacuated, too, and just forgot to tell anyone.

Cabin cruisers, motor yachts and fishing boats headed west in flotillas. Mega-yachts, too, just as quickly as crews could be flown in to drive them back to their owners in Jupiter, Palm Beach or Miami.

Meanwhile, cruising yachtsmen were jockeying for secure moorings in Hope Town, Man-O-War and Hawksbill Cay, all popular hurricane holes, or deciding to risk a mooring in Marsh Harbour or a tie-up at one of the marinas.

By the time it was certain that Helen would make landfall in the Abacos, the Parker inquest had been cancelled, Radio Abaco shut down all programming except for storm warnings and evacuation notices, and it was too late for me to leave the islands.

I got my ditch kit together: passport, money, prescription meds, my wallet containing my Blue Cross/Blue Shield card – and put it all in a wheely duffle along with enough drinking water and clothing for three days. I packed canned goods and unperishables in a canvas tote, and added a can opener. Manual. I found some long-life milk only two months past its sell-by date, so I chucked that into the bag, too. My sleeping bag topped everything off.

Over the last of Molly's chicken and a casserole of green beans, Molly and I discussed what to do. There were no designated shelters on tiny Bonefish Cay. Two women riding out a hurricane alone on an otherwise deserted cay didn't seem like a good idea to me, even if we were both able-bodied gals described by everyone who knew us as 'spunky.'

Our designated shelter was the Hawksbill Cay All-Age School, but Molly taught poetry there from time to time, and wasn't convinced it'd be any safer than staying at home on Bonefish.

277

'Trust me when I tell you, Hannah, I'd rather ride out the storm in *Pro Bono* than in the Hawksbill All-Age School.'

An alternative was the St Frances de Sales Catholic Church in Marsh Harbour, but we didn't know anybody there.

Then on the Cruisers' Net that morning, a welcome announcement. Jaime Mueller (who claimed he never listened!) called in on open mike to say that the Tamarind Tree Resort and Marina could be used as an evacuation center.

'He just wants to curry favor with the locals,' Molly grumbled.

'Curry away,' I said, delighted. 'Any port in a storm.'

'Not quite any. My late husband was a builder,' Molly told me. 'Let's check the Tamarind Tree out.'

'What I really want to check out, is that shack in Kelchner's Cove. Since we'll have free access to the grounds, do you think...?'

'Snap out of it, Hannah! Hurricane? Remember?'

'There's a party pooper in every crowd.'

Twenty minutes later, it seemed odd to find the turnstile up and the gate to the exclusive resort unattended. When we found him, Lou, the gate attendant, was dragging pool furniture into the fitness center with the help of another staffer. Sitting on an empty planter ten feet away, watching, was Alice Madonna Robinson Mueller.

'Hello, Alice,' I said.

Her tears had dried, but they'd left tracks of blue-black mascara down her cheeks. I was going to ask her what was wrong when she said, 'Oh, hi, Hannah. Who's your friend?'

'This is Molly Weston. She lives over on Bonefish Cay, too. We're hoping to ride out the hurricane with you.'

'Oh, goody! It'll be nice to have a friend staying here.'

'Looks like you've been crying. What's wrong?'

'Nothing, really. It's just that Jaime can be such a *stinker*! I wanted to go home, *begged* him, but he said if he had to stay, I had to stay.' She folded her arms across her bosom. 'And now it's too late.'

'Well, if it's any consolation, Alice, I'm stuck here, too. My husband's back in Maryland, totally pissed off that I didn't make it out in time.'

Alice hopped off the planter, seemingly cheered by this news. 'Jaime says this place was built to withstand winds up to one hundred and eighty miles an hour. Can you imagine? I've already got my space picked out. Come and see.' Like a camp counselor on a field trip, she led us into the dining room where I'd last eaten lunch after my talk with Gabriele, down a narrow corridor and into an elegant, mahogany-paneled club room decorated in British Colonial style, more reminiscent of the Raj than the West Indies. Small items that could easily become projectiles – silverware, glassware, vases – had been stored away, leaving only tables and chairs. Ceiling fans circled slowly overhead.

'I'm behind the bar,' Alice said. She pointed out her mattress, pillows and blanket; a pile of *Vogue* and *People* magazines; and something that made me want to take her in my arms and whisper *there-there* into her hair – a teddy bear so well loved he was nearly hairless.

'What a lovely little nest you've made for yourself, Alice,' said Molly.

'I couldn't bring everything, of course.' She started to tear up again.

I picked up her hand, squeezed and held on to it. 'We're going back home to pick up our things now, but after we return and get settled in, let's sit down and have a nice chat. Okay?'

Alice managed to dredge up a smile from somewhere and plant it on her face. 'I'd like that a lot, Hannah.'

'What a sad little creature,' Molly said after Alice had scampered off to retrieve something else she'd forgotten from her cottage on the point. We were wandering around the club room, casing the joint. 'Poured concrete floors,' Molly said, testing the carpet with her toes. She laid a hand flat on the wall. 'Solid concrete construction here, too.' She leaned back, checking out the ceiling. 'Reinforced trusses, two-by-six and not two-by-four, that's good.' She pointed. 'And they're nicely camouflaged, but can you see where they used hurricane straps to tie the roof to the walls? That should prevent lift-off!'

Even I could see that except for the picture window overlooking the pool, all the windows had been constructed, Bahamian-style, out of wood and high-quality plexiglass. They became their own hurricane shutters when lowered and dogged tightly down. 'And another plus?' Molly added. 'The doors open out, and not in.'

As we strolled back toward the main gate, Molly pointed out that in a town where trees, telephone poles, boats, golf carts, air conditioners and even other buildings could rise up and fall down on you, the Tamarind Tree had an advantage. It sat practically alone.

It was a no-brainer.

On the way back to Bonefish Cay, we stopped at Hawksbill Hardware – 'If we don't have it, you don't need it' – and bought spare batteries for my flashlight and the last two cans of Sterno.

'What's CNN saying?' I asked Molly on the VHF radio a bit later.

'It's coming, it's bad, and it's tomorrow. Over.'

'I'll come and help you, then we can secure *Windswept*. Over and out.'

When it was *Windswept's* turn, everything that was outside had to come in. A flying coconut can do damage enough – I'd heard of people being killed by them – but a flying barbecue grill?

I disconnected the gutters from the cistern to prevent wind-driven waves of salt water from sweeping over the roof and contaminating our drinking water. With Molly's help, I lowered all the windows and dogged them down tight while she hooked them to the window frames on the inside. I flipped all the breakers and turned off the power. And I hauled down the flag.

Molly went to fetch her ditch kit, but I had one last task to do.

Pets weren't allowed in shelters, I'd heard, and I wanted to say goodbye.

The last time I'd seen Dickie had been that morning. I'd been sitting on the back steps doing kitty shiatsu along his spine, when he suddenly stiffened. The fur on his tail puffed out as if it'd been stuck into an electric socket, then he leapt from my arms and streaked off into the bushes, a coonskin cap on four legs.

'Dickie!' I called now, hoping he'd come back. 'Here Dickie, Dickie, Dickie!'

I'm not sure why I was bothering to call as I'd never known the skittish animal to answer to his name. I filled a bowl with kibble and wandered around the back yard, rattling as I went. 'Dickie!' But he failed to appear.

I followed the path that led from my house to Molly's and back again, rattling and calling, but the silly cat was AWOL. Still holding the bowl, I sat down on the steps and began to cry. 'Damn you, cat,' I sniffled. *'Please* come out!'

Did Dickie know a hurricane was coming? Did some electrical charge in the air tip him off? Was he off in some hurricane hole of his own?

Swiping at my eyes, I clumped back into the house and rummaged around in the cupboards until I found a couple of mixing bowls. I filled one with kibble and the other with water and crammed them in the crawl space under the house where Dickie liked to hide. He'd survived more than one hurricane, and I hoped he'd survive this one, too.

Finally, I locked up.

As I clicked the great big padlock in place on the front door of our home away from home, I felt an overwhelming sadness. I was abandoning this friendly house to the mercy of the wind, and I wondered if I'd ever see it again.

With tears still in my eyes, I plodded down to the end of the dock to wait for Molly.

Looking out over the water, I began to worry. It was still sunny, but the Sea of Abaco was kicking up; the wind blew whitecaps off the tops of the waves like heads of foam off beer. We'd left it too long.

'Here, put this on,' I said, handing Molly a life jacket. While she strapped herself in, I put one on, too. Michelin Man and the Pillsbury Doughboy, we bumbled down the dock and scrambled aboard *Pro Bono*. As an extra precaution, we threaded lines through our life jackets and tied ourselves to cleats just in case *Pro Bono* decided to throw us.

'Hold on!' I shouted, pulling back on the

throttle.

'Wheee!' Molly hollered. 'Hi ho, Silver!'

Pro Bono roared out of its slip, reared up and took the reins in its teeth, *thrump-thrump-thrumping* over the tops of the waves, getting us to Hawksbill Cay in one piece, but leaving us feeling bruised and battered.

Once inside the harbor, the wind abated. Gator had suggested I tie the boat in a thicket of mangrove near the island's dump, so after dropping Molly off on the dock with all our gear, I headed for the dump. I aimed *Pro Bono* into the mangroves, revved up the engine and rammed her in, head first, as far as she would go. Then I tied her off to the thickest branches with every rope I'd been able to find.

When I finished, *Pro Bono* looked like something out of a bondage fantasy. To be on the safe side, though, I dropped an anchor off the stern and tied it on tight. Just as I was finishing up, Gator came alongside in his dinghy and ferried me back to the government dock.

When we got back, Molly had already loaded our gear on to the back seat of Gator's golf cart. She perched on top of the pile, flexing her muscles like Superwoman and singing into the stiffening breeze, *I am strong, I am invincible, I am woman!*

Forgetting about everything for a moment – Paul, Dickie, Frank and Sally Parker, even the approaching storm – I laughed until my sides ached.

Twenty

HURRICANE HELEN STRENGTHENED OVER-
NIGHT TO A CATEGORY 3 HURRICANE WITH
WIND OF 100 KNOTS. CONDITIONS IN ABACO
SHOULD BEGIN TO DETERIORATE THIS EVEN-
ING. EXPECT 100 KNOTS OF WIND FROM THE
NE, WITH STORM SURGE TO 12 FEET, FOL-
LOWED BY SOUTH WIND TO 80 KNOTS AND
CONTINUING STORM SURGE AS HELEN EXITS
TOMORROW.
Chris Parker, *Wx Update*, Bahamas, Thur 4, 10a

It seemed odd to be preparing for a hurricane
when the sky was blue, the sun shone, and the
winds blew no more strongly than usual. If you
didn't listen to Barometer Bob, download your
weather from the Internet, or have CNN
nattering away *ad nauseum*, you'd think it was
a fine day for sailing. Hey, ho, the sailor's life
for me! Out you'd go, then *blammo*!

At one o'clock, however, Radio Abaco reported that Hurricane Helen had made landfall on
Eleuthera with wind gusts up to one hundred
miles per hour. She continued to steer our way.
Most of her staff had evacuated over the

weekend, but Gabriele Mueller had stayed behind with a skeleton crew of volunteers to help prepare the resort for the coming storm. Although she was holed up in her father's office rather than in the club room with the rest of the peasants, she appeared around two o'clock on Thursday just as everyone was getting settled in. She wore a beige, v-neck, button-front Calvin Klein sundress I'd seen in the window at Nordstrom, and Tommy Bahama flip-flops with a flower on the toe.

'Welcome, everyone,' began her walk-and-talk. 'I'm Gabriele Mueller. My father asked me to apologize for not being here with you today, but he's returned to San Antonio to be with his young children. I speak for my father and my brother – who's out with some staff securing our grounds but hopes to be with us soon. I speak for everyone at Tamarind Tree Resort and Marina, when I say I hope you will consider this your home for the time you are with us.'

Gabriele had reached the bar. She continued talking, trailing her hand along the polished wood as if checking it for dust. 'Of course we're hoping that the storm will pass through quickly and do as little damage as possible, but in the meantime, the bar is open.' She spread her arms gracefully, like Vanna White on *Wheel of Fortune*, showing off a prize. 'There's plenty of ice, water, and a limited supply of fruit juice and cold beer, and although the kitchen isn't available, Jeremy Thomas here...' – a big smile

286

for Jeremy, one of the college boys who had shucked his TTR uniform in favor of shorts and a wife-beater tee and had been busily schlepping bags into the shelter for Alice Madonna – '...Jeremy will do what he can to make you comfortable.'

She smiled, bowed slightly, and wafted off in a cloud of ylang-ylang and patchouli.

After Gabriele had retreated to her sanctuary, Molly and I helped the staff move the outdoor furniture inside. We turned patio tables upside down, nested chairs and placed them on top, then used the tables to barricade the double doors leading out to the patio bar.

Two of the canvas loungers we saved for ourselves, dragging them to a corner of the club room near the gas log fireplace where Molly and I had set up camp. 'This feels like Girl Scouts,' Molly said as she unfolded the lounger, adjusted the back and spread her blanket on top. 'Maybe we should sing "White Coral Bells."'

I arranged my lounger next to hers, retrieved a paperback novel and a flashlight from my duffle, then slid the bag underneath my chair. 'I vote for "Do Your Ears Hang Low." Can you believe they still sing that in Scouts? My granddaughter, Chloe, was driving me nuts with it not too long ago.'

I tossed the paperback on the lounger, sat down, and arranged my rolled-up sleeping bag behind my back like a pillow. I wriggled in, testing for comfort. 'This should do nicely,' I said, plumping up the bag with my fist, 'but it'd be nicer if I were wearing a bathing suit sitting by the side of the pool.

'Where *is* everybody?' I asked after a moment.

Molly shrugged. '"If you build it, they will come." Gator went off to fetch Justice. I saw him a while back building a cave underneath a table. And Alice Mueller seems to have gone off to hire a decorator to spruce up her little spot behind the bar.' She frowned. 'Which brings up an interesting point. What happened to all the booze? Those shelves behind the bar used to be lousy with it.'

'They make good projectiles. Wouldn't want to be killed by a flying bottle of Jack Daniels. You'd never live it down in North Carolina.'

Molly chuckled. 'There's Gator, now,' she said, pointing.

We watched as Gator shook the folds out of a blue tarp and held it over one of the shuttered windows while a staffer secured the tarp to the wall with generous lengths of duct tape. One done, they moved on to the next window. Taking it down would be hell on the wallpaper, I thought.

'What's Gator done with Justice?' I asked. 'I thought pets weren't allowed in shelters.'

Molly chuckled. 'Everybody breaks that rule.' She pointed. 'Justice is under the table. You can just see his nose.'

'I thought there'd be more refugees by now.'

'There's hours to go yet,' Molly said. 'But we've got some powerboaters in the corner over there. They put blankets down to reserve the spot, then went off to get their stuff together.' She grinned. 'I hope it's beer. Ever been confined with a bunch of stink potters when the liquor runs out?'

I laughed. 'Not pretty.'

'The sailors will be the last to show,' Molly continued. 'They're down at the marina now, checking their anchors, adjusting their lines, and swearing up and down they're going to ride out the storm on their boats. But, they'll change their minds at the last minute, come staggering in, wet and wild, just as we're about to bar the door.'

'Except for Gator, I don't see any of the locals, Molly.'

'You really expect to?'

I thought about that for a moment. Right. After fighting Mueller's development tooth and nail, if I were a local, I wouldn't be caught dead under the rubble here either. I'd be up at the All-Age School settling in with my friends and my family. And the food would be better, too.

I reached in my duffle and pulled out a bottle of Myers Rum. 'Recreational beverage.'

Molly pressed her hands together. 'You *are* a love!'

I popped a can of pineapple juice, filled a plastic cup to the halfway point, added a glug-glug of rum, and handed the cup to Molly. She took a sip and melted into the cushions. 'Ummm. You think of everything.'

'Just conserving our water.' I mixed an identical drink for myself and leaned back against my makeshift pillow to sip at it and wait.

I had closed my eyes and drifted off when my handheld radio crackled. 'Scarlett, Scarlett, this is Rhett. Come in.'

My eyes flew open. Paul? What the hell?

I sat up so quickly that my head swam. I reached under my makeshift cot and dragged out my duffle, pawing through it looking for my radio which continued to say, 'Scarlett, Scarlett, this is Rhett.'

Next to me, Molly struggled to sit. 'Paul's in radio range?'

'Evidently.' I finally found the radio in an outside pocket of the duffle where I'd put it so it'd be easy to find.

'Scarlett...'

I mashed my thumb down on the talk button, stepping on his transmission. 'Rhett, this is Scarlett. Over.'

'Hannah, this is Paul. I'm with Henry Allen. We're in his plane and we're coming in for a landing.'

'What? In this weather? Are you out of your freaking mind?'

'Don't argue with me now. We're just north of Scotland and should be touching down on Hawksbill shortly. The crosswind's pretty stiff, but Henry's confident we can make it. Out.'

I tucked the radio into the pocket of my shorts. 'Where's Gator?'

'Hannah, you're not going out...'

290

'Of course I am! What if he crashes? Oh my God! Gator!'

The wind blew hot, churning the water of Poinciana Cove into white froth like Armageddon.

I stood next to Gator on the muddy banks of the runway, panting after my hundred-yard dash, desperately scanning the sky, hoping for a glimpse of the bright-yellow speck that would be Henry's Savage Cub. To the northwest, cirrus clouds were strewn like spun cotton across the blue sky, but dark clouds had settled over Man-O-War to the south, building layer upon layer of gray.

'Can they land in all this wind?' I shouted to Gator.

'Henry's done it before!'

Wind whipped noisily over my ears, but still I heard it, the drone of an engine, steady and strong. 'There they are!' I yelled as the plane came into view.

The Cub headed straight for the runway, flaps down, wings dipping right, then left. With its chrome yellow struts and black trim, the Cub reminded me of a giant bee. It lifted, then dipped, lifted then dipped; with each dip my heart thudded against my ribs. 'Come on, come on!'

I watched, fingers tightly crossed as the Cub closed the gap between us. I could see Henry now, struggling with the control stick as the plane slipped right on a sudden gust of wind. Henry won, and the little plane steered straight for the runway again. The big tires skimmed the water, sending up rooster tails. It skipped, bounced, then touched down lightly at the end of the runway.

My arms shot up, and I started to cheer, but the cheer caught in my throat. As I watched in horror, another gust seized the Cub by a wing, spun it, flipped it, and sent it sliding sideways into the cove.

I ran forward, flat out, with Gator pounding right behind. We reached the end of the runway in time to see the plane, with Henry and Paul still in it, settle back in ten feet of water with a gurgle and a sigh, its wing lying broken on the starboard side. The propeller still spun.

'The door's on the port side,' I yelled. 'Help me get them out!'

I splashed into a sea as warm as bathwater. When it got to my waist, I started to swim, reaching the plane in a dozen strokes as the wind and the tide bore me out. Through a curtain of rain I could see Henry in the pilot's seat, struggling with his seat belt.

When had it started to rain? The drops fell faster, splattering coldly on my face as I hung on to the fuselage and worked my way around to the port side. A wave broke full on my face and I swallowed a mouthful of salt water. Coughing, I braced my feet on the wheel support, grabbed one of the struts and pulled myself up until I was standing on it, trusting it would bear my weight. In the single seat behind Henry, Paul slumped. Blood oozed from a cut on his temple.

I grabbed the door and pulled, but I couldn't get it open. 'Help me, Henry! Where's the handle?'

Henry moved, and suddenly the door was outside the plane. It slid past my legs and tumbled into the sea, which was strangely flat and calm where the fuselage sheltered it from the wind. I watched it sink to the bottom. With the door gone, I grasped one of the seat supports for balance, leaned in and spoke to my husband. 'Paul! Paul! Are you OK?'

Paul squinted at me groggily. 'I think so.'

'Can you swim?' I asked as I struggled to help him with his seat belt.

'I think so.'

Gator had joined me by then, bracing one foot against a strut and the other on the side of the plane. As Gator struggled for balance, Henry tore out the pilot's seat cushions to make room to work. Leaning over the auxiliary stick, he helped me extricate Paul. Together we handed him down to Gator who eased Paul into the water, holding on tight to his belt. I watched him float my husband slowly to shore, fighting the wind and the waves every stroke of the way.

'What the hell were you thinking?' I wanted to scream at Henry, but this didn't seem like the time for it.

'Are you ready?' asked Henry.

I nodded.

'After you,' he said.

And I jumped in.

Getting back was much harder as the weather was against us. For every two strokes forward the waves would push me one stroke back. I wasn't sure how strong a swimmer Henry was, so I kept checking to make sure he was still with me. Stroke, kick, stroke, kick. Turn, look back. It seemed like hours before my feet touched sand and I could stand up and wade on to the beach where Gator was sitting next to Paul. He'd propped my injured husband up against a piece of driftwood.

I fell to my knees in the sand, crying with relief, checking Paul's wound gingerly with my fingers. 'You scared me half to death!'

Paul looked at me, then closed his eyes. 'Don't cry,' he said.

'I'm not crying, you idiot. It's the freaking rain!'

The corners of his mouth twitched in what might have been a smile. 'I was worried about you, Hannah.'

Gator eased his hands under Paul's armpits and urged my husband to his feet. 'Let's get him back to the resort.'

The rain stung my face, the wind slashed at my hair as I lifted my husband's arm and eased under it. 'Is this what it feels like to skydive in the rain?'

Gator snorted. 'A few minutes later, Henry, and you wouldn't have made it.'

Henry's head wagged and water dripped off his earlobes. 'That's as close to death as I ever want to get.'

As we straggled back to the resort, supporting Paul who stumbled along between us, I said to Gator, 'You know that mini-sub that Jaime deep sixed?'

'Yeah?'

'He lied. It's out there. Under the plane.'

Twenty-One

SATELLITE WIND DATA, AIRCRAFT RECON-
NAISSANCE AND LOCAL REPORTS CONFIRM
HURRICANE-FORCE WIND OF 100 KNOTS IS
LASHING ABACO. EXPECT A WIND SHIFT AS
THE CENTER OF HELEN PASSES IN A FEW
HOURS, BUT A CONTINUING BLOW AS HELEN
CONTINUES TO INTENSIFY THROUGH THE
NIGHT AND WIND IN HER EAST-QUADRANT
WILL BE AT ITS HEIGHT.

Chris Parker, *Wx Update*, Bahamas, Fri 5, 10a

Rain blew sideways into the club room as we
stumbled through the double doors. It took both
Gator and Henry to pull the doors closed, lock
them and drop the hurricane bar into place.

'Anybody got a first aid kit?' Molly shouted
when she caught sight of Paul.

'It's in the kitchen,' Jaime called out. 'I'll get
it.'

Molly hustled off to the restroom to dampen
some paper towels, while we settled Paul into
my lounge chair and covered him with the
sleeping bag. Kneeling next to the lounger, I
rested my head on Paul's chest, grateful for the

strong, steady heart beating against my cheek. 'What were you thinking, Paul?'

His hand found the back of my head and rested lightly on my hair. 'Henry'd flown his wife out to Lauderdale a couple of days ago, but wanted to get back to the park. The captain goes down with the ship and all that.' A laugh rumbled up from his chest. 'We'd been in touch ... well, it seemed like a good idea at the time.'

'I'd listened to the reports,' Henry said from behind me. 'I was sure we could get as far as Treasure Cay airport before the storm hit, and I was right. But the skies looked good over Hawksbill, so we decided to come on in. Rookie mistake.'

Beneath my cheek, Paul stirred. 'I don't think I've properly thanked you, Henry, for a masterful job of flying. Sorry about the plane, though.'

'That's what insurance is for.'

When Molly returned, she took the first aid kit from Jaime, motioned everybody out of the way, and got to work.

'Better hurry before the power dies,' Jaime advised. 'I've just come back from checking the generator, and we're running low on fuel.'

'I used to be a nurse,' Molly said, dabbing lightly at the cut on Paul's forehead. 'Once we clear the blood away...' She leaned closer, patted Paul's knee. 'You'll live. Won't even need stitches.' Using a pair of scissors she found in the kit, she cut a strip of adhesive tape into a butterfly and used it to close the wound. 'You'll have a headache tomorrow, but that's what aspirin's for!'

'Aspirin?' Paul frowned. His eyes shot toward the empty bar. 'Don't we have anything stronger than aspirin?'

'I can make you a Bahama Mama,' I said helpfully as Hurricane Helen began to howl, took hold of the doors and rattled them against their hinges in her fury. She threw rain against the roof, hard as marbles. She clawed at the hurricane shutters. There was a screech of tearing metal as something was ripped from the roof and carried away.

I fixed Paul a drink, then sat on the floor next to his chair with my back against the wall. The whole building seemed to vibrate, humming like a cello. I pulled my knees up under my chin and hugged them, making myself as small a target as possible as the wind screamed like the engines of a 747 preparing for take-off.

'Gotta go while there's still a restroom to go to,' I whispered to Paul after a while. He mumbled sleepily.

'Wait for me,' Molly said.

I took her hand and headed toward the Ladies' room with the wind pushing against our backs as we staggered drunkenly along the narrow hallway. 'It's a wind tunnel,' I shouted as something crashed against the roof. I flinched and we jumped back, pressing our backs against the wall. 'Something's open somewhere.'

I dragged Molly the last few feet along the wall, and we fell through the door into the restroom.

Inside, it seemed quieter. I entered the stall gratefully, feeling safer somehow as I closed the door and threw the latch. Stall, inside restroom, inside building, with me cocooned in the center like a Russian nesting doll.

Yet Hurricane Helen had long fingers. As I sat down, she stirred the water in the toilet, sloshing it up against the sides of the bowl. On the inside of the stall, someone had posted a sign: *If it's yellow, let it mellow. If it's brown, flush it down.* Classy. I was feeling grateful for the Tamarind Tree Resort power generator so I could read the sign, and thankful for their desalinization plant, too, as I did what I had to do, then flushed.

When Molly and I got back, Paul was napping. How he could sleep while the wind roared and thundered like an oncoming locomotive, tearing at the roof of the building like some wild beast trying to get in, I'll never know. I waited until Molly was safely back on her lounger, then said, 'I'm going to check on Alice.'

I found her stretched out on a blanket in her hidey-hole behind the bar. Somewhat surprisingly, Alice seemed to have left her size five-and-half Manolo Blahniks on the floor under her bed and put on a pair of sensible white sneakers. She wore white jeans and a green t-shirt that said: *I love vegetarians. More meat for me.*

'Why aren't you sitting with Jaime, Alice?' I

299

asked as I sat cross-legged on the blanket beside her.

'I'm not speaking to him.'

Although I could think of a thousand reasons, I couldn't resist asking why.

'I put my foot down, Hannah. I teared up and I put my hands on my hips and I said nuh-uh, no-way, fuhgeddaboudit.'

I felt like I'd tuned in to the middle of a sitcom, lost without the script.

'He gave me this ring, and now he wants it back.' She leaned sideways, bumped her shoulder against mine. 'I think he wants to pawn it.'

Alice offered her right hand for inspection. On her little finger, she wore a small emerald and gold ring. 'Jaime needs money?' I asked as I admired the ring.

Sally Parker had owned a ring like that, I thought. My stomach churned.

Alice shrugged. 'Who. Freaking. Knows. Every time I mention money, Jaime tells me to shut up. So I do.'

'Where's Jaime now?' I asked his bride. 'I haven't seen him since he brought the first aid kit.'

She reached for her teddy bear. 'He's probably with his precious sister, hiding under daddy's desk.'

The lights flickered once, twice, then died. As Jaime had predicted, the generator had run out of gas. 'Are you going to be OK?' I asked Alice as I squinted at her into the dark.

'I think so.'

'Do you want me to stay with you?'

'I'm OK. I've got Mr Patches.' She grabbed the bear's paw and helped him wave goodbye to me.

'I need to go check on my husband, Alice, but if you want company, just bring Mr Patches and come join us.' I patted her knee, comforting her just as I would a child.

I made my way back to Paul largely by feel, guided by the beam of the flashlight Molly had turned on. As the storm continued to rage, I straddled the end of Paul's lounge chair, thinking about Alice's ring. A thin gold band with an emerald perched on top. There must be thousands like it in the world.

Yet I was convinced Jaime had stolen it from Sally.

As I stared into the dark, my eyes slowly adjusting, I wondered if I should confront Jaime about the ring as I had about the boat. I scanned the room, but didn't see him.

A Coleman lamp burned in the corner where two sailors huddled, reading in its light. I could see Gator's Nikes, a ragged disgrace to the brand, sticking out from beneath his blanket as he slept with his head under a table, curled up next to his dog. Every once in a while a flashlight would play eerily over a face as it was flicked on, played around the floor as if looking for something, then switched off.

Helen continued to roar, uprooting trees and hurling them against the building *thump-thump-thump*. Rain dashed against the windows as if

301

someone were throwing gravel, while over our heads, the roof moaned and popped. I looked up, convinced we were going to lose the roof, and grateful when I couldn't see daylight.

I nudged Paul. 'Move over, sweetheart.' He stirred sleepily. I squeezed myself on to the narrow lounger beside him, nestling against the warmth of his thigh. I pulled the sleeping bag tightly around us, and as the wind continued to howl like a demented soul, I prayed.

Just as suddenly as it had come, the noise stopped. I awoke to a deadly, silent calm.

Hurricane Helen's eye.

Sometime during the storm, Alice had made her way over to us. She had sandwiched herself between Molly's lounger and mine, clutching her blanket and Mr Patches. 'How much time do you think we have?' Alice asked. 'Before it comes back, I mean.'

I consulted with Paul who was wide awake now, too. 'Thirty-five minutes, give or take.'

Jaime appeared out of nowhere and met Gator at the front door. Together, the two men lifted the hurricane bar and threw the doors wide, flooding the club room with grayish-yellow light. Justice frolicked out, presumably in search of a tree. Considering the intensity of the storm, I thought he'd be doomed to disappointment.

Alice had been watching the dog, but she suddenly said, 'There's something I have to do.' Before I could stop her, she dropped Mr

Patches on the floor, aimed a venomous glance at her husband, and ran out the door.

Jaime stared after her, fists clenched at his sides. 'Alice, you crazy bitch! Come back!'

'Do you want me to go after her?' I asked Jaime.

Jaime pawed the soggy carpet with the toe of his shoe. 'No, I'll go talk to her.'

I bounced up and down on my toes, shaking the knots out of my calves, watching Jaime disappear through what was left of the garden.

'Want to go for a walk?' Paul asked. He'd come up behind me.

'Are you sure you're up for a walk?' I asked, staring pointedly at his bandage.

'Sure I'm sure. I need to work out the kinks. Been lying down too long.'

Hand in hand, we walked through the open door and into the artificial twilight of the storm.

When I saw the destruction Helen had wrought, I couldn't believe the building had survived. The Tamarind Tree gardens had been ripped bare of plants – lignum vitae, sea grape, casuarinas, bougainvilla, hibiscus – scoured by the wind off the face of the earth. The few palm trees that had survived were bent double. Others, less resilient, had lost their heads, snapped off about ten feet above ground. One enormous trunk had crashed down on the pool bar, reducing it to rubble. Other trunks lay higgledy-piggledy around the grounds like enormous matchsticks tossed down by an angry god.

We walked down the path, hardly speaking,

climbing over limbs, wading through piles of wet debris. When we reached the resort gate, the guardhouse had disappeared. The turnstile pointed straight up, twisted like a strawberry Twizzler.

'Want to go into town?' I asked, curious to see how the settlement had fared.

Paul checked his watch. 'No time.'

Back at the Tamarind Tree, the staff were still policing the grounds. The wind blew hot and gentle as we helped with the cleanup. We picked up fallen coconuts and branches and tossed them into what was left of the golf cart shed where we hoped the wind couldn't find them.

I was helping Jeremy Thomas check the shutters, securing all the dog downs when the wind began to rise, blowing hot against my neck.

Jeremy banged his fist against a shutter, testing it. 'Inside.'

I went.

'Where's Alice?' I asked Molly as I pawed through my duffle looking for the Fig Newtons, dreading the return of Helen. We'd already had one hour of hell. Wasn't that enough?

'I don't think she's back yet.'

I ripped the cellophane off the package and held it out. 'Cookie?'

'Thanks.'

'Where's Paul?'

'Bathroom.' Molly took a bite of cookie and

chewed. 'Said if he wasn't back in five minutes, send out a search party.'

'Ha ha.'

Alice Madonna was a two-cookie worry, then a three. 'Should I go look for her?' I asked Paul when he came back from the bathroom. 'What'll happen to her if they bar the door?'

Paul's arm snaked around my shoulder and squeezed. 'Give her a few minutes. She's silly, but not stupid. She'll be back.'

Paul was right.

Alice came back, but she was not alone. She scurried through the door staggering under the weight of a purple leather bag, earning a frown from Gator who was waiting at the door, counting heads, to bar it. Alice headed straight for her corner and sat down. I couldn't see her face from where I sat, but as she passed me, framed in the light at the door, I suspected she'd been crying. Her sneakers, once white, were water-stained and covered in sand.

I wormed out from under my husband's arm. 'Let me see what's bothering her.'

I crossed the room in seconds and popped behind the bar. 'Hey, Alice, mind if I join you?'

She shook her head 'no' which I took to mean yes, so I sat down.

Her legs extended straight out in front of her, she held the bag on her lap.

'I just couldn't take it any more,' she sobbed. She wrapped her arms tightly around the bag, and it was then that I noticed it wasn't a bag. It was a pet carrier.

'It'll be over soon,' I said, thinking she meant the storm.

She stared at me, tears streaming down her cheeks. 'He said I couldn't keep it. I asked him why, why, why?' She started bawling. 'He's such a bastard!'

'What are you talking about, Alice? The ring?'

She sucked in her lips and looked at me sideways through her long, wet lashes. Slowly, she opened the hatch of the carrier. I started when an exuberant puppy leapt out, a white and gray mop of fur that stood up on its hind legs and joyfully licked the tears from Alice's face.

No, not a puppy. The dog was a full-grown, brindle Scottish Terrier.

'Isn't he darling?' Alice giggled, her tears vanquished at last. 'Jaime said I couldn't bring him into the shelter, that dogs weren't allowed. What a liar! Gator brought Justice in for heaven's sake. I couldn't leave my little sweetie all alone in our cottage. Poor thing was terrified!'

Dread clutched at my innards, but I managed to say, 'Where did Jaime get the dog, Alice?'

She shrugged. 'I don't know.' She lifted the animal up like a doll, nuzzled his fur and said, 'Mommy wuvs her widdle Beckums.'

'Beckums?'

'Beckham, as in David. I think he's hot.'

She kissed the dog on the nose. 'I couldn't let Jaime take Beckums away, now could I?'

'Why would Jaime want to take the dog

away?'

She plopped Beckham in my lap, picked up my hand and placed it between the little dog's shoulders. 'Feel that tiny lump there? It's a microchip. Jaime said it could be traced.'

I stared at Alice stupidly. Jaime had Frank and Sally's boat. Jaime had Frank and Sally's dog. And Jaime had probably given Alice Sally's emerald ring. I wanted to call the police right away, but we were in the middle of a hurricane, so it would have to wait. I'd have to tell Gator instead.

Alice leaned her head against the bar and said dreamily, 'If he'd throw a helpless little dog over a cliff, Hannah, can you imagine what he'd do with his own baby?'

The eye had passed, and Helen began to tear at us in earnest. She howled and shrieked like an enraged dragon, lashing the building with the flat of her tail.

My ears popped and my teeth ached as the eyewall swept over us and the air pressure changed. I grabbed Paul's hand, my anchor. He'd keep me from blowing away.

'I think Alice is pregnant,' I said, holding on tight, my lips against his ear.

'That's good,' he shouted over the storm. 'Isn't it?'

Before I could answer, Gabriele appeared. Across the room, she and Gator were up to something. 'Anybody seen Jeremy?' Gabriele screamed over the roar of the wind. 'Hell-oh! I could use a little help over here!'

Gabriele helped Gator push the table he'd been sleeping under against the door, then she marched over to roust out the boaters. Six or seven of them began dismantling the pile of furniture, setting the chairs aside fire brigade-style, so they could get at the tables to make barricades.

Meanwhile, Helen sat on the roof like an F-15 fighter jet, all engines full throttle. I heard a shriek as nails lost their hold and the plywood that had been covering the picture window tore away. Pale light entered the room; the plexiglass began to flex with the force of the wind, growling and howling like feedback on the speakers at a Black Sabbath concert. And yet it held.

'Away from the door!' Gabriele yelled, her hair flying.

Helen wanted in. She thumped and rattled and knocked at the doors. I could see the door frame flexing under the pressure, the hinges straining. The doors banged and bowed and managed to hold on until with one last desperate crack, the hurricane bar splintered. Helen ripped the doors away and entered the building.

Suddenly I was on the floor, clawing at the carpet. Salt water mist filled the air and I struggled to breathe. 'Paul!' I shouted, but the wind tore the words away.

Eyes stinging, I looked around for Molly. She sprawled on the floor next to me, whimpering. I crawled over and covered her body with mine.

The room became a wind tunnel as Helen screamed through like a banshee, picking up books, bottles, cups, coolers, even our lounge chairs and hurling them aside in her fury.

'Hannah!' A table was inching toward us. At first I thought it was Helen's doing, then I saw Paul underneath, pushing it along. He shoved the table against the wall, and I helped Molly crawl under the makeshift barricade where we huddled together for protection.

I didn't think there could be any trees left, but Helen found them. Trunks crashed and thumped against the building. Raindrops drummed on the table over our head and I realized the roof was leaking. I tilted my head and looked up. The ceiling fans spun like windmills gone wild and light streamed through cracks in the rafters.

Across the room, Alice began to scream, 'Stop it, stop it, stop it!' I hoped Jaime was there to comfort her.

It felt like hours before the winds abated, but according to Paul's watch, it was only forty minutes. When the wind died and we were sure Helen had gone, we crawled out from under the table, dirty, wet and disheveled, like survivors of a war-torn country after a ceasefire.

Paul and I stood up, took inventory of one another. Nothing cut or broken.

One of the boaters had been struck by an airborne chair, injuring his arm. After we made sure she'd suffered no injuries herself, we let Molly hustle off to nurse him.

I was about to check on Alice when Gabriele

stumbled into the room out of the hallway, hair loose and wild, a flashlight in her hand. 'Has anybody seen my brother?'

From a corner behind the bar, a small voice began singing: *The eensy weensy spider went up the water spout; Down came the rain and washed the spider out...*

Twenty-Two

CONDITIONS MODERATE RAPIDLY TODAY AS
HELEN EXITS, WITH SOUTH WIND BELOW 50
KNOTS BY MIDDAY. CLEAN-UP EFFORTS CAN
BEGIN STRAIGHTAWAY.
Chris Parker, *Wx Update*, Bahamas, Sat 6, 10a

The sun came out, shining on a settlement I
barely recognized.

With Justice in the lead, Paul and I straggled
back to town behind Molly and Gator, weaving
through piles of debris, stepping over logs, and
sloshing through puddles up to our ankles.
Everywhere residents were emerging, dazed
and blinking from the shells of their ruined
homes. Where walls remained, jagged holes
stood as reminders of doors that had once wel-
comed visitors, or windows that had once been
open to the tradewinds, flower boxes blooming,
curtains gently swaying.

Golf carts, generators, and air conditioners
had been picked up by the storm, whirled about
and discarded, sometimes hundreds of yards
from their original locations. Behind the hardware store, a delivery van had overturned; the

driver's-side door yawned open, the seat missing. Next to it lay, incredibly, one of Tamarind Tree's tiki torches.

The Pink Store, I was relieved to see, had suffered little damage. The slats of the jalousie windows were twisted and bent, allowing water to blow into the store, but Winnie's pharmaceutical shelf appeared to be the only casualty. The wind had toppled it, sending boxes of Tylenol, Dramamine and cold tablets tumbling, bottles of shampoo, Pepto-Bismol and Benjamin's Balsam cough mixture, too. They lay in two inches of water on the floor, a soggy jumble.

Winnie was already at work, sweeping everything out.

'How'd they fare up at the school?' I asked.

She paused in mid-sweep. 'Trying to make it.'

I turned to Gator for a translation. He waggled his hand. 'Means so-so.'

'Anybody hurt?' I asked Winnie.

'No, praise the Lord.'

A few yards down the road, Tropical Treats hadn't fared so well. Hurricane Helen had hurled a generator through its roof. It landed smack-dab on the ice cream freezer where crushed tubs of ice cream oozed and dripped, forming multi-colored puddles of ice cream soup. 'And I was going to buy you a rum raisin cone,' Paul teased.

I poked him in the ribs. 'Rain check.'

The marina was worse than I feared. As it came into view, Gator grunted. His dive shack had disappeared, tie-downs and all. The dock had twisted and heaved, planks were torn away leaving gaps, like missing teeth. Some floated loose below, knocking against the pilings.

Paul, Molly and I picked our way carefully down the dock while Gator stayed behind, kicking desultorily through the debris that had been his place of business.

One sailboat had sunk. Three others were still afloat, but all had parted company with their masts. One mast leaned crookedly against a piling; another had been hurled through the window of the marina office. I stuck my head inside. File cabinets had toppled, their drawers yawned open. Papers, magazines and books lay in a sodden, pulp-like mass on the linoleum.

I worried about Gator's boat, *Deep Magic*. When I'd last seen her, she'd been tied into a slip, held off the finger piers by a web of lines strung from port to starboard, like a giant cat's cradle. Three anchors had been set off her bow. I headed in that direction, calling to Paul and Molly over my shoulder, 'I'm going to check on *Deep Magic*!'

I saw Gator was already aboard his boat, grinning hugely.

I ran down the dock, cheering wildly. 'She's OK! She's OK!'

Gator patted *Deep Magic*'s console. 'Good old gal. Never let me down yet.'

'Can you give us a ride back to *Pro Bono?*'

'Dunno. Depends on the engine starting.' He twisted the key and the engine sputtered, rumbled and then growled to life.

'Where's your dinghy?' Paul asked, coming up behind me.

I glanced at *Deep Magic*'s stern, embarrassed that I hadn't noticed. The davits were twisted and bent where they'd tried to hold on to Gator's dinghy, but lost it in a tug of war with Helen.

Gator shrugged. 'It'll turn up. They always do.'

I tugged on Paul's sleeve. 'Do we have time to check on *Wanderer*?'

Gator nodded. 'Go ahead. Things I need to do.'

'Want to come?' I asked Molly.

She'd plopped herself down at the end of the dock, legs dangling over the water. 'I think I'll stay with Gator, Sugar. I'm absolutely beat.'

'I can't imagine why,' I teased.

Poor Mr Pinder! His boatyard was a disaster. One powerboat had been blown off its jacks, toppled into the next, which fell against the next ... over and over they had tipped and toppled, like a giant game of dominoes. 'This breaks my heart,' Paul said, surveying the damage.

'*Wanderer*'s not here, thank goodness,' I told him. 'Last time I saw her, she was in dry dock. C'mon.' I grabbed Paul's hand and together we managed to climb over the debris that separated the boatyard from the marine railway. The space that *Wanderer* had once occupied stood empty.

'Where's *Alice in Wonderland*?' I asked one of the yard hands who was bent over, picking up wood and other debris and adding it to a big pile near a dumpster.

He straightened. 'Jaime Mueller thought she'd be safer tied up to a mooring ball.'

'Where?'

The yard hand pointed, but I didn't see anything in the harbor but empty water.

The yard hand shaded his eyes and squinted. 'Ooops. So much for safety. Doesn't look like she made it, does it?'

Five minutes later, we boarded *Deep Magic*.

Gator eased his boat into the harbor, proceeding slowly, steering a careful path through the floating debris. As we cleared the marina I stood up. 'Over there!'

Gator spun the wheel. 'What? Where?'

'That mast sticking out of the water. I think it's *Wanderer*. I recognize the radar dome.'

As we neared the obstacle, Gator cut the throttle, drifting as close as he dared. I held on to the gunwale and peered over the side, my eyes following along the length of the mast all the way to the bottom where *Wanderer* indeed lay. She appeared peaceful, undamaged, as if she'd simply turned over on her side and fallen asleep. A parrot fish pecked at the transom where it said, *Alice in Wonderland*.

Molly leaned on the gunwale next to me, chin resting on her hands. 'The End,' she said, wistfully, capitalizing each word.

Gazing at the sunken boat where we'd spent so many happy hours, I said, 'I'm not so sure about that.'

I crossed the deck and stood behind Gator as he shifted into reverse and backed *Deep Magic* away from *Wanderer*. 'What about the mini-sub?' I asked him.

'What mini-sub?' Paul wanted to know.

I explained about the now-you-see-it-now-you-don't mystery vessel. 'Sometimes I put two and two together and come up with five, but this time I think I'm right. As weird as it seems, I think Jaime Mueller was using that submarine to run drugs. Nothing else makes sense.'

'Something funny was definitely going on at that beach,' Molly added. 'You'd think it was a top-secret military base the way Mueller guarded it.'

Gator motored past the settlement dumpsters that had disgorged their contents into the harbor, picking his way carefully through floating garbage as he rounded the headland at Poinciana Point. Miraculously, Henry's airplane seemed to have survived the blow, if you discounted the broken wing. It had been sheltered from the worst of Helen's wrath by the trees of Poinciana Point.

'I'm having flashbacks,' Paul said as we neared the plane. He shivered.

I took his hand and squeezed three times: I. Love. You.

With Gator at the controls, *Deep Magic* nosed in, eased out, nosed in as we searched the water around the Savage Cub for the blue mini-sub.

'Gone,' I said at last. 'Do you think it's been swept out to sea by the storm?'

Gator shook his head. 'Not if that plane wasn't. That mini-sub's gone, someone drove it out of here.'

'Well, lookey-lookey!' Molly caroled in my ear.

I followed her gaze. Whatever had been in the Kelchner's cottage had disappeared, too. Nothing but a cinderblock foundation remained. Everything else was gone, gone with the wind.

We were heading back to find *Pro Bono* when I noticed something floating off Poinciana Point. At first I thought it was a tree limb, or a piling. I blinked, refocused, but still couldn't turn it into a piling. 'Paul, what's that?'

'Part of the airplane?' He shrugged. 'There could be anything floating out here about now. Even a body.'

Paul was joking, but as Gator edged closer, I saw that it *was* a body, floating face down, arms splayed.

Gator noticed it about the same time I did. 'Bite your tongue, Ives.' He guided *Deep Magic* closer, cut the engine, and coaxed the boat sideways until the body lay along the starboard side. 'I'll need a boat hook.'

Paul pulled a boat hook from the rack and handed it over.

I watched as Gator used it to hook the victim by the belt. 'Help me, Paul.'

317

'You want to lift him into the boat?'

'No. I want to turn him over.'

Leaning carefully over the side, the two men tugged and pushed until the body rolled slowly over. Looking up into the sky with sightless eyes was what was left of Jaime Mueller.

I gasped, sat back. It wasn't out of surprise at the identity of the victim – I had been half expecting that. It was because Jaime's entire left leg had been torn off at the hip.

Gator buried his face in his hands. 'Shit, man. I counted heads. Thought he'd made it back after the eye. Drowning's a helluva way to die.'

'This is the last time I go out boating with you, Gator Crockett,' Molly scolded. 'Every time I do, we turn up a body.'

'The police...' I began.

'I hear you,' Gator said.

I took a deep, shuddering breath. 'We just can't leave him here.'

'We can in a way.' He passed the boat hook to Paul. 'Here. Hang on to him for a minute.'

While *Deep Magic* bobbed erratically on the restless sea and Paul tried to hold on, Gator went rummaging in the box where he kept his equipment, coming up a few minutes later with a dinghy anchor. He made a rope fast to the anchor, then looped the other end through Jaime's belt and tied it securely. Then he threw the anchor overboard.

'Now we call in the pros,' he said, picking up his microphone. 'Dive Guana, Dive Guana, this is *Deep Magic*. Come in Troy.'

Jaime Mueller's would be one of five bodies claimed by Hurricane Helen. *Found floating by a fisherman off Poinciana Point. Sharks may have contributed to Mr Mueller's death, The Abaconian* would report.

But, I had seen the fury, the tears in Alice's eyes.

I knew that Jaime was dead before he even hit the water.

Whoever recommended the mangrove was right on the money. Except for minor scrapes, *Pro Bono* had survived. In a matter of minutes we untied all the lines, climbed aboard and with a farewell wave to Gator, headed back to Bonefish Cay.

Molly's dock was canted up and missing some planks, but still useable. Likewise ours, although we'd lost our favorite bench from the end of the pier. Branches, palm fronds, coconuts, even whole bushes, littered both yards and trash would continue to wash up on the shore for weeks. Paul hurried to check on his pet banana tree and when I heard him cheer, I knew it, too, had survived.

Inside the house, it was if the storm never happened. 'Molly was right,' I told my husband. 'These houses are bulletproof. We should have stayed here.' I pawed though Mother Hubbard's cupboard, checking each can, looking for something that might do for dinner.

Paul opened the refrigerator, but there was no light to greet him. No milk, no cheese, no leftover spaghetti, no ice for his Bahama Mama. The corners of his mouth turned down in a pout, purely phony. 'I guess it's time for me to set up that generator.'

Before she left the island and the battered Tamarind Tree Resort and Marina, I paid a call on Gabriele. She met me in the dining room where a simple cold lunch was being served to the worker bees she'd hired to put the place in order.

'Soft drink?' she asked. 'Our kitchen isn't yet open.'

'A Coke if you have one.'

We sat in lounge chairs by the side of the pool, which had been drained. Workers swarmed around in the deep end, shoveling debris out of the bottom and putting it in plastic sacks.

'I'm sorry about Jaime,' I said.

'Thank you. He wasn't much of a brother, but in my own way, I loved him.'

I took a sip from my can. 'I'd like to talk to Alice. I promised her lunch, but looking around here, I think it will have to be at my place.'

Gabriele blinked and looked away. 'We sent her home to Texas. Jaime's death came as a great shock.'

I'll bet. There were only two people who knew what really happened on that headland overlooking Poinciana Cove during the eye of the storm. Alice was one, and the other one was dead.

'During the storm, Alice hinted that she might

be pregnant,' I said.

'She is. Due in April.'

'That should be a comfort to her, don't you think?'

'Al vivo la hogaza y al muerto, la mortaja, Papa says. Live by the living, not the dead.'

I sat quietly for a while, thinking. My late mother would have agreed with Rudolph Mueller.

'Did Alice take the dog with her?' I asked.

'Beckham?' Gabriele smiled sadly. 'Yes, yes, of course. The paperwork was a nightmare, but she wouldn't be separated from Beckham.'

There didn't seem to be anything left to say, so I wrote my address on a napkin and extracted a promise from Gabriele that she'd give it to Alice the next time she saw her.

'One thing else, Gabriele. Promise me you'll take care of Alice?'

She considered me with cool green eyes, nodded, and walked away.

I invited Molly for dinner. Afterwards, we sat on the porch, sharing a chocolate bar by candle-light.

'We've worked it all out, haven't we, Molly.'

Molly put a square of chocolate in her mouth and licked her fingers. 'You should write a book, Hannah.'

Paul lay in the hammock, only half listening, I was sure. 'Worked out what?'

'Jaime Mueller was running drugs,' I said. 'The plane would fly in from Colombia or somewhere, they'd off-load the drugs into the mini-sub and toodle over to the United States. Underwater.'

'*Way* under the radar,' Molly added. 'I saw it on CNN. The Coast Guard and the Navy are making it so difficult for boats and planes to get through that drug smugglers are turning to submarines.'

'Right. Jaime was the kingpin. The late Craig Meeks, Jeremy Thomas and maybe even trigger-happy Kyle were his accomplices.'

'Who...?' Paul began.

I held up my hand, still holding the chocolate bar. 'Wait a minute. I'm coming to that. When Frank did that underwater dive, he saw the sub. Maybe he even watched it go out. Trouble was, Jaime saw him, too. So I suspect Craig and Jaime murdered Frank and Sally and stashed their bodies under the lobster trap.'

'And after he sailed *Wanderer* back to Hawks-bill Cay,' Molly added, 'Jaime bumped off Craig Meeks.'

'Wait a minute,' Paul wanted to know. 'Why would Jaime kill Craig?'

'Maybe Craig was OK with the drugs, but not with the killing?' I shrugged. 'Anyway, I figure he killed Craig to keep him from talking. Set his body on fire so it looked like the poor sap died in the wildfire. That's why he was so eager to volunteer. Ugh.'

Molly chimed in. 'But Jaime kept Sally's ring, and the dog Duffy, and gave them to Alice.'

'Right...'

'Now that's what I don't understand,' Paul cut in. 'Stealing *Wanderer* and trying to cover it up was dim-witted enough, but holding on to the dog and that ring was just as good as saying, "Hey, look! I killed those people."'

'Yes, except Jaime never expected the bodies to be found. When they were, he panicked. Alice told me he asked for the ring back, but she refused.

'As for Duffy,' I continued, 'Jaime probably thought a dog is a dog is a dog, until he discovered the microchip under Duffy's skin.' I paused long enough to pass the chocolate bar around again. 'And then poor Duffy had to go, too. Alice told me Jaime threatened to throw the dog off Poinciana Point during the eye of the hurricane, but I think Jaime went over instead.'

Paul rolled on to his side, setting the hammock swinging. 'She killed her husband over a *dog*?'

I shook my head. 'It took me a while to put it together, but earlier in the week Gabriele mentioned that Alice had been under the weather. Then something Alice said during the hurricane finally clicked. "He said I couldn't keep it." At first I thought she was talking about the ring. Now that I know she's pregnant, I'm pretty sure Jaime was pressuring his wife to have an abortion.'

Paul climbed out of the hammock and came to sit on the bench beside me. 'The boat, the ring, the dog. It beats me how Jaime could be so stupid.'

'Guys like Jaime think they're above the law, like they're born with a get-out-of-jail-free-card clutched in their chubby little hands.'

Paul shook his head. 'But still...'

I raised a hand. 'Why would Michael Vick risk a multimillion-dollar career with the NFL by staging illegal dog fights?'

'I read it in the *News & Observer*,' Molly said. 'A twenty-two pit bull operation.'

I covered my mouth with my hand. 'Eeeuw!' Then forged on. 'And there's hotel maven, Leona Helmsley, who believed that paying taxes was only for "the little people".'

Next to me Paul was nodding vigorously. 'Martha Stewart went to jail because she wanted to save a measly seventy-five thou.'

'I rest my case,' I said.

'Can we back up a minute?' Paul asked. 'Who's Jeremy?'

'He's one of the staffers at Tamarind Tree,' Molly explained. 'He was around when the hurricane started, and he went out during the eye, but we didn't see him at all afterwards. Gabriele came around looking for him.'

'So, if Jeremy is gone and the mini-sub is gone...'

I threw my hands in the air. 'Case solved!'

'Not exactly,' Molly added.

'Oh, yeah. I forgot to mention that Gator notified the Coast Guard to be on the lookout for the sub. But if Jeremy was dumb enough to take it out in the middle of a hurricane, it's unlikely either he or the submarine will ever be found.'

'Did Gabriele Mueller know what her brother was up to?' Paul wondered.

'I don't think Gabriele knew, or Alice either. I'm not so sure about Jaime's dad. He might have known, but simply looked the other way.'

'With Jaime gone, what do you think will happen to the Tamarind Tree Resort?'

I shrugged. 'Whatever Gabriele wants, I imagine.'

It had been several weeks since Hurricane Helen blew through, and things had returned more or less to normal. The Pink Store reopened at once, although pickings were slim until the barge steamed in with fresh supplies. The Cruise Inn and Conch Out reopened after a week with an all-you-can-eat conch fest which Paul and I attended with Molly and half the population of Hawksbill Cay.

The power came back on after six days, and we celebrated the return of the Cruisers' Net to our morning routine.

Pattie confirmed what we'd learned through the grapevine, that Marsh Harbour had fared surprisingly well. Boats, docks and marinas had sustained moderate damage, but nothing like the havoc wreaked by Jeanne in 2004. Mangoes and Snappas were still closed, but planned to reopen soon, and the Conch Inn was serving dinner in the upstairs bar until their downstairs furniture could be replaced. Groceries, hardware and appliance stores were doing land-rush business, but most happily of all, Mimi called in to report that the horses had survived the hurricane as they had for centuries by taking refuge in the forest.

Paul picked up Daniel as usual each Thursday. Daniel chopped and trimmed and raked, making huge piles of debris on the rocky headline which he'd burn some day, but only when the wind was right.

One afternoon I sat on the dock drinking iced tea and watching Daniel do his Zen-like thing with the rake, and I was remembering Dickie.

I really missed that cat!

I left his bowl in the usual spot, but he never came to eat. Every time a bush rustled, I searched for him. I walked the beach, dreading that I'd find his body washed ashore.

Maybe I should adopt a potcake.

I sighed, waved to Daniel and went inside to wash a load of laundry.

When I came out carrying a basket of wet clothes, Dickie lay on the steps next to his empty food bowl, calmly rearranging his stripes with his tongue.

Twenty-Three

IN A DANGEROUS NIGHT OPERATION ON SATURDAY, US COASTGUARD OFFICIALS CAPTURED A SUBMARINE STUFFED WITH SIX BALES OF COCAINE WITH A STREET VALUE OF $30 MILLION.

A COASTGUARD SPOKESMAN WAS QUOTED AS SAYING A TEAM OF SPECIAL AGENTS WERE DISPATCHED ON SMALL BOATS TO SURPRISE THE SMUGGLERS AFTER A US NAVY AIRPLANE SPOTTED THE SUB IN INTERNATIONAL WATERS ABOUT THIRTY MILES OFF THE COAST OF FT LAUDERDALE.

TWO SMUGGLERS WERE ON BOARD THE TWENTY-EIGHT FOOT STEEL AND FIBERGLASS SUB, BUT THE COASTGUARD WAS ABLE TO CAPTURE THE SMUGGLERS BEFORE THEY COULD SCUTTLE THE VESSEL.

ARRESTED WERE JEREMY THOMAS, 23, OF PENSACOLA AND ERIC MYERS, 21, OF OCALA. THE US SHIP THAT NABBED THE TRAFFICKERS ARRIVED IN THE PORT OF FT LAUDERDALE TODAY WITH THE DRUG BOAT IN TOW.

Florida Sun Sentinel, Sept. 6, 2008, P. B1

Twenty-Four

EL MIRADOR LAND CORPORATION, DEVELOPER OF THE TAMARIND TREE RESORT AND MARINA, AN EXCLUSIVE BAHAMIAN ISLAND RETREAT FOR THE SUPER-RICH, SAID IT FILED FOR BANKRUPTCY AFTER FAILING TO SECURE NEW FINANCING, DEMONSTRATING THAT EVEN THE RICH CANNOT ESCAPE THE COUNTRY'S CURRENT ECONOMIC TROUBLES. SPOKESPERSON GABRIELE MUELLER SAID THE CORPORATION FILED FOR CHAPTER 11 PROTECTION WEDNESDAY IN FEDERAL BANKRUPTCY COURT IN TEXAS. THE MOVE CAME JUST TWO MONTHS AFTER THE RESORT SUFFERED EXTENSIVE DAMAGE IN HURRICANE HELEN WHICH SWEPT THROUGH THE ABACO ISLAND CHAIN IN SEPTEMBER.

IN A STATEMENT TO THE ASSOCIATED PRESS, THE CEO OF EL MIRADOR LAND CORPORATION, RUDOLPH MUELLER, DEVELOPER OF THE TAMARIND TREE RESORT, SAID HE HAD BEEN UNABLE TO SECURE FINANCING ARRANGEMENTS WITH ITS CREDITORS AND BONDHOLDERS. THE COURT FILING SAYS THAT TIGHT CREDIT MARKETS HAD MADE IT DIFFICULT TO RAISE MONEY TO PAY OFF

DEBTS AND MAKE NEEDED REPAIRS TO THE RESORT. HE PLANS TO REORGANIZE ITS FINANCES AND EMERGE FROM BANKRUPTCY 'AS SOON AS POSSIBLE,' THE STATEMENT SAID.

OPENED IN EARLY 2008, THE RESORT HAD BEEN PLANNING AN EXPANSION WHEN THE CREDIT CRISIS HIT WALL STREET. THOSE PLANS, AS WELL AS PLANS TO DEVELOP OTHER LUXURY RESORTS IN SOUTH AMER-ICA AND THE CARIBBEAN ARE NOW ON HOLD PENDING RESOLUTION OF EL MIRADOR'S FINANCIAL WOES.

The Dallas Morning News, Oct. 16, 2008, P. A1